GALOS; Z J

SHORT STORIES
PART TWO
BOOK III & BOOK IV

BOOK III
THE MUSES

BOOK IV
ORION'S LOVE NEST

Impressum

Bibliographical information of the German National Library.
The German National Library indexes this publication with
the German National Bibliography. Detailed bibliographical
data may be derived from the Internet website
http://dnb.dnb.de

©2020 GALOS; Z J
©2020 Galos; Z. Illustrations

Producer and publisher: BoD-Books on Demand,
Norderstedt

ISBN: 9783752628609

Contents

BOOK III

The Muses

An Icy Storm in Midsummer's Day

It became again a togetherness with a variety of virtual touches, talks and loving. It's a circle, vicious, enjoyable, exciting, depressing, high-flying, and a final fall from the sweet cotton clouds. He went through the process and he disliked it in the end, yet he is out again to do the same workings all over again. Only, just now, it's different to the times he had before. He has learned, thanks to his friends and a good Muse. How good has she been though? Was it quite an experience in practical psychology? He has suffered and being the hunter, he became the hunted. Not by the sheer personality of this Amazon he was wrestling with, but the mental games that ended brutally, due to the slaying of the Amazon by her master: Fate. Indeed, he was perturbed as she thanked him for his compassion, he even wondered who she'd propose for him as a replacement for her. Someone intelligent, he said to her and she laughed hollow with a sarcastic taint. However, in the end it all took its toll on him and rendered him emotionally unstable. He recalled her words: We can do this, but you have to be strong. Would he be? It took him six month after her passing to reach a reasonable positive mind again, and only then was he prepared to search for a new female Muse again.

The storm has subsided and the air smells fresh again. The leaves glisten, washed and cleared from the air-pollution's sticky film and the pellets of hail that has melted into the clear-blue coloured water in the swimming pool. Its water feels warm to the touch, as does the stored energy in the surrounding flagstone pavers, which had heated up during the day, had radiated into the pool. He wished he could have a swim longing for skinny dipping.

Since the woman with the long braided hair from next door does not watch him any longer, this action has lost much of its attraction. He had enjoyed being watched. Subconsciously it had turned him on; he could sense her eyes on his cock, when he sat down on the warm surrounding paved area drying in the sun. Perhaps he had fallen asleep once in a while and the sun had an effect on his arousal. She had desired him, showing it in many ways. He was though seduced by her beckoning, but something inside held him back. Finally, he had made up his mind not to get involved with her, a female minister of the Anglican Church. But, she was highly attractive, sexy, at least from behind, with her beautifully braided hair that reached down to the top of her bums. Gosh! He thought and imagined her hair opened. He saw her lying naked on her bed, covered only by her auburn hair. Now, those moments were behind him, however, an unfinished desire that was ill-directed, not entirely the true state of his heart, but along his desires for a comparable sexual partner.

Then he met Nimis online and she seemed immediately to him that she could be his saving Muse, Ana's answer to his lively imagination and wishes. Initially he was head-over-heels in love with her, but she kept a secretive aura around her being. He thought about seeing her in real life, before he would place any judgement towards his inflamed feelings. He wouldn't be happy living apart from her and she was not into sex online. It was then that he desired to see her at once.

En route to a job he had been commissioned to do, fate had redirected him to London. What an opportunity to see the city the way he wished to see it and not as a side-kick to some egotistical man, he had to travel with last time, part of a team-research work.

There it was laid-out for him and the game of Nimis started taking hold of his consciousness. Her secretive style apparent through her sun-sign and the way she presented herself, intrigued him. She wasn't after men, she had at that time stated categorically to him. Well then, he thought, another Amazon, indeed. This time Achilles did not step into his armour to fight Penthelesia. This time he let subtle feelings take their course and at a moment of stirring, he dialled her mobile number; yet as she answered his call, he hung-up. She knew it was him and she understood his pride not to give in and beg her for sex. She responded to him the day after he arrived.

This was a different world; he did not expect anything, but love he did give her. It seemed unrequited love to him, but she took it. He could sense her deeper seated emotions, as she couldn't cover-up towards him. She took his words, his poems, and his letters, his hand, and his kisses to her cheeks. Then he heard nothing further from her. She had a sparse way with communication, as if she was counting the words she wrote, while he was smothering her with adoration. He was his usual self again – overflowing, but he guessed that she had developed a taste for gender-love, after a huge disappointment with a male partner. She had indicated that to him and he wondered about further indications.

He didn't mind her gender affairs, but he also told her that he could do to her just the same and even more to satisfy her. Would she wish to finish her present affair, before she was ready to be involved with another man?

"If I decide to get involved with you," she said and stopped to think, but then continued "May is also involved with a married man." He assumed it was her girlfriend.

"Married or not," he said, "is it pleasure you seek?" But she not in a state of mind to pursue this discussion, just enjoying the superficial pleasures he offered her whole-heartedly. "Maybe some other time then," he moaned, but he dreaded the thought of delaying such a pleasure of love – he had a gutfeel that it could be turning out to be great – judging about the way she had reacted to the touches of his hands moulded on her feet. In fact he could sense it to be tremendous.

"I am a passionate woman," she murmured.

Darn! He thought, why does she refuse a good man like him then, making love to her?

She knew it could be unusually great with him, as a woman knows instinctively matters of the heart, but she was not at all in a state of mind and body to share lust in a stealthy way. It wasn't what turned her on. She was a straight-forward type of conditioned woman and she wasn't the heroine who has a secret life of an aspiring novelist.

As he touched her breasts, she pushed his hands off and then he slid his fingers to her vulva; she protested: I don't do that if I'm not married – he thought to understand from her murmuring.

At the start she had sent him a poem, but since then she had never sent him another one. It was a good poem and he encouraged her to write. Pity, he thought, she has such emotional depths and she doesn't make use of her talents. She rather wastes all on her insatiable drives to feed the desires of her gender-oriented relationships. For her a bit of clitoris is everything, he mused, as for him the pussy, so he couldn't blame her. He thought of her as a clever woman, avoiding the onslaught of men, being single and stunningly attractive. All she wanted was a soft touch now and then, being satisfied by another woman. All she wanted from him was a great foot and neck massage. He did not mind. He loved her. He could give her a massage and get aroused quite easily. Pity that he could

12

not take her top off that night; he was enticed, horny, and he desired to fuck her beautiful breasts.

That was his closest erotic event he ever could aspire to get with her. He could feel that she was closed-up considerably to a man touching her sexually, even if he was gentle. Her wearing of a sports-bra hindered the sexual sensation at that magical moment he desired sharing a great skin contact with her. He couldn't imagine that she would not be aroused to his touches to her breasts and his kissing and sucking of her nipples, he wished to see and have her this way at least.

The next day he could have done it perhaps technically easier, as she wore a soft top. He was though tired-out, repelled by a giant wave of tiredness that surged through him like the climax he'd expected with her but never had. Falling almost to his knees, he sunk onto the softness of her bed that embraced him and he fell asleep. Here now, he wished to sleep with her and his mind was already reaching half way; he was overcome by thoughts that censored his actions, which had been genuine the night before. What a tragedy in the sense of wasted efforts to have love made enjoyable for two well-matching partners!

He saw Anne's face. Her words still reverberated in his mind: We do not have much time! Then, as he thought back, he noticed that out of five years of a stealthy relationship, three years remained most memorable ones: The first year as an opening with many discussions and agreeing about the rules, the second, as a timid love but a promising start with interest of meeting in real life, the third, to transfer virtual love into reality. The fourth year was a highlight of twenty days and one of fucking and being in heaven all the time. In the fifth year she suffered a decline of her sexual powers and was fading away physically. Then there was the shock of her untimely death, like that of an infant. This was the reason why he was almost mad about Nimis. How could she resist a good loving? Did she not see it, or didn't she feel it? Did she not need it anymore? Can't she share her emotions equally with women and men?

His eyes already tiring, have begun shedding tears as he writes. He needs to apply eye drops immediately. His erection does still function most mornings and he can be off to a sexual height quite easily, stimulated by the appearance of her sweet face, but would she care about that? He has given up on her a few times now, after she had avoided to sleep with him and now what has she got? More desire? To him it was like an outcry of his own fear of his libido's loss and the last clasp to a woman, named NIMIS, but then she hopefully will remain a friend.

He had wished her to become his lover, but she isn't a woman who could deal with clandestine love, perhaps. Then, what about her visits to her women friends? Of course, it had to be discreet. That's all, everything else will destroy too much and he sees now the values of it, as she had first-hand experience. He thinks: I have been spoilt by the dedication of Anne, who was there for me daily. But unfortunately in the apex of his sexual love with her, she vanished amidst tears that tore his heart into two; but still it could be saved and mended. Something of a good surgical suture by other skilled hands still remained, he could be pasted together again and looking for a soulmate. One, who matches with oneself is always difficult to find. Will he ever find another one?

Facing the death throes of a beloved one, the lover will be on the procrustean bed of his pains; pains that arise as he is incapable of doing anything to save her, as love has ceased to be possible and the only healing available. Perhaps compassion will serve as soothing strokes to the heart, intact at periodical states of her consciousness.

14

Then, as coma sets in, he is already far away, due to his commitments and his traveling, which raises his desperation, rendering it that much greater, without the slightest means at his disposal to have been of help, although he muses about the fact of having felt the need of being present at her death bed. Would that have helped? He has a bad conscious that he isn't present. In the throes of his inner struggle, her soul-sister's voice would still rebound in him: "It is better if you don't come, remember her as she was rather." Indeed, the last image of her remained the strongest, as he can see her still up and writing, her first cousin present; she would be on her feet, acting prolific and even smile, as her cousin says: "Could you read a poem for me?" Addressing him with curiosity in her eyes. And as he starts, Anne says: "But that is personal."

"Well, all my poems are personal." He says selecting one with less graphic descriptions of lovemaking. When he finishes, her cousin says: "Lucky person for whom this poem was written, awaiting him to reveal his lover. Anne just scribbles on and he is asked by her cousin to read another. Finally she asks him for his typed manuscript and she reads all the poems, devouring them, visually stirred by emotion. "She likes your poems," Anne says at the same time, as she thinks the same. "I will do now an unusual thing…"- he leaves the sentence unfinished thinking about taking the two women to bed. That certainly would ease the apparent sexual tensions. After all we are partners in crime. But he does not say that aloud. Her cousin looks at him with beady eyes and swallows hard. Suddenly she gets up and leaves for the kitchen.

And now the year has ended and Anne is still vivid on his mind, so much as he will not need a video clip of her to recall the way she moved and smiled.

Sometimes he wishes to sedate his emotional life that kept pitching-up his innermost and let her go for good. After all, she said good-bye to him already and without saying the words like in a movie, she enticed him to make love to her. While it was already physically painful to her, to him emotionally. He didn't imagine such a shocking sexual love ending some months ago.

Now he has already said 'Happy New Year' to Nimis, wishing to have spoken to her at least. He was emotional and he couldn't. He doesn't know where she is and he is not feeling happy to reach her at a place and a time disadvantageous to her. He senses that she would like him to be single, so he would be eligible for her. He, on the other side, wishes to be free from obligations, the best way to love and live, as Anne had taught him. The storm is over at the old year and a new one will be in the making again. And Nimis, what about Nimis?

*

Gargoyles

His mobile phone rang. "Guten Tag, mein Freund, ja!" Glens laughed as he conversed with the German words he practiced every time he called him.

"Guten Tag," he replied "Have you finally come to tell me you are building a house?"

"Not yet," he said, "but I am with a client who needs some ideas for an alteration of her roof."

"Well, if it's a challenge and I'm paid, I'll do it."

"She's close to your home, Zarco." Glens concluded, dictating him Sandra's ten digit mobile number.

He struggled with his short story's angle, he needed to finish for a writing competition, when he recalled to call Sandra. He left his mobile phone number on her answering service. Ten minutes later she called back. Her voice had a slight twist ending nouns and sentences. She sounds like a trendy, fashionable with-it artist-amazon, he thought. She agreed to see him in an hour's time.

He arrived at Twenty-First Street and searched for number 69. His mind reduced the numbers: fifteen, six, he mused. A game he learned from a former Muse. Six sounds like sex. His mind played games of sexual positions, he saw in a French movie the night before. He parked his Merc 124 in the shade of a plane tree and waited. Halfway through, writing a poem to his new Muse, she appeared in her turmeric-yellow sports Merc. A Mercedes lover also, he noted.

She opened the plain steel door by remote control and he walked behind her car into the narrow driveway. She stepped from the low seat of the sports sedan by the time he caught up with her.

"Hi," she tensed-up, her face showed stress. She unlocked the entrance door and he stepped behind her into the lounge. "Sorry about the mess," she said," I have been busy at my shop." She moved ahead in her tight red hip jeans. He noticed her slender hips, unusual for a woman in her late forties and he enjoyed moving behind her, as she led the way around her house with an artistic feel in the interior decoration

"I like your unusual environment," he said absorbing the natural look of a brick wall, steel frames with cut-in patterns for a huge mirror. She noticed his interest

"I am eclectic in my taste," she said opening the glazed double steel door from her dining area. Water from three spouts tumbled into cone shaped receptacles filled with brown pebble stones, cooling the air. The splattering noise soothed the mind. The wall at the back, entirely framed with steel angles and steel mesh, held the brown rounded pebbles like a riverbed run dry.

"A bit of a contemporary Alhambra, he said and glanced at her as she turned.

"I like natural steel, as decay changes its surface." The rusty streaks, usually avoided by popular designers, Sandra used in a new aesthetic movement that emphasized the natural beauty of industrial products without conservation. "Your stone wall relaxes the mind, as one can meditate here," he commented watching her reaction, "even the colours of stone and rusty steel complement each other." Sandra smiled. She continued to show him around.

They passed the huge mirror framed in a wide welded steel frame, with cut-in flower decorations, hung on a natural brick wall, its plaster scratched off. He observed the cut steel frames with lines that appeared darker like scars of inflicted wounds on the skin of iron, covered with scales of brown rust. Further to the left of the yard, Sandra had placed two bouquets of twisted iron rods that appeared like a forgotten bunch of flowers, a lover had left behind.

Sandra fitted into the environment of rusting reeds and stained brown pebbles with the natural painter: Rust on a high roll, has chosen her as a Muse. It had invaded her environment at the periphery of her unusual domicile. Sandra appeared as an alert Amazon, sharp, without cutting him up, pointed, without piercing him. A woman with a deep throbbing artistic vein, without drowning anyone who disliked her evocative choices of decoration.

The fascination with her environment set his artistic half into an instant life, he could not control. Dissolving from his body, it presented itself for discussion and an artistic debate to face her. "Zippo," his artist-half said and stretched out a hand. "Nice meeting you Zippo," she took his hand and her curious brown eyes passed down his body. As he felt her scrutinizing his body, his spirit walked with Zippo and disappeared into the pebble-wall to take on a body of brown pebbles and rusted iron. She floated to the slotted mirror frame and her artistic self disappeared through the slots into the depth behind. Zippo followed her through a flower slot.

"It's an unusual name," she said.

"Yes, it's related to fire and lighters," he laughed.

"How come?" She tilted her head.

"It's the way I paint my inflamed pictures."

"You like fires?" She stepped back.

"Well, let's say my spirit does." She eyed him with big mystical curiosity that resembled her black iridescent Burmese cat, who watched her movements with huge green eyes.

Self-assured and restless, Sandra moved ahead and stepped through a glazed steel door that led to a wooden decking around a plunge pool. She stood in the semi-shade with a ray of sunshine crossing her face in a band that illuminated her hazel eyes. A tinge of sensuality flicked through her gaze, as if she could suddenly read his mind, while he thought of her emerging from the bedroom next door in the nude, taking her invigorating dip. He saw her slender figure and her well-shaped breasts, as she stretched and dived coming up for air. She pushed water from her mouth and breathed in pushing herself-up on the edge of the timber deck, her nipples hard points on the discs of brown areolas. He thought of the brown pebbles, the rusted colours, and he related them as the basic design element. He would crown the sectional elements of the wooden garage doors with them. A half-smile appeared on her profiled lips, her fingers touched his by accident, as she moved them across the layouts of her house with the proposed changes.

Step by step the figures of Zippo and Sarah returned from the slots in the mirror frame hung on the rough brick wall. Swoosh, swoosh, they danced like ghosts wafting through the space between their seated bodies and the brown wet pebbles in the stone wall with the three water features.

"I like your Chinese cupboard," Zarco said as his fingers ran along the highly polished dark-grey lacquer with white decorations of flowers and leaves, highlighted on the lacquered surface.

"I'm an eclectic person, Zarco," Sandra said moving to the main bedroom. The white floor in a cement finish, decorated with a darker band around her king-sized bed, felt like a marble floor to the feet.

"It must be nice to bare feet," Zarco said, as he imagined her walking barefoot on it. Sandra looked at him with her half-smile, he interpreted as not too interested in him physically at that moment. He felt though that she as a sensual woman might be interested in any individualistic beings, men or women.

The bedroom ceilings resembled white painted cement boards above a white exposed timber support. The industrial character became aesthetically acceptable through its structure masked with a layer of white paint. A glazed section at the gable end let natural light deeper into the space. The glare, absorbed in the matt white paint of the ceiling, bounced back as a pleasant natural illumination.

"Well," he said, "I like the stark arctic white against the dark brown-purple of the bathroom walls." She smiled.

"One could disappear in the bathroom," she turned into artist model Sarah again, circling her index finger for him to follow her. He turned into Zippo and followed her into the bubbling Jacuzzi. "Ahh, how wonderful you look, Sarah." She descended onto his lap, a goddess, born from the rusting steel and floating on the purple foam.

"The stair must go," Zarco said.

"Whereto?" she replied and frowned.

"It's like a knife, cutting through the heart of your carapace you retreat into." He moved his hand as if he would emphasize the slashing of someone with a knife.

"Swoosh, swoosh," the sound of slashing blew from his lips. "I think it supposed to be against a wall," he said and paced through the room to find a position.

"That's what the Feng Shui-man said as well," she retorted with excited eyes at him having touched this crucial point. The art of placement of objects and elements seemed to be touching them both.

"Sure," he said, "placement art is always worth listening to." She nodded. "I'll show you the rooms upstairs." She spoke while she moved up on the wooden treads in her elegant way, swinging her hips slightly. He watched her rhythmic gait, his aesthetic and artistic other half emerged at her side. He gazed at her back. Her hip-slacks slid down and showed her smooth skin and when her pants pulled tight around her flexing legs. And he stared at her well-shaped bums.

"See?" Zippo said "She is sexy, no?" The voice said aloud and it sounded like a dialogue with her. She turned, smiling at him and climbed the stair. "This stair needs maintenance work, Sarah," he said.

"Indeed," Sarah replied "the stair must be sanded down," she turned at the landing. "The floor gave-in." She frowned. He bounced up and down on the flexing timber.

"Not much support," he said. Sarah looked frightened.

"Yes, it's all rotten," she carried on showing him the two small bedrooms.

"Indeed," he said and recalled the playful note of a colleague teasing him with sparkling eyes: "We have to do more research, Zarco!"

"Yes," he replied and looked into the play of her eyes shooting off sparks as an invitation to a pleasurable game. His mind memorized Sandra's walk up the stair, as he intended to find a typical movement, emphasizing her character. In time it'll come to him, like a poem, or a piece of prose writing. Given respite, while it will percolate through his artistic filters, the concept's creation will take shape: A painting first, as she's definitely a model for more than a poem, or a short story later perhaps? Or whatever his creative delving would be.

He looked at her well-shaped breasts she pushed them out, opening the door and he waited for them popping out at the top, as she stretched back waiting for him to touch them. He was mesmerized by her beautiful figure. She is my client, he thought, how would I continue? He felt

22

tempted to touch Sandra, but then all would be finished for the business. She might refuse my advances if I take the goose now and loose the golden eggs, she would stop working with me and I would have to resign from the job. I would lose a good opportunity proving my artistic talent and furthermore I would lose out on a necessary income.

It's sex or income, make your choice Zippo, he talked to himself aloud, as she emerged from the mirror frame's leafy slots. He grinned. "Damn you Zippo," he could clearly hear his voice, as his other half became jealous of him being so close to Sarah, while he had to watch. She smiled as he looked up from observing the aching floor-boards as their eyes met and he returned her shining gaze.

He had dealt with business women before. Tricky, he thought, as she asked for a quotation for his work. "I have to go," she moved down the wooden stair. He followed her, less enticed as on the way up. He packed the floor plans and his sketches and left. He mused about his multi-layered impressions, as he moved outside her house along the tight driveway, bewitched, intrigued, along a path to artistic impressions in architecture, some-thing that had evaded him for a long time. Since he had taken up writing poetry, meeting his Muse, his other half. No other woman had called him: My Man.

He took his digital camera snapping pictures. The black cat with mesmerizing green eyes appeared in front of him, watching him from a safe distance. The mannerism of Sandra's fingers, her intonation of words, stretching the last syllable of nouns, resembled the cat's moves. Her slick movements as she walked between an array of liz-ards, reptiles, and snake replicas in wood, metal or stone.

23

She kept them on parquet floors, concrete floors, and around the house on the dark timber decking around the plunge pool.

The cool colours of her bedroom represented her main character: The innocence of her spiritual soul attacked by the darker side of her brown-purple artistic nakedness. Zippo could see her: One half dressed in a deep purple leotard with slots and cuttings in the stretch fabric, to show her delicate porcelain skin. The other side on her left, with the bleeding heart of an artist, denuded from the cloth. Drops of magenta dripped from her heart down to her thighs like tears.

The black and white figure reminded him of soulmates, the matching 'other half' – The Dionysian versus the Apollonian spirit – darkness against light, positive thoughts against negative ones. He attempted to stretch the list of contrasts forever in the same breath as he admired her bathroom contrasting with her bedroom; her dark grey and silver Chinese cupboard against the rough brick face and the rusted slotted steel framed mirror.

He returned the second time with an engineer, whose comments he listened to in accordance with his conceptual design. CC, the engineer, knew the place from the previous owner. While he talked about general matters with Sandra, Zarco took some pictures with his digital camera. Some he captured with her portrait at the edge of the frame. He behaved like her Burmese cat pawing around a bowl of milk. He felt not superior to CC and his former knowledge that invaded his delicate relationship with Sandra wouldn't bother him. Feeling challenged by CC, the engineer and Glens, the builder, he thought that she would still place him above them as her choice of artist. Zarco made it clear to her that she intrigued him and he wanted her. Would she consent at the end of the job? Her Burmese cat broke the ice, as she sniffed first at his lowered fingers and then his feet, before it crawled up and moved behind his seat and then settled behind his ears on his shoulders. Sandra took it off him into her arms and it snuggled at her breasts curling around her. She looked at him and Zarco felt as if Sandra, who cuddled the cat, would cuddle him in this sensual act of intimacy. Then CC, who was a cat lover, cuddled the cat, but rougher than Zarco did, who it preferred to snuggle up to, and then CC left. Sandra talked to Zarco reflecting on his ideas.

The condensate water on the glass of cold water stained the moss-green painted surface of the wooden table top. He wiped the run off drops with one hand and moped them up with a tissue from his pocket. Her strong sinewy fingers touched his, as he sketched for her his idea of a new elevation. A partly finished torso hung across a mirror at the entrance. Sandra's? Her sculpted fingers gave it away. He began to love her physiognomy. He wondered how she moved when she made love. The door to her bedroom stood open, but he could be wrong with all his assumptions about her. Was she out to be excited in role playing? Possess and being possessed, but given a chance she would ride him. Being a business-woman made her tough. Is it now all about commands and orders? He mused. However he had to chuckle inside, with his poetic descriptions of her 'Jewellery box-home, she glowed, he was literary at present in the driving seat.

"It's late, I must be going," she exclaimed suddenly, "I'm opening a shop in Pretoria." She gasped. He still wanted to keep her for a while, fascinate her with his story. They talked on. He told her about writing a book with its hero being an artist. He wanted always to become an artist. Through her inspiration, his love for painting surfaced suddenly stronger than ever.

"Your space is inspirational to me!" He concluded: "On a quest finding my 'Other half', I made a step forward, realizing my artistic calling through the genre of painting." He finished with her, packing his sketches into his X-clusive Books' plastic bag. He rose. "I'll give you a call." He left.

He arranged a meeting with Glens, who wanted Sara to be present, but Zarco told him that this meeting would be only informative. He outlined the scheme to Glens, but he sensed that he wouldn't talk about Sandra with him. No personal matters. All chit-chat with Glens would do nothing more than wedge a rift of doubt between himself and Sandra. Somehow another story unfolded, as Glens started to mention another woman, he also knew from a previous job. Glens used her as a metaphor and Zarco would add two and two together.

"Jody had an operation, did you know?" Glens spoke with a stern face. "I wasn't aware of that," he replied, "is it a serious matter?" He looked at Glens, whose face coloured pink, as if he would have caught him red-handed with another man's wife. Glens turned into a steel-chameleon and placed himself on the new façade of Zarco's design, just below the roofline. He looked magnificent.

"Yes," he gulped, as his face coloured to a darker pink.

"Gore hit her and broke her jaw." He averted his eyes.

"Impossible," Zarco said, but nurtured his curiosity, enticing Glens to spill out more. Glens finished his tale with details and the two yearlong shaky relationship with Jody and her violent hubby, Gore. Zarco realized that he heard this story from the third viewpoint already: Spouse, wife, and lover. Eyeing Glens as he talked, once set onto his track as a stealthy lover, he couldn't be stopped. Glens switched-on like a cross-country runner, took short cuts, and telling half-truths. He could hide all his personal drama behind his stories; yet bragging indirectly about his sexual prowess.

"You are getting older, Glens," he said and watched the fired-up tradesman turned builder.

"Memory fails first and then slowly the other lower human compartments." –

"No!" Glens protested, as if Zarco hurt his pride that lay between his thighs..."the department down there is still in good working order."

Zarco smiled as he sketched in his mind all characters that sprung from the art of a sculptor, assembling steel scrap metal welded together. Create a set of animal, he could use as gargoyles and depict the story in fixing them to the corners of Sandra's house. He had ignored all the chit-chat before, but now the rusty steel animals became alive.

He recalled the chameleon, where Glens sprung from, just about Sandra's bedroom. He pointed at the rusted buckled figure: "I use these as protective elements to your house, extending lizards, crocs, and mambas."

He showed Sandra their positions, watching her smirk, comparing her to her cat. Yes, he would fix her to a corner too. He turned CC into a bristly gnome, Gore into a dragon, Glens into the confused knight, the gardener into a chameleon. What would he be, the invisible scribe, living in the decorative cuts of her steel mirror frame watching her dinner guests?

If Sandra turned into the slick lizard on her table, he would join her as the other lizard. Lazing in the sun and lying on top of each other at times of inner heat.

The third time he came to see her, she did not appear. He parked his car under her plane tree and waited. Then the gardener appeared. He finished his writing: Seeking Anna. Assuming her to be at home, he dialled her mobile number. She opened the gate and he rushed to the entrance door. She received him dressed in her gym gear. Her tight pants showed off her slim figure, her top zipped-up, kept her generous breasts in check.

"Sorry I'm late," he said. Sandra looked pale without her make-up. He noticed her dark brown eyes. This is Sandra natural, he mused, observing her bums as she moved ahead of him. She wants me to concentrate on her body parts, she knows I would admire, he thought. Well, she had succeeded.

"You came for the plans?" He nodded and she confirmed "I have phoned the former architect for the originals, but the firm has none."

"Sloppy indeed," he murmured, "usually one approved copy has to be kept."

"This is the only copy I have," she spread the drawing onto the parquet floor. "Please don't lose them, otherwise I am left with nothing."

"I'll copy them and bring them back to you." He looked at the paper prints on the floor she'd left spread out.

"I have a busy morning here," she said "we are painting the chairs."

"It's a nice colour," he commented, "like magenta, indeed." The stocky woman painting her chairs moved the brush irritated being observed, spraying dots of oil paint across Sandra's only plan copies.

"Oh Gosh!" Sandra rose checking her track suit for paint. He followed suit.

"I'm sorry," said the stocky woman with a frown. Strange character, Zarco thought, obviously her friend.

"Do you want to talk to me?" Sandra said, and as he nodded, she moved. "Let's go over here." She pointed to the soft couch opposite her TV-wall. The cupboard with a curved shape and brushed steel elements suited her natural style. He called it 'Punk interior style'.

"No cat here today?" His hands probed the cover. He sat down and spread his sketch from the upper floor.

"I found a solution for your staircase," he said, rose, and she followed. He stopped at the steel door that opened to her wooden decking surrounding the plunge pool. "Here," he said and pointed his hands to describe physically the position to her.

"I see," she cooed, "Yes, I like it!"

"It's the best place, my gut-feel tells me. I took time to consolidate all ideas and overrule the spots recommended before. I am convinced now!" He moved back to the soft settee and checked the plan on the table against the position he had described.

"You'd like some coffee?"

"Yes, I like some," he followed her to the open kitchen.

"I have no milk," she said.

"Don't bother, black is fine." He sipped his coffee immediately, while he explained to her the proposed upper floor layout. "OK," she said.

"I draw it up like this," he concluded.

"Let's have a party then." She stretched.

"Well, I'm sure it's still too early."

"It's never early for a celebration…have a drink meanwhile, all's there on the sideboard. Please help yourself, I'll go and change."

After his second drink a man arrived, dusky and well dressed. He introduced himself: "I'm Sandra's ex."

"I am Zarco, her architect." Sandra came down the stair. She greeted her former husband like a friend. "Let me show you the new design, Fred." Sandra unrolled the originals from Zarco's protective carrier and explained roughly the scheme. Fred seemed to have little interest, but once Sandra had finished, he asked her what she would like to drink. "Gin and tonic, two ice." Fred came back with the drinks, while Zarco rolled the drawings together again. "I must say," Fred started suddenly, "the design is unusual and original, certainly better than the scheme of the other architects."

"My husband is old-fashioned as far as houses are concerned." Sandra frowned. "However, I think it'll be just great." She smiled. "Cheers," we toasted to each other. More guests arrived and soon the cold and hot buffet as well, one of Sandra's associates had organized.

The party was in full swing and he noticed through the lounge window that Sandra had an argument with her husband outside. Somebody came to refresh my drink. I had enough and wanted to go.

When Sandra returned, she had another drink and walked about chatting to some friends. As she came across Zarco, she asked him if he could check out a new formed structural gap behind her bedroom wall. Zarco followed her upstairs. On top she turned suddenly and kissed him. Zarco kissed her back, but felt suddenly weak in his knees. He told Sandra. "It's not from kissing, is it?" she laughed. "No, I think it's the drink…"

"I hope it's not that darned…" Zarco did not hear her last words any longer, as he collapsed onto her bed. Sandra closed the door and walked down to the kitchen to check on her associate who made the catering arrangements.

"Hello Sandra," her right hand associate greeted her, "we just ran out of drinks."

"Well, let's close-up, I want to turn in."

"Have you taken him upstairs?"

"Don't be silly, he felt ill, somebody must have spiked his drink."

"Nonsense. Let's have one for the road," Hilda, her associate said. Sandra felt flushed after the drink. "My god Hilda, you have a heavy hand!"

"Well, whose glass is this?"

"I don't know." Sandra sniffed at the drink. "It smells potent!"

"Let me taste it," Hilda said and took a swig. "Not bad, it would be a pity to waste." She downed the drink. Ten minutes later she ripped her clothes off and jumped into Sandra's small deck-pool outside.

"Come on Sandra, the water is fair." Just as Sandra took off her clothes and prepared to join her, Zarco arrived from upstairs. "Come join us, you'll need some waking up." Sandra laughed.

"Thank you, I'd love to, but it's late."

"Well, have a short jump-in then." Suddenly Hilda seemed to be unwell and collapsed. Sandra called for help. Zarco held her up and they both rescued her from drowning. "We have to lay her on the couch," Sandra said. Zarco fetched a bedcover and they laid her on it. Together they pulled her into the nearby lounge. "it must have been her drink," Sandra murmured.

"Tell me about it," Zarco said.

"But you recovered."

"I stopped in time, as I noticed that it affected my vision. I had one black beer and felt sick, but collapsed afterwards." Somebody rang the bell outside.

"Who the hell could that be at this late hour?" Sandra checked the spy hole. "It's the neighbour." She opened the door. Meanwhile Hilda recovered too and Zarco brought her a glass of cooled water to drink. After some sips she went back to sleep.

"What happened?" He asked.

"Let's have some coffee," Sandra said "and I'll tell you later." Zarco phoned his spouse to let her know that he was a guest at his client's residence and would not be driving home tonight. On intuition, he took Sandra up to her other bedroom and they made love languidly. In the morning Sandra had made already breakfast, the coffee and croissants tasted just wonderful. He felt good and thanked her for the night.

"We would not have given up making love just for these damned KO-drops, would we?" She said.

"Oh you found out?"

"My husband did, as I asked him to check your glass, you and Hilda drank from."

"And the culprit?"

"Damned Matilda, one of my business associates, who disliked your plans. The KO-drops that matched your glass were inside her handbag they found lost in the park across the road. No idea what happened to her. It's Africa," she concluded philosophically.

"I'm glad we are alive." I kissed her good-bye, said hello to Hilda and drove to my studio.

*

Seeking Simone

"If I could pour my heart out to you," she says and he senses her sad mood that floods her heart now, "I could cry with you," she continues and his eyes gather moisture in their corners. Her sadness has transgressed into him. He is unhappy, but he tries to hide this time his feelings from her. He wishes her to be happy, but how? Then he remembers the friend she had before, she had told him about, and who became possessive of her. He elbowed himself between her feelings she had for her girlfriend. That made her unhappy. "He took away my happiness," she told him at the beginning of their friendship. "I will never take away your happiness," he answered, as she looked at him with her big dusky eyes that shone in the evening light. "That's how," he thought by himself, "that's how I could keep her reasonably balanced and joyful. Indeed! AyAy, his passed away friend and Muse reborn, all over again. Then he made a mental note to refresh his memory with more research into amphisexual behaviour.

He isn't concerned about her being loved by another woman. It's better than messed about by suppression and losing her complex nature. He says nothing, just listens to her enjoying her presence and getting drifted away into a pleasant feeling, by the way she appears to him as a natural sensuous woman. She is good for him, as she is relaxed with her and he relates to her. She would listen to what he has to say and she leaves him the same room he'll need for his creativity, to emerge onto the innocent sheets of paper, he fills with symbols and letters to her.

Suddenly, some fear had gripped his heart like an ice-cold hand someone stretches out to take, as a sign of friendship. He has taken the hand and it was like ice in this immediate shock that has to be absorbed on behalf of more important personal values than that unfortunate physical imbalance.

How much is Simone involved into underground work? How much does she know about urban terrorism? He has picked-up on a theory that, as it will be created by those power structures that rule the world, in order to stay number one against the secondary forces, we are all to be made pawns, bystanders and onlookers sharing the guilt of blood as a collective.

He recalls his friend's lectures about the late Middle Ages, when Vienna was on the verge of being taken the third time by Turkish forces of Sultan Suleiman. Of course they have heard about this decisive battle for the dominance of Europe, every scholar has learned about in secondary education. However, fate had decided against the half-moon then and Europe prospered as a basically Christian stronghold. That's why we are here now, Leon, his friend and helpful engineer would jokingly refer to, every time he saw him. And they had to laugh that freed them from their thoughts of another type Europe, which Leon painted in gruesome colours being a staunch believer of Judeo-Christianity. He misses his pranks and restlessness for some time now. Finally, when he phoned his home, his son was on the phone: "My father passed away last Friday."

He wished to know from Simone about her involvements into structures and forces that swept the underground below our feet of consciousness and determine our future. But, she would be taciturn, say nothing. I have patience, he thinks, but I cannot stand Simone's silence for the long run. And how could he get closer to her? She keeps him at arm's length from table and bed. He has appealed to her intelligence and he got euphemism. He has applied to her artistic side and he drew a lemon. Then he wrote her letters and poetry and he thought that he could approach her heart. Perhaps he did, but she would not show the slightest enthusiasm. There's a lack of communication with her, different to the way he used to communicate with his last Muse. This isn't a continuation of his interactions with AyAy, his past counterpart and sounding board in the world of letters.

This is a completely new ball game, or what game will it be? Perhaps that game with a feathered ball? One has to hit hard to get bit through the air, whistling past the opponent's ears, but at times it would need delicate treatment at the net to topple over the net, onto the opponent's side. This is a story that leaves him suddenly stranded for three days out of seven, stranded in the big city. He draws his mind to other matters on hand: Art and beauty, architecture and building, painting and poetry. And he sets out to find the links that supposed to lift him above the grounds of reality, he dislikes, as he cannot consolidate his imagined world with the world outside his being, wishing continually to create it the way he sees it to be right.

He wakes in the middle of the night. He is wide awake and after he had made himself a cup of tea, always available in hotel rooms, he sits up in bed and takes his notebook and ink pen starting off in a flash:
I woke in the middle of a Saturday night. I felt warm and excited. I switched on the night light above my head. This wasn't a dream. The noises of coupling next door recalled a scene in my mind. I envisaged the desired lovemaking with Simone; I had formed in my mind for some time. I wanted her, but more than that, she gave me little opportunity to partake with her feelings, she held back for some other reason. On the other hand, she also missed the

chance to let me show her my pent-up side of feelings I harboured for her.

There was a deep vein of erotic richness that flowed through this mountain of desire rising in me. I came prepared to be with her in any way love extracted from me, to bring that across to her. But she was not here. The grunts and coos next door increased to a climax. The woman cried-out in sweet agony, a prolonged sound of pleasure bordering on pain. I thought of Symi and one of her friends she had described to me with an indicative style. I thought of them to make passionate love, maybe even be asked to partake, but yet was excluded by this plate glass wall between them and me. I had been punished just to listen and view. I felt though part of this lovemaking. A feeling of rising warmth pulsated through me. I wondered why Symi decided not to be with me and miss out on a good chance of a lifetime. But perhaps I had great expectations like everybody else. Though, we matched certainly more closely as many who made love tonight, besides us, who missed-up on this chance. I was a normal and healthy person in love; I would even please her with whatever she found fulfilling. Was I in love? I was in more than one way attracted to Simone; I wanted to be in love with her. Something just moved between her expressions about this barrier and me to overcome it, of course. I felt to break this barrier down, bit for bit. But then, how does one remove a barrier gently, without the noises and the dust?

I suffered the disappointment of her promises, she made in the initial moments of our conversations on our mobile phones: "I'll see you during the weekend. Phone me tomorrow at one."

She phoned me before I had a chance to dial her number: "Where are you?" She always asked that. Why was she so keen to know my movements? I told her truthfully.

I could have lied to her, but that's not my way of meeting a woman I am fond of. This was an adventure for me as much as it was for her routine. I sensed it: "Meet me at the station in …and she rattled down the descriptions of trains, stations, and routes. Finally we agreed at Richmond station, we settled a time. Usually she chose the afternoon. Simone was not usually keen to be somewhere early morning. Perhaps she had many personal matters at hand to deal with. Now, as she had shown interest of meeting me more often as she originally intended, I felt an analysis of my consciousness, stating: "Fly back to 'Jozy' earlier, GO!" I panicked, as I had suddenly these mixed feelings, controversial and unexpected. I turned in my bed, having fallen asleep again in between noting down my thoughts into my journal, I had bought at the British Museum showing the Portland Vase as a high point in art and beauty.

It was now quiet next door. Stillness. I looked at my watch: It was ten to five in the morning. It was the 12th of June. I had met Simone at Richmond. She had phoned me on my cellular phone: "I'll be late a bit, stuck in traffic."

"All right," my replies were laconic. I knew I could love Simone the way she imagined, the way it would make her cry-out with pleasure. But Simone wanted her man to be free. But is freedom not in the mind? The past did certainly count to some degree, but then, nobody is really free. Was Simone not possessed by the love her girlfriend could evoke in her? Simone had an aversion to be possessed by anybody and I recalled having heard that from AyAy before. I just wished to love her.

The train station at Richmond looks like most stations of the National transport system. I place my ticket into the validating machine and exit to the hall. I dislike waiting outside the station. The hall is a gathering point of arriving and leaving persons: A boy fetched by his mother, a girl-friend by her girlfriend. Maybe a lover by a lover, all lined-up now like sheep to catch a bus or take a taxi. My phone rings: "I am here," she announces and I step outside to see her at the opposite side, as she waves me from her opened window of a sleek silvery car I recognize, as most people in position will drive. An independent woman, filled with vitality, adventure and talented, no doubt, even if she is projecting somebody she is not, but whom?

Who is Simone? Is it wealth she wants? It's love, is it? She opens the central locking system of the doors and I step inside her comfortable air-controlled driving world. I greet Simone and bend over to kiss her cheeks in a sign of friendship, which she accepts fleetingly. This time I kiss her three times, "like the French do," I say to her. "Yes," she says and smiles. A mysterious smile. She has mag-netism and is attractive, drives suddenly off with pa-nache. She is a skilful driver. But how could I break the barrier down to reach her as a person? How could our budding friendship be enhanced? I have to think of the couple from last night making love. How could lovemak-ing be enhanced time after time? How may we enter love and then keep it alive?

While I watch her profile, the slightly protruding upper lip, the fleshly lower lip seems to be in constant dialogue with the dominating upper lip that keeps it in check. I wish to touch her lips and arouse a sensual response in her. I certainly feel that Simone is passionate. Then I think of rather stepping a bit back. This is dangerous. I could not emerge out of this relationship unscathed. This would be a trifle too much for my tested heart at present.

I feel waves of desire for her, but let it all slip. The con-scious mind jogs along. It's made a sucker for such situ-ations. I let my feelings stand in front of my being and I enjoy these moments with Simone. I could not care about the others, I'm feeling self-assured and in control of my-self. It is strange and she says: "What did you do?" Simone starts the conversation, while she zips along the roads, well-known to er. She's a keen driver, as if she would be professionally involved being a constant mover. I tell her a bit about myself, bits that come to my mind and may be of common interest. I observe her neckline and then her body. My eyes scan her appearance, her fine fingers that grip the wheel, profiled, slim and sinewy, plucking away on me, as if she would steer my body movements. I shift in my seat. I feel warm. Kew Gardens, I read a road sign. I notice the wall of the Botanical Garden. She drives down to the river. There are boats on the Thames, just like on the century old depiction that hangs on my wall at the hotel. The shape of the boats has changed together with the attire of the crowds. The atmosphere remained.

Her favourite pub is filled to capacity and she drives on slowly. Then further down, she parks her silver arrow. Close to a side-arm to the river. The water level is low due to the damming of the river arm. We walk alongside the river bank on a path that winds down alongside pretty residences. I keep my arm around Simone's shoulders. At times she touches my fingers. Then we walk as if we wish to find a place forlorn enough to stop and I wish to kiss her, but there's always something that comes as a hindrance to the intimate act. At an overhung tree I stop her, kissing her on an impulse. I want her now, but she carries on restlessly. She avoids slowing down, stopping and letting me express my feelings with kissing her. She isn't ready yet. "I want to feel your hand in mine," I say to her as she walks now on my left side. I take her right hand that feels warm. It feels good. We both enjoy this human warmth. We walk quietly hand in hand for a while. I am getting heated-up, my palms moistened-up slowly. At that point we reach the Crown & Bull, the pub, we have been to a drink for the first time we met. It seems to be familiar to us now. I wait for Simone to join me as soon as she finished with a visit to the lady's room. She must have a busy social life. She takes a while, perhaps she answers a phone call. I sit down in a corner that reminds me of a Whistler painting's atmosphere. I tell her as she reappears. We sit behind the lead-lined glass windows in the diffused light of a late afternoon. I ordered sandwiches, prawn with Marie-sauce. The taste is delicious; she wolves her sandwich down, almost being careless. A spot appears on her white skirt. Is she nervous? I need excitement in my life and she tells me about her lover. Suddenly she starts telling me about her life from the age of sixteen. She is as much excited about love, as I am. I feel being involved with her intimately, but I have learned to distance myself quite fast, or do I wish I could, as it is another love she is infatuated with?

AyAy taught me to distance myself quite fast. She believed that it will eventually serve me as a base to be a good writer, but then I've always wondered why. We talk about our loves and Simone talks a lot today. I enjoy listening to her. She's compassionate to friends and passionate to her lovers: It has to come out, it has to come out eventually, she says and her hand is turned to a fist that hammers her chest, to show me her state of excitement.

"I am fond of you, Simone," I tell her. "I wish I had an opportunity to make love to you.

"I need someone like me," she says and her large eyes capture me, devour me, make me melt down and get weak in my knees. "I am here," I say. "But you are married," she replies. I am amazed she would wedge that between her and me now. It appears to me a good excuse for her Sapphic love to be concluded.

"Love has many layers," I continue. "Love is good in itself. We can love as long as nobody will be hurt. What's the point of being married or not?"

"I had 200 responses to my profile on the Internet," she says shining with her eyes. I wonder where I feature in the assessment of prospective lovers.

"I see," is all I am able to mutter, "but I would have been disappointed if it was only me who reacted to your ad!" She smiles. "You are an unusual man," she continues and I return the statement to her. I watcher hands. She has a beautiful ring on her left hand. "Turkish," she says. I admire the emerald set in between a heart-shaped white gold mesh embedded with small diamonds. "I have lots of rings," she says and I immediately have a picture of a woman that has an army of lovers surrounding her, for the pick of her choice, a female Sultan.

I sense that I have a handicap. She toils with my state of being married, although it's of no importance to her. She's dominant, demanding and she is rushing through life like a sudden breeze that catches the curtains in an open window, blowing a sail.

"I'll see you Monday then," she states as a matter of fact. "I have some appointments tonight." She pauses, then adds: "Perhaps if something will change, I could see you maybe tonight."

"Well, you could always phone me if you are free," I say dryly. "I have planned nothing much." She takes me in her silver arrow to the station entrance at Richmond. I recall the times of Virginia Wolf. I can see her oval shaped face, stirred-up with racing emotions, as she hurries along the station to catch a train to London, her dedicated husband trying to get her back. Then I recall her tenderness towards her girlfriend. Somehow this does not seem to fit to Simone. Strange, something is not fitting here: A square peg in a round hole?

The short and promising time of a walk that supposed to become the background to a budding intimacy, has now suddenly dropped away. It feels like the change of a stage in a play. Darkness has settled in for a while. Simone seems to be preparing for something else already, one of her choices out of the 200 responses?

"I was involved with a man, after Joe, my husband died. It was at first good, as he cared and loved me, but he was becoming very possessive, so I ended the relationship."

"You are dominant and strong," I carry on with the cue. "That's why I came to you." She looks at me with her huge dusky eyes that are an exaggeration to AyAy's eyes, doubting me. My romantic notions have been quashed. What did I expect? Coming to see her and she would instantly embrace me like a king? Yes! But it's different, she refuses to be involved yet. She has other reasons.

"I love good sex," I tell her. How should I know if she matches to me, if I cannot be with her in bed? She mentions my commitments, but then what does it matter in good sex? She seems to be the one who is possessive. Indeed. I get out of her car. We kiss as friends. OK. There's nothing more to this. I'm sad. She is sad for some reason too. What is this all about? She drives away in her usual zippy way. I see her as a successful business-woman, somebody who is above the purely emotional state, a harridan, or hetaerae? Cultivated, top class entertainment. I feel nothing. Empty. I walk to the train. I do not even write poetry as I used to. London does me no good, but I am fond of Simone. I am quaint and her company is pleasant. I seek her for that. This is a perfect duality, ambiguity, we poets feel more intense, being at home in its intricate web, being in a groove of creativity at the twilight of our fragile and exposed existence.

I enter the new hotel, I was given to move into, due to a snarl-up on booking a hotel nearby, whose friendly clerk arranged for me. I don't mind it's a nice place. There's a queen size bed that is wonderful, with a large window opposite that has curtains in French-blue. I take a shower and lie in the fresh white linen. It feels good. It's seven and Simone prepares for her social dinner. I send her a message: Wish you were here in this room, the wide bed, tonight! Then I sleep a bit. I wake at eight and she had not yet responded to my message. Well, somebody more interesting occupies her time, or he is better off than me.

Simone is demanding, a gatherer of wealth. I place my black Lee onto my naked body and the Nike weave-top, all black. I love black clothes, since I was in Athens. I go down to reception to ask for the internet code. The young lady receptionist does not know of it. She asks me though if I speak Hungarian, having come across my name. We enter into a lively conversation. I am ashamed that the vocabulary from my mother-tongue remained so poor. I battle for words; it's like my love for Simone: Shards, broken pieces, the story of my love-lives –
It's early in the morning, six o'clock. I feel stirred, wish to sleep some more if I could. I am stirred again. Simone stirs in me sexual feelings that melt into this calyx of an unusual love and I recall the famous poet's words, I read on the brass plaque in front of Westminster:
To carve out dials quaintly, point by point,
Thereby to see the minutes how they run:
How many makes the hour full complete,
How many hours brings about the day,
How many days will finish up the year,
How many years a mortal man may live.

How many days – just two of them left now to still see Simone? I wonder if she would feel what I can indicate to her, without falling all over her and eating her up pips and

43

kernel and all. Smack my lips dripping with her aromatic juices of life. How much do I want Symi, how much! In between these ancient walls of kings and priests I feel free, imprisoned only by the thoughts that fly in circles around her being, carving out the erotic image of her body, denude her with my magical notions, delightfully taking off her last piece of clothing, her champagne laced panties that still are hung on the ivory handle of a tall window. I hear the coupling noises, the panting, and the cries drowning in a sea of delight. It's unbearably hot, we burn, and the misting mirror reflects her face where my sticky hands touched it. Her eyes appear large and mysterious, her open lips suck me into her throat, her searching tongue, her oyster-lined thigh lets me slide and slide, as I have lost control. It's my end. I feel the millions of beatings that clock-up like a huge consummation, a mountain that'll burst for the body it holds, and the debris of this explosion will rain down onto the streets of London and cover people, buses, cabs and cars. The molten lava will rise and place even the Thames to a frozen standstill. A huge cake of a negative cast has been cooling off, and now it's lifted by magical machines off the mind and shrunk to a miniature toys. It's cast in endless procedures, day and night along the river, where we walk in Kent.

The souvenir shops are full with them and I buy one for Simone. "Merci beaucoup", she whispers and shows me her perfect row of ivory-white teeth that bite my heart to pieces, gently, steadily, like the dusky girl with huge dark eyes, chewing me rhythmically upon her gums, lips closed, moving sensually up and down, then opening them slightly just now and then. I feel a sensation, I felt with Simone before when she let me hold her hand. I am stirred and excited, gently, steadily, sweet like her kisses tasted when she kissed me. Once when we were alone, along the winding rive, somewhere between the romantic cottages embellished with garden gnomes and dwarfs and the fantasy world of this rich cultural sediment.

I stop at Westminster heading across the streets to the Abbey. It is though today closed for visitors. I walk around and come across the Jewel Tower, I just detected on my own. Then I take a walk along the banks of the Thames towards Tate and Clore. Ahh! Magnificent art!

Song without Words, Frederic Lord Leighton: The sorrowful woman in a loose top forgetting her uncovered breasts, longing for her lover. The servant-woman leaving, amber, wide-hipped, while her madam redlines with one foot below the other, touching her toes as if she would think of touching her distant lover, close to the gentle flow of water dispensing into a blue pot that reflects the colour of her richly draped skirt, the light-blue top almost a loose cover to her musing about love. Love and Death by G.F. Watts with a progress of the inevitable, but not terrible death, partially, but not completely overshadows love! Love with crushed wings vainly defends the House of Life. Death advances calmly, with a lowered head, trampling down the wild roses in its path, but avoiding stepping upon the dove's nest near his feet. Does this cast death in a more positive light? Is it the truth that dwells in the innermost?

Watts has painted his interpretation of themes I am most concerned about: Eve Repenting – she shall be called woman. Eve Tempted – the woman making music appears to be futile. It's a notion of despair, like being filled with love for somebody and one cannot merge, although one is so close to that love.

Love as Altruism and Compassion – but I had my share of that already. I wish I could live again. "Simone," said this voice in me, "don't turn into a laurel tree! The more I

45

undress you, the more you cover yourself with lush sprouting vegetation, along the winding river's banks.

I follow you from one room to another and hear your steps in front of me and along the river banks of the snaking flow of the Thames. I corner you in the Jewel Tower, but it's only your voice, telling me something about a possible meeting, but where?

In my restless sleep, I have torn off your dress and kissed you with fire, my hands running down your body to your thighs, spreading them gently apart.

I am reminded of Tudors and Stewarts, with portraits of unknown women, who show us their beauty and their power over men? I know you have powers over me, Simone, but then let it rest, have a day off and let me celebrate your beauty. Let me just for once adore you. There's much love I could give you and there' the way I know that'll lead to your heart.

I am tired of this pictorial pilgrimage to bodies and faces. I am seeking to be with you. My carapace will fail me, but my heart still beats for you. This is the sorrow of Zsolt- Werther, a married man, for a widow, but I am far from a physical suicide and I don't intend to jump into the Thames, as Paul did into the Seine. In what form are you appearing for me now? It's a material form, but in the image of transformation it turns into your spiritual form, or part-form: Shards, arms cut-off and lower limbs missing. You step forward in your soft-flowing night dress. I cannot see your head and limbs in a pitch-darkness, only an indication of your breasts and torso, your strong and bleached-out opening thighs –

'Unblemished by this love let me live, or die within it,
Perhaps even know, grant me honest fame and enticement
Of passionate love, or grant me none.'

46

Does Symi know about Pope, the poet?

Reading pope's statement at the Reynolds gallery in the Tate, looking up the evolution of man, I have to muse instantly: Like my love has started with a bean, one pixel added to another and then with the objects that did lie in the way – The pin, the needle in the fridge, the tube of vitamins, the tin-box clad in plush interior, the tube that shoots like a bullet through the belly of Mrs London.

Francis Bacon and the view of a woman in lust, her sex exposed I travel-up, I came from, back again. We all travel-up a woman, a man, once we have come-out of the tunnel. Die; go back into the funnel to enter the universe? This is painful and ugly, super naturalistic. I am still an aesthete at heart. The sculpted, near natural flesh, has its beauty and pictures of slaughtered and burned flesh are horrible deaths.

Piper's buildings with a human expressions, I quite relate easily to. Stone that cries-out and talks; stone that is man.

'All that is sold melts into air'. Karl Marx.
'All that is love solidifies, crystallizes from our air'. zoltanzelan.

Wadsworth's granite quarries, flow of stone in an architectural sense, the generation before me, aesthetic arrangers of natural objects, machine parts to embrace a new aesthetic vortex. The poet's inner voice stirs up:

'My soul evaporates at the images I keep of you, Simone,
Like Turner's steam and air and the whistling wind
And the salt crested sea.
I will live here in these rooms at the Clore and sleep
On the polished wooden parquet floor.
Will I then grow closer to you, nearer then and without
Much ado appear to you in my spiritual form you still
will deny of its possible existence, virtual perhaps you
Will, but virtual is then better than physical direct,
Indirect physical, direct only to the eyes, enabling us

To state all our emotions staring out in the brain,
But what about my spirit, my soul, my puff of air
That lets me jump about and leap into excited life?

Will my life be sketchy, unfinished, like the unfinished canvasses of the great impressionist's father, master and genius? Will they appear to us as the true spirit behind the artist? Will it be that in my unfinished state of my wordy expressions I will be remembered too? Will it happen that I was born to great loves that remained sketchy, passionate, but unfinished to a master's eyes? Love cannot ever be finished; love will always stay unfinished, eternal, mystical, the greatest knowing to all, just as much as the biggest mystery. Simone, I've spent all night desiring you, all night to be followed again by all day, which I spent loathing around the river bank, Millbank, moving like a hare through the galleries, and I'm not even chased by a dog, but a pack of dogs that are thoughts, thoughts in various disguises. I feel love and sorrow, lust and pain. What will this day still bring me? And the landscapes shape the air, the spirit, and the dust of pleasure will merge into it and build excitement that again will shape the love we will act upon, its movements and this ball of clasped limbs and heads, the combined melting of our bodies'.

'The babbling water recoiling in vengeful power', Samuel Rogers, the poet, speaks out, while Turner, the painter, adds the colour and depicts the innate powers to his canvas.
'The shepherd on Tonaro's misty brow
And the swart seamen sailing far below
Not undelighted watch the morning sway
Purpling the orient-till it breaks away,
And burns and blazes into glorious day!'

John Ruskin's loveliest engravings echo the poet's verses and fill the heart with the beauty observed, as we take each day for granted.

I buy a notebook for Simone to write her thoughts into. Something specially designed from Tate: Flowers, life, happiness, love and romance. She could transfer her love into these innocent pages, love them, kiss them and process them, if she feels like a power-house of a woman.

If desire is about a screw, why don't you screw? This gremlin shouts into my ear. Because for me a screw is connected to love, and desire to pure lust, as brother and sister-souls, that's why my gremlin's sister shouts into my other ear. Has the trilogy of love: Lust, Love, and Spirit, had once that extraordinary experience in me? I scratch my head, but then AyAy comes to mind, followed by Simone too, who is still hesitant to such an experience. Of course she has many friends, and being in a fortunate position enabling her to choose. I ask her if she has whittled down the selection of possible protagonists, to a few people who want her, and is she then happy for the times ahead in which her libido could still last? And then? Then we talk, she says to me and smiles, as if she's the happiest woman on earth.

And then she's off, somewhere, invited to a party. Shen does never reply directly to my messages or letters, but later she phones me. "I'll see you perhaps after the barbeque", she says and adds "I'll phone you." She never has times or dates fixed. And I carry-on with my lonesome walk through the containers of culture, galleries I will enjoy. Now and then, a young woman who is curious about what I write or sketch, will come close to gaze at my notebook placed on my knees. I will hold it up for her and permit a comment on my impressions, or address her. Some young women reply with interest in art, but the teens reply only with a few words and take flight, as if they would try avoiding a conversation. Simone phones me that she isn't far away from my domicile. I am still in a reflecting mood: Westminster, Jewel Tower. I relax for a while at a seat with a table placed upon the fresh green lawn. I write.

I have just walked the 15th century interior, as more people arrive. I take my notebook and stroll across Victoria Park toward the Thames. The Tate and Clore galleries are just a short walk ahead. How wondrous the architecture with Tate's Classical lines and the colourful Clore building fitted to it with n such harmony, to rather enhance than to cry-out too loud. Its rainbow coloured facade stir the expectation of the great master's paintings behind, vivacious and contemporary. I think of Simone's colourful youth fitting to my advanced and ageing body's dull physical appearance. In mind, the age comparisons fall by the side, if there' an immediate vibe of understanding. Yet the uncertainties, the mind wishes to explore and understand, are returning at all times. There are no barriers from my side and I sense Simone's reserve to give her own self to me fully.

She talks about this man she knew, who took care of her after the death of her spouse. Simone never rests. She rushes about, as if she would try tenaciously to recover her tracks, she just left behind. This is a link to her way of moving about in her silver-streamed car, being at any given moment anywhere, if she decides so on the spot and what she feels doing. Like now. It's Sunday and my last evening in London. I had an early morning and had not slept well last night, although my bed is excellent and the comfort is good. I get up and tend to my morning's ritual of a shower and thorough cleaning. Since I have lived in the hot climate of a Greek summer, I have adopted this procedure, besides AyAy always wished a clean body, obsessed with a fright of catching some infection from traveling on public transport vehicles. Washing in hot climates is an obligation, as we touch many objects on the move, especially in public life.

I love to lie in bed to dry after a shower and let the body settle, stirred up from the sharp spray of water jets to awaken it to its rosy state. I tend to reflect in words my night before and also my dreams that mingle with the harsh realities of the outer world. This is my twilight time of a usual morning, the misty no man's land, where I may roam about free and unbridled, paint my thoughts on the

50

monochrome canvas of a mysterious morning, and create a picture from within, into this shock of waking where one gathers the fire of first thoughts. Then, as a piece of poetry or a letter takes off, soon the galloping horses are untenable with their race through this planet's arena that never stops to spin. I feel the adrenalin's rush, the exhilaration that'll sweep my body with its pulsating venom. All rises fast into the clear morning's air, light as a feather and just as speedy as the lot of apocalyptical riders who are thundering past. It will float for a while in midst the stirred-up dust and then settle slowly with gentle movements of a random dive onto the smooth and crystal-clear ground that resembles glass, in colours of blue, green and purple. How far will it perform and shape to take Simone's dancing moves, and finally show legs, midriff, with torso and breasts moving towards me, in a rhythm that stirs desire in me?

It is not Simone; it's a peacock that struts proudly along the illuminated floor with a majestic move and a dance of pride I gaze at and gasp admiring the scene. I wonder if she has indeed changed into this paradisiacal bird, just to foil me, foil my intent to seduce her, and foil my intention to love her. Does she place no value on a poet's love; no value on a man's love, who is genuine and straight-out with his choice of words?

I remain in a state of an erotic limbo.

Breakfast I keep short, continental, and the first walk in the open garden at the backyard of the place reveals to me to dress warmer today. I take my dark-blue raincoat and slip from the corner street towards the station, with its light steel-roofed space and pleasant natural illumination. Crowds are already milling as usual, save for the late night return.

The tube takes me to Green Park, where I change from the Piccadilly line to the Jubilee line. One stop and I'm at Westminster. The crowds in a constant stream flock towards the Abbey. I sit in the green courtyard amongst the trees and ancient buildings, once castle to the kings. I write my 'Realities'. It started as a journal poetry and

51

*slowly grew into an Elegiac poem. There are many reali-
ties for me. All are layered: All with their respective order
of importance. All are in a preference that's changing
from time to time. Now, with Symi along with her friends
and her social circle, I feel that this time my life will be
diametrically opposite to my past life in Greece. My floating state of being, disjointed and exploded at the tragic
end of a friend's untimely death, has now started to heal
here in the cool, but pleasant climate of the British Isles.
Here, where the cultures are well preserved, history
maintained at innumerable sites, and even available to
members of a heritage club for a discount on return visits,
to be joined by the seriously concerned. I will join.*

*Simone has a talent to phone me in midst of my deep-
est thoughts: "Where are you?" I tell her. I'll have to finish
the train of thought as I stroll along the Thames, with its
steady flow that streams towards the sea. I have lost my
sense of time, but the steady walk clears my mind and
rids me of all thoughts I do not wish to harbour any longer.
I have spent much time to think about AyAy's advice and
her thinking about the way how to go about writing, besides one's choice of words. What were her last
thoughts? Family, loved ones? I wish I knew. I wonder if
she was concerned about my life of ups and downs, my
love-life or the state of my writing.*

*Perhaps both, as she gathered herself notions and ex-
periences to follow her own path of writing. "I do not want
you to go to another woman," she said, meaning another
Muse. But she said it in a whisper, her words sinking with
the gravity of her sadness. The words came hardly across
her lips, as there's not much to say any longer, when a
terminal illness is feasting on one, like a leach, and medication will render one numb and become immobile. Of
course she has helped me to grow as a poet and acquire
a notion of what good writing is all about. We have exchanged our life's stories and talked about our loves.
Now, as we are open books for each other, we have experienced good sexual love and perhaps the discovery of
my innermost being has suddenly been left with a void, I*

hate falling into. My compassion with her is still love and yet I wish to fall across the beautiful lass downstairs at the flower shop, touch her base-midriff, rip-off her clothes and make love in the bed of all flowers, cry-out and let AyAy hear my climactic cries amidst heavy breathing. But is this fair to her? I never could hurt her this way openly in such a crude and uncouth way, although the idea is outrageously gripping me fast and I proceed down to the shop for a talk with the lass. Then AyAy will compromise in her way she thinks, or perhaps consulting one of her many friends, especially the one I dislike from all the others, as she had shown her to me on a photograph: In her light and Nordic appearance, she oozes to me the sweetness of her poison that flows from the pertness of her lips, and it's enhanced by sinister flickers in her green-grey eyes. A sudden cold rises from the base of my spine. This is however my gut-feel and perhaps rash judgement, although my gut-feel is never far out.

The walk along the river is wonderful. Space has been generously created by its bisection of the city. A giant hand had moved all buildings to their respective spots, so one could breathe freely. I always had difficulties with breathing, that's why my senses enjoy these freed-up spaces. I see Simone's face and her dusky eyes express her immediate feelings. How wonderful they are, how magically inverted with that dusky glow of magical powers she showers upon my face, down to my chest, and warm me-up instantly from head to toe .She could well see that I'm in limbo with my sexual awareness. She is aware that I'm a floating feather, whenever she sweeps along in her silver arrow. As I settle down in the cradle of her being, I feel growing with her as one being, one person. We are like twins of one heart and one soul. I touch her hand, it's warm and sinewy, and I hold it for a long time, even if I get nervous that I cannot get through to her yet as a lover. As a friend I'm accepted, possibly even more, but she wouldn't tell me. She obviously will need more time to find out herself, how she will carry-on in the mainstream of this society's tradition. I am an artist and I admire her for her beauty and sensuality.

It's early morning and I think of Simone. I think of her all the time. She has captured my entire being and I'm in her hand.

Visitors still flock through the entrance of the Tate like a bunch of moths attracted to the glow of richness in art. It's a great experience each time. This time, I enter from the side of the Classical building. I am fascinated by the Classical painters and take photographs with my digital camera, but without a flash, as requested. Especially drawn to the Pre-Raphaelites' paintings, I take my time there, as their expression of eroticism fascinates me. This time I admire Watt's bust of Daphne, his love depicted, not just his model who sat for him. I sense it.

Sitting at Baglios on Nelson Mandela Square, back in Africa of the South and in the midst of a hum of worldly noises, I reflect on my present life. The present enrichment of the soul that has burst forward in a sudden spurt, after this marathon of a personal trip to seek not only a publisher for my poetry, but also Simone, has no beginning and no end to it. The giant bronze statue of the president smiles upon the small square that serves as a playground for children, and at one end towards the Sandton Library at a space used for exhibitions. Yet, having had my share of noises, this Square remains the one worthwhile visited one in the urban sprawl of Johannesburg. There's the only reasonable assembly of beauty within this place for social intercourse within its continental atmosphere. Kids love the giant statue of Madiba and run through between his legs, which display his shuffling styled dance move. Some kids, just detecting their walking, feed the doves. A small and wiry Far Eastern boy is disappointed that his contemporaries from the South African fellows chase the doves away, with their four-wheel bikes and roller blades, in a rather crude manner, as he had just won the trust of the doves by feeding them. Black Nubian women swing their shapely hips past in a gap between chairs and adjoining tables. Their faces are aglow with self-assurance, corn-row beaded fine wiry hair, and symmetrical faces completely relaxed. Someone offers African face-painting for a five Rand donation. The Japanese kid still feeds the doves patiently and with tenacity, fending off the biking kids. The birds seem to trust him as they all follow his slow walk, picking at the crumbs he leaves like a trail behind. The level fountain's jets are switched off. Around them a series of Italian scooters are displayed: 'Vespas' mainly, well-known around the world, like cappuccino. I wish to have that frothy drink just now, but the waiters seem inattentive, even to raising my hand. They hardly cast their eyes on the customers, however, I still have time and I can wait. Then crowds are not different to the place I stayed in London, except there are more dark faces here. Perhaps one would think less civilized, but I get the feeling at Mandela Square that the spirit of aged past president still hovers here, creating a new melting pot for all different people, the rainbow nation, as he envisaged and had laid down the foundation stone for it, right here at this commemorative Square to be cherished. Now he is watching, immortalised in his greater than life statue, hopefully forever over his nation.

I found I couldn't live in this turmoil of an emerging nation that let us have our undeserved part of suffering for it. Injustices, we are aware of, have occurred in the past and were dealt with in the wake of the Truth and Reconciliation Commission's task, which cannot be better described than in 'Country of my Skull'.

We, as professional backbones, here to help everybody, in spite of race and colour, supporting many good causes to advance the education of the less fortunate, have not deserved the full brunt of the violent arm of confrontation-tactics. We have not deserved the fanatics, as nobody would. The principle of good and bad is written into every being from birth, as is the condition for intelligence. Is it? Is doing something good the same as doing something bad, undistinguished by an emerging youth who had never any home-education? Is love the same as hate? The differentiation is related to the set of morals we are brought-up with. Of course, if both parents have to work all day, or are not present to fend for their families, we all would be in the same position.

The enhancement of the good, as we are taught, pointed out to us in contrast to the bad. We develop our senses along these moral structures we take from our parents and they supposed to correspond finally with our genetic inheritance. I carry on writing:

Matters in love are different. Love is a dimension taught by our parents, mainly by our mothers. The slow-flowing spring of its appreciation will reach our souls along the ways of learning. The oscillation height of our first love encounter, marked by love's highs, often is associated with death. The first kiss and then the first sexual experience will be rushing through us with the spring that turned into a torrential stream, tearing deep markings into our being. Do we mature in love or are we just swept away? Do we reach the safety of land and step up one stone at a time, one level to the next, until we reach the top? What top? The top of a pyramid-shaped structure that we aim to reach as the epitome of our human existence that'll transform us into a demi-god stature, we may reach in a struggle for self-realization. Or we might never reach even part of this structural height at all.

As love is connected to suffering and pain, not many of our contemporaries live-up to stand in queue of an inner enriched world with creativity. This process will be challenged by its clashes with the outer world's realities in a shock event. A rebirth will be induced every time. 'To die and to be reborn is very difficult', DDr. Fritz Perls stated in his 'Gestalt' therapy. The jazzy young generation strolls past, all self-assertive on the outside and physically attractive, gym-toned bodies, with a new untenable frame of mind entirely.

When I met Simone, I was rather enthralled with her beauty. I my leisure time, I could admire her photographs she had posted me on the Internet pages, where people seek people for friendship. It was also by accident that the program, AyAy had sent me before her death, would yield my attention to Simone. As I activated the mailbox again I saw her immediately, she stood out from the crowd. Everything changes. It changes faster as we get older, although it's a repetition of previous matters, as all history is. The shapes and names are different, and the vehicles used to achieve it have become speedier, also in matters of love. There' the speed of selection, as this spinning wheel of fortune is spun everywhere. The mere coincidence of meeting someone matching is thus increased and lies in hundreds of multiples in front of us, depending on your input. Still, it's a coincidence to meet a sympathetic person with human warmth and an inner beauty radiating from the eyes. The spirit of adventure is combined with the qualities of a matching soul and mind, heart and body. It becomes an immediate powerful cocktail if the mixture happens to be right.

I wrote to Simone immediately and I liked her response. There was a woman who had lost her beloved spouse in her late forties, attractive, intelligent, and a responsible human being. Of course she would try to find a matching person sharing her life with. However, I was thinking of Simone as a person, not about anything further. But as I approached her and listened to her voice, the mode of her talk, I experienced a continuation of AyAy's spirit. The way she looked free and unbridled at life before her. This sudden attraction to her assured me of my adoration for her that could turn to love.

I knew inside that I'll meet her, come my time. I told Simone my notions and feelings in my letters to her. I wrote a poem that came off suddenly with ease and rolling from my heart. It's the usual part of a poet who falls in love.

But then she held back, burnt by my sudden exposed feelings through my letters. In conversation, she has certainly secrets in her heart, she wishes to hide and overcome, but I feel that she wishes to tear down that wall of secrecy quite soon. It renders her tainted with something that stops her to reach another stepping stone in the development of mature love. Then she sends me a poem, she wrote about her personal belief. It sounds more like a translation of Zoroaster's teachings. I know this from my school days touching on Nietzsche. I have not read his philosophical essays any further, due to many misgivings from society after Great War, but at present I might just read on. Even Istvan Kertesz bought an edition for a good price, he wrote in his diaries. And who hasn't read his book 'Kaddish for an unborn child', his prayer for an unborn child? I read my German edition with bated breath and as long as my eyes let me read, until they just folded up. I think that I have lots in common with him, the way we think and write. Of course I was happy for him to be selected receiving the Nobel Prize for Literature in 2004 and will enjoy reading his acceptance speech.

I find sweet and also bitter-laced words for Symi in the poetry she induces in me. She has become a Muse to me overnight. An explosion had incurred in me that rippled through the Internet's airways to reach her. What does she feel?

I write to her letters, calling them 'The Peacock Letters', as the peacock is a symbolic image to the Royal Throne in Persia, now called Iran. Ayatollah or not, I am an artist who has a right to think freely, and the symbolic image of the real peacock appeals to me, besides it is enormously aesthetic. The colours are beautiful, as religion could never be, as it is man-made, the peacock isn't. However, I respect people's believes, as we all believe in something and should have a right of choice. I believe in beauty and love, as there's nothing greater or better in the whole universe. One thing is certain: Love embellishes our qualities of being human; everybody knows that who was in that mode and cherished that state of feelings.

I know that from my time I spent with my Muse, even for a short while, before she was taken away from me by fate. But she told me, before she passed away, to find another Muse through the Internet. "An artist needs a Muse to stay creative," she said. For seven months, while I was depressed, I did nothing. Then, after an extended time of grieving, one sunny morning in Africa, I pressed the one button that brought-up the face of Simone.

I have written quite an amount of words that deal with this relationship in the realm of the electronic world. Now I desire her and want her. I follow my heart as AyAy had taught me and also encouraged me to do. After such dedicated time of mourning she had approved it, as any woman and any spouse would. As always, she would be my spiritual guide. She taught ne to keep an open mind, to be tolerant and see love's multitude of layers, a book one could experience turning the pages. Then she said: "Step back and reflect about it taking an immediate distance." That was the hard part where I needed the help of others, friends, Muses, and lovers. It's though endless like the universe and wholesome to a poet's heart.

I copy my letters and poems to a disk. Some I write down for editing, I will send them to a publisher. Will she help me? I have trusted her immediately, perhaps blindly. Am I a fool? This is the crux of the poet, he is open to his intuitively selected loves, just to be disappointed times, just to be misunderstood, just to be ahead of a love he has often consumed already, without any knowledge of the person he had selected. It could be that he had lost his sense of gut-feel for a moment in heat. Symi might be shocked, as she lives a quaint life within a selected circle of friends, and she is well-looked after.
I write to her that I'll come. She tells me is selling her other flat and will travel to America soon. I write:

It seems that we will be missing each other, as I have to pack house in Austria. K, B, and I pack and pack, there's no stopping. Often I swear inside. What for is all this? K has found a sudden motivation to sort-out my mother's possessions, decide about the useful, the beautiful, and the decorative from the practical. B assists, but she is not feeling well. I have to believe what K does is right. Originally I wanted all to leave to R and K's who moved in. As they were heaping all to throw away to a dumping place nearby, I became upset about my Mom's belongings treated in such a disrespectful way. I could hear mother's voice telling me that my father bought all these items of furniture with his savings, he put aside from his earnings in the army. It was for their engagement. I dislike R and K's attitudes. Not that it's all for nothing, but also there's hardly any appreciation for it. I spit-out in anger, but then excuse them for their uneducated simple-mindedness.

This is life as a dark pit, all three generations who lived here will fall into and vanish. I might manage to survive with the help of K's mental strength and her motivational talk. I query it. She needs this and that. I tell her that in case we'll die, she will inherit all goods we move now. It appeals to her, as she might have thought these scenarios through already, as soon as I have approached her about this move. She seems not to be touched by it. The face of a cool businesswoman appears, then again, as I mention something I would like, she says: "Take it, take it," as if I would still chase after a dream that could become true one day – A home in Greece indeed? –

Since a few years I plan such a move with B, as we both love Greece and the blue Mediterranean Sea, the warmth, and the dry climate of the mainland. There is space and also the possibility to obtain a small piece of ground suitable for our project. But I feel that life will run out on me and it has turned out to become a race toward the last laps of one's existence. I sense it. I enjoy a speeding car and a challenge, the same way as Simone races along the English countryside. The same way I rush about the realms I have created and arranged my thoughts through protagonists who I try directing into a play. I haven't succeeded yet, but perhaps one day I will.

Simone is what? What does she do all day, not having to commute to work at all? I encourage her to write, as she shows talent. She's too emotionally involved into many happenings with too many people. I do not mind at all. My concern is her happiness that'll affect me positive too. I could give her more than she ever will get from any *marriage. That's a fact. As for herself, she has to decide hr future life-style. "Perhaps I'll get myself a bearded collie and walk him daily," she says to me. But it also means to care for such tender animal, a trusted friend. I roll this thoughts over, as I sit in this tin-foiled jet that transports us speedily to Europe, then across the Dark Continent. I seem to have lost contact with Simone, as my mobile phone will not pick-up her number at all. But sometime after those three weeks of stillness I reach her. Has she returned from her overseas trip? I could never be sure with her. I take her reports as fact, true or not. After an absence of five weeks, she had thought I will not live-up to my word. She's rather surprised by my visit, as if it would be an unfortunate time it came as a physical reality into her life. Well, I do not ignore her, but she does ignore me, although she messages me almost at the same time, as the plane had set to a standstill. "Do not think I ignore you, I just had no time. I do not want you to think I do not care." Whatever the true meaning of these messages might be, at least she acknowledged my coming. I take the tube to Earl's Court. The area is Middle Class, close to Kensington's Upper Class. Yet, I do like the casual atmosphere, living next to people who are communicative and tell the truth. But what truth do I like? The quaint and grey every day's truthful ongoing, or the sensational and colourful?*

I think it's the way truth sips out like bubbles from a glass of soda with someone I just met and wish to have a deeper interest in her personality? Personalities could be cast-iron character-hindrances. In this instant the poet is speaking, while the man behind has to turn to white lies to leave the poet his space, he will need to be creative. This is the sacrifice he has to pay to enable the poet researching his book, which life dictates to him. There is the voice of his Muse in his ear again: Go sail to the British Isles, it's your mission!" And he asks his Muse: "Why to those Northern Isles?" And she will not return an answer, just like Simone. "I don't know where the trade winds will take my boat to," murmurs the poet. I will just follow then my inside world that is guided by the words of my Muse, even if I have to find stories and incidental happenings that'll protect this realm against the new Barbarian invaders, the mean radicals and the chance-takers.

The first day I check-in at this family hotel in Berkley Gardens, just off Earl's Court Road, I am told by the charming young receptionist that my confirmation had been cancelled. I feel not only at the end of my wits, surprised and kicked-out of town, but also abandoned by Simone. The end? However, the young man listens to my pleas. Once he had made a few phone calls, he finds a room for me in the Dutch Hotel, but meanwhile I am welcome to stay in the basement room for a few days. The room is spacious and pleasant, it is cool without an air conditioner, which suits me. I thank him accommodating me and spend all afternoon on the phone, establishing links to publishers and banks. By late afternoon I am exhausted and I proceed to the outside world, exit at reception and take to the right. Just about a few minutes later I am on the busy Earl's Court Road. I see Pizzeria Dyno's and I am looking for a table, order a pizza and a glass of wine. An elderly lady with a blue scarf on her head sits nearby. Her head is bent down, she appears to have snoozed-off, but then she also talks in that position. I finish my food, pay, and get along. All I want now is to lie down and sleep.

This won't be either Aphrodite or Artemis, but for once she did try and felt sated, but she could not respond. What is she then? A ghosting image of a woman that rules with her existence from the side-lines of the town's social order, drowned in the heritage of protocol? Another victim of racism. A victim of a social order that hasn't yet stopped the abolition of slaves? Social slaves, nonetheless. There are small pockets of the megalopolis of this earth, where the truth shines for those who realize the purest voice of the people, the grass-roots of a social pyramid. The base where there's no space for lies.

Darn, why all this cloak and dagger moves by Simone? Finally on the last day she shows some human facets, and somehow she's now what I have missed for the last four days. "Are you afraid?" I ask her.

"No," she says, "it is that the play before it will be more exciting than the actual deed of love."

"Really?" I reply astonished, "but haven't we played yet enough?"

How far does one play before, all one's darn short life? Is then death the highlight of one's love? I'll muse. I cannot get to Simone at all, I cannot grasp the way of her thinking. There is hardly any time left, no time at all, I sense. She has not yet realized that the days of my visit are soon over, when physical excitement could have brought us joy with love's delicacies, enjoyed with smacking lips, it could have made us alive with the magical glow of love. Besides, where does one find a matching partner that easily, like in this present once a life-time chance?

She doesn't move, appears to be shay and still disappointed by some screwball who saw her as an object for his sexual desires and satisfied himself, leaving her dead at the roadside for lust. And now she doesn't believe in a man any longer. She has to overcome the shocks of being used and appear as fair game, recreating her healthy attitude towards sexual enjoyment with the partners who are reasonable and pleasant, who accept her personality and her specific likes. She has to change her attitude fast, if we suppose to get-on with each other and reach positive heights next time. Will she be there?

It's Tuesday, already nine months since AyAy's death and I had no luck to get hold of Simone. I hear voices of an elderly woman at the end of the telephone line. She tells me in broken English that, - "Ha, - Who?..."almost as Simone does her 'Ha!' She sounds like a disciplinarian to me. I sense her curiosity though – "my daughter – in an hour…"

"OK," I reply. "I'll phone back." I proceed to the entrance of our property and I paint the steel gate meanwhile, dark-blue.

It looks like it could rain. It would be the first rain of the oncoming summer season. It's the ninth day of the ninth month since AyAy disappeared and transformed herself into this child again, called Simone. The homecoming is set, I think I love Simone, but will not press her, as she is a Mercurial soul, and although she appears shy to the outside, inside she's brewing like an awakening volcano.

From a short interplay I understand that Simone is passionate, but that it might be too late for some extraordinary sex. Presently she still avoids men, hooked-up with a girlfriend. I don't mind, I find women making love exciting and rather stimulating. I am not repulsed and when she's bored with it, she'll find great variations with all I have to offer. My love for her at present might be only existing in my fantasy, however, fantasy and dreams may fuse and turn into reality in sense of flesh and blood. It might be not too late for me yet? Does AyAy take responsibility for guiding me? Yes, I think so, as I feel her strongly. She is here all the way, the result of her vibes are clearly visible after one happening.

I'm happy with Simone and she has a soothing effect on me that I need at present to stay sane. I could have died, exploding like an overheating star, indeed. I would have disappeared from earth and yet fate has still some surprises in store for me. An Unusual woman, Simone, indeed. There is the immediacy of a relationship showing on our faces, our bodies eager to be touched b each other. I have touched Simone already, but she did not wish to have sex with me. I respect her and that's the basis for a great friendship already. All I have at present are guesses, again being a happy child, as she could be my mother, I adored. Oedipus? 'Oedipus Poeticus', indeed.

Physically she is a magnet for me, and I'm drawn to her like I was to AyAy. But by now AyAy has told me to move-on and be with her this way. I have asked AyAy for a good-bye screw and she bent down for me. She was asking me to finish, as she could not stand the normal thrusting paces any longer. I pained her inside of her body already, riddled with terminal cancer. As I pulled-out of her she was bleeding. Frightened, I said "That's not me, is

64

it?" She sighed "No," she answered back disappointed, "that's me!" That was the end of our sexual relationship, physically, but the mental relationship still carried-on. I still loved her and was loyal to her, although I wished to go to any hotel and fuck my brains out with any woman available, even a sex-worker, I told her. "No, don't!" She exclaimed with fright in her voice "Your heart must be in it." Despite all, I was in the turmoil of a rebellion against her terrible sickness that was eating her up, as I was unable to do anything against it I chatted up a few women, but AyAy's voice was always there: "Don't! Your heart must be in it!" She was right, after all.

I lived for one month in her rooms at the seaside cottage, writing my story about love and pain, and one story about an unusual love, indeed. AyAy was very ill by now. As I wanted to see her, share my compassion for her, I even took the hardship of getting-up at 5:30 am, take the bus at seven to town, where I waited two hours until 11:00 am, as she needed time to get ready. I bought some presents and near her flat some flowers in the shop that served mainly the visitors to the cemetery on the opposite side. She was still in bed. Her cousin Ata came to the door. I knew by instinct that these were her last months on earth and our togetherness would end. But then, will it? Ata said that AyAy is ill, but as soon as we had settled down talking about literature, AyAy appeared from her bedroom. "Zed does not believe that I'm gravely ill." She said in a low voice. "Well, I do not know," I replied "as you are a poet and an excellent actress." Indeed, I was angry with her that she spent lots of time with other people, and perhaps even if I was selfish and unfair to her, I demanded more access to her alone, which she seemed to avoid. We had a great sex-life and now all turned to ashes in a sudden incineration of feelings, right in front of my eyes. I still felt aroused touching her, hurting her with my healthy libido as she was sliding downhill fast.

I read some of my love poems to Ata and she gasped, but liked them, sighing when the words were truly emotional and sexual. But she listened to the end. I wrote her a poem that day in the bus on my return to AyAy's cottage.

One month of messages in communication with AyAy. One day she wrote: I have to go to hospital until I will get better. The death sentence as a procedure, I thought, but didn't say to her. She gave me the hospital's name, I have forgotten by now, but I wrote it down into my diary. "Mai is here," she messaged me. "That's nice AyAy," I messaged back, to greet her. She loved Mai and I couldn't blame her for such a delightful girlfriend. I envied Mai being able to be there, while I couldn't. I hear myself muttering: "This is the end any day now." But AyAy hung onto life. It was then that I had to return to Africa and stopped by at her place. Ata told me not to come to the hospital, rather remember her as she was. It broke my heart not to be able to say good-bye, but then we all would have just cried. It was then that I remembered my mother's last moments and I could not get home in time to Austria either. This was now the second time, and why was it to me even more painful? This is difficult to answer, as it is always one of the most painful moments in one's life.

Fortunately B and I met D, who was at that time in Athens. I was glad to be with him for a while taking my mind off matters that affected me gravely. How deep and grave, I didn't know et. But now, nine months after AyAy's death I finally came through to Simone and I was happy again in different ways. The wounds of an unusual love had not healed yet, but I had found a new friend, I dare not to lose, come hell, and come fire. She is a deer-eyed cool personality on the outside, but she burns inside. Fire and ice, just like another version of AyAy. How well I recall her still. On a short video-clip I have conserved her voice with a private strip tease for me. I cannot play it without becoming emotional and then wanting to love her, turn to self-love, satisfy myself in front of her, as I did many times live with her in the video-chat programs we engaged in. She wanted something on the side before she died, and it flared up into something greater than expected, she told me once.

An unusual love, an Affaire du Coeur had developed from a friendship through literature and poetry, in a burning search for self-realization, and it ended up in the love for artful expressions in words and drawings. Then the poet lamented and he wrote:
Tonight the ninth of the ninth
Month since AyAy died
I held you tonight.
Tonight I could kiss you
And adore your sighs
When my fingers slide
Down on you
And my lips follow in a trail
That arouses you.
In a trail of passion
Where I will slide upon
With great ardour –
Cause you delightful moments
And let you be the one –
The one I want to love.

Tonight.
This is the day of many days
That came to me as a surprise
Almost in a trance of words
I lost you in their maze
And searched for you.

The voice on the other end
Reminds me my Gran
Self-assured and used to
Excise command for a huge
Family
That is now strewn all about
The globe
But she's strong-minded like
You are
Perhaps more like your father

Though.
But I can feel and not say aloud
As I have known you for a while
Simone albeit short
It seems for a long time you are
Familiar to me.

The days are short and yet
Shorter until I have to say
Good-bye and follow
My poetic friends
I wish to introduce you to
Their deep emotion sensed
Reading their creations also
To you.

My heart is overflowing
You can stir so much in me
Welling emotions even
Over the telephone
Across the Atlantic
Passed continents that ooze
Blood and death
You said to me you believe
In nothing
But I don't buy that yet
As I believe in love.

On this milestone of my final
Laps in life I still see a horizon
Quite far
How lucky I really am
To travel alongside with you
Albeit you having some days
Of your busy life off
Spending them with me
Days that could become weeks
And then months and perhaps
Even years
That gilded me with all the

Silver-rays
You've showered upon me.

It's near-night again in Africa
And I think of you –
Time in
Time out
As long as I will hear your voice
As long as I'll sense your warmth
Your smile –
We'll laugh and share
Precious love.

*

Myrta's Eyes

Just on the second last day of his holidays his pet-silver bracelet broke in two, he once bought in Paris, fashioned on film star Belmondo's jewellery. The concierge at his hotel suggested he paid a visit to the jeweller opposite the hotel entrance.

"Unfortunately I cannot do it for you," the stocky jeweller commented, looking at the broken wrist chain. "I'll recommend you take it to Myrta, she has soldering equipment that's better than mine. I think she could do it." I took the chain back. "Just don't tell her that I've sent you," he added as I was already leaving.

He went down the village road where most souvenir shops were located. He saw the sign with decorative letters above the entrance door to her shop. He could hardly read the flowery style writing. 'Myrto's, or Myrta, there were too many garlands obliterating the Greek letters.

As he entered, the shop was filled with customers. "I will come later," he excused herself to a young woman with soulful dusky eyes. "Just look around meanwhile," she smiled at him, "I'll be shortly with you." She busied herself with two customers who bought souvenirs for their friends at home. Her captivating smile had made him stay. He liked her instantly. He looked at her showcases. Her handmade jewellery looked interesting, showed imagination and some pieces reflected her creative spirit. The more he browsed, the more he liked Myrta's creations. He continued to study one showcase in particular, the silver trinkets were modelled on scenes from Greek mythology. He would buy one for Pam, his spouse. But then, he thought, he would be obliged to buy one for Kim, his sister-in-law, who stayed with them. Then the sisters would compare and criticize, make a fuss, and wish to know where he bought it and perhaps go back to Myrta and exchange it for something to their specific liking. No, he said into his breath, I'd rather stick it out here. They would be by now already on the beach, have a last swim for their holiday in the Cretan sun. He began to like his stay at Myrta's shop.

Now and then he looked-up and watched her talking to customers, in Greek, in English, and in German. He lauded himself to have escaped Pam's manipulative ways of cunning him into going shopping together. No way, he thought, it has been already such a challenge to have to bear her overpowering organizing character, but Pam wanted her to have a holiday here with them. Perhaps she would keep that way in Kim's good books for later favours. Who knows, he mused He was away now and they would not know where he was. He felt a surge of freedom, how strange, he had to smile. Well, he thought, he had agreed for his holiday – Kim had called cunningly a 'ménage-a-trois' – in French, a triangle, a threesome. She might have wished for perhaps, but she only played that in her mind. There were good-looking men around the pool bar at lunch time and one Greek man was casting eyes on Kim, but she shied away meeting him. "Well," she said to Pam, "would you not like to introduce me to him?" Pam laughed, "Go and talk to him, he's all eyes over you." Kim sulked as the man left again. "Another opportunity missed." Zervas had to laugh inside. Typical for ageing Kim, she doubts being still attractive to men.

He had accommodated Pam's wishes, to behave sweet to Kim, as they had to visit Austria again in the near future and she would invite them to her home to stay. "Well then," Pam said "she couldn't deny her sister staying with her husband for a week or so." That's Kim, the businesswoman-sister, Zervas thought. Kim always had a probing mind, looking for her advantage, cunningly suggesting alternatives to any plan one brought forward, so she'd make some profit out of others. Zervas, the artist and poet despised her for this character trait. Let her be dominating on trivial matters for the time being, he thought, as she had taken this opportunity of being offered a bed in the holiday accommodation of her sister, especially at this well-appointed holiday village on the south-eastern coast of Crete. She took the last minute invitation with a greedy mind and would have swallowed them, if Zervas would have joined her bed. But he didn't for the second week of their stay, when she arrived. How much did they depend on her? He would find that out later.

"Hello!" She came towards him in midst of a few foreign faces, offering him a warm smile of welcome and a curious look in her dusky eyes. "Can I help?" He was still startled by all his thoughts about Pam's family, he quickly put by the side. This woman's approach with gentle and sensitive manners soothed his stirred-up mood and he had an urge to kiss the back of her close-by hand, but that would have looked ridiculous and out of place, an intimate gesture without the right moment.

"Yes," he said, looking into her eyes that were a deep hazel, and amber and almonds came to his mind. "Look at my bracelet," he continued "Its clasp is broken."

"I have no time now, but if you wait I will look at it in more detail."

"Of course," he replied, not minding her busy day selling souvenirs and jewellery to visitors and tourists. He felt his knees weaken and he looked for a seat. The only seat in front of the counter as occupied. There was a small desk with a backrest she used as a workbench. It had a small bentwood chair at the front. He sat down, with his eyes looking across her workbench filled with innumerable pieces of jewellery, silver wires, all kinds of rings and materials she used to solder and work on her object d'art. Then she had a comment. She came across the room to him. "Could you still wait a bit longer?"

"Yes," he said, "just finish your sales, I will wait." Hee eyes changed colour. The left one was staying dark and sad, while the right one turned lighter. He thought of being deceived by the ambivalent lighting of natural sunlight and the reflections of shadows that run across her back wall, like then waves which rolled in from the nearby sea. He was bored, stood-up and walked to a nearby showcase. He saw some silver items that fascinated him. Amber pieces worked into a silver pointed lance-shaped arrow serving as a bookmark. That would be a present for Imis, he thought, I'll take one tomorrow. The customers had left, one by one, and she was available again. As soon as she had started to evaluate the damage on his bracelet, he handed her some parts that had been broken off. At that moment a woman appeared, Nordic, blond, greeted her by name and he immediately disliked her tone of voice. He did not appreciate the woman barging in, besides the sharpness of her tongue irritated him. Yet he had to be diplomatic. He introduced himself "Zervas," he took Myrto's hand, it felt warm and slim.

"I am Myrto," she said and held on to his hand, but he understood Myrta. "This is Gudrun, a friend," Myrta said, still holding his hand. "You have a Greek name?" He sensed Gudrun's androphobe vibes. The sharpness of Gudrun's voice indicated a fight that was brewing. Myrta spoke some words in German, to soothe the tension building up. "My name is Joe, but I adopted the name Zervas, as it suits to my ancestry. They came from Crete." He paused and looked at Gudrun with a triumphant look, not being Nordic. Gudrun avoided his gaze. "That's all very interesting," Myrta said avoiding the hostile stance of her customers overflow into the usual debate of the bad times at the Great War. The jealous glances of Gudrun amused him as much as Myrta. She stood at Zervas' side with her white cotton voile dress and he could feel her closeness so tactile that his body stirred, as if touched by her, enveloping him with her physical being. He did not mind any longer being attacked by Gudrun, he had no feelings for. As long as Myrta liked him, he felt content and balanced. In his mind he could see that Gudrun intended to challenge him in a half-intellectual way, he disliked. Zervas contributed some historical facts to her stirring discussion on political developments, and he commented on from his viewpoint. Myrta always intercepted to defuse the loaded guilt-complex of Gudrun, as she put it indirectly to him that she considered herself taking his side. He didn't know what Gudrun intended with her negative stirring, ignoring her comments, and then it hit him: She was attracted to Myrta, the same way as he was!

"Myrta," Gudrun said with some words of endearment in Greek, as she addressed the pretty jeweller who had moved toward the opposite side of him. She stood with her back against the early afternoon sun, where the sun-rays were eating away her voile cotton dress. Her beautiful legs were outlined and he could not tell if she wore a thong or not, but definitely no panties. Myrta, a beautiful nymph born from sun and sea!

Her thin layers of cotton draped around her body started moving towards the window, where the slight breeze in this bright light waved her cotton veils like a sail. She stood like a model on a boat that furrowed the sea, undressed as the cotton wound itself tightly around her slim body. She had the streamlined look of a Nereid diving out of the Blue. He became aroused. Gudrun snapped for air and Myrta smiled. She came across to him and stood so close, their bodies touched as she leaned against him.

"It's nice to have someone say: Ich liebe dich "– I love you – she said in German. He felt his mouth going dry, his heart beating louder, and he knew she had him stirred with her romantic notion by the way she had exposed herself, observing his reaction. He sensed that siesta time was coming and he had been told this from both women. He felt left being stranded. "I have to go," he said.

"Come back tomorrow after ten," Myrta said immediately. "All right Myrta, I will. Have a pleasant afternoon." He turned at the door. "Auf Wiedersehen Gudrun," and he left, without turning around. His inside, stirred-up, made him flee the shop. "Ich liebe dich," he mused, only meant to add to it the second part, she said in a whisper: "Nice to hear that," she meant it said from a man who was cheated from making love to her. His body was aching for her. Of course it was a normal human reaction from a man falling in love with a woman instantly. It was as if she had despised Gudrun, who wished to satisfy her sexual greed with her. Beautiful Myrta was sensual, with a magical power in her eyes, her right eye being different to her left one, which made her even more attractive. He sighed, he wanted her.

He spent the afternoon at the pool of the hotel. Kim and Pam were sun tanning and sinking into a lazy doze. He was reading 'The Last Temptation', and wondered about the literary style Kazantzakis could storm-up into. He stopped reading to rest his eyes on the arriving holiday makers. As a young woman passed, he gazed at her well-shaped body, fascinated by her swinging gait, and he had a sudden intuition for a poem. He started penning. It was for Myrta. It was a good poem, he could sense that immediately. Finishing it, he felt thirsty and commuted to the bar to have a local draught beer. The red-haired woman serving chatted with him, then offering him a Raki, as he didn't know that drink yet, a locally brewed spirit acting as a chaser to his beer. He felt a bit tipsy.

"You start to drink early," a woman's voice startled him from thinking about meeting Myrta.

"Well, it's just a tot," he replied. She spoke a perfect German, as he found out. She told him about her life in Greece, where she was staying, where she worked, and why she chose to live in Greece. A liberated woman who played hard? What was she indeed after? She told him about love she preferred, almost a factual story, as if romance had been cut-out of her life. She wished to live it up and enjoy both, women and men. Her aim was pleasure at all times, immediate, the more the better. Her outlook on life was the result of the individual pursuance of her parent's interests, who were separated. She thought of that as a gift in the New-Age of alienation. All rather civilized in manner and allowance of her family ties that were to be observed, once the law had stamped its approval, and she and her mother went to live in Greece, while her father and brother stayed back in Germany. Everybody was now to himself, pursuing individually happiness, she defined as a free state of being, free to love.

Is it that we are free in love without contracts? Does love not wind its cocoon up in the Web they consciously fled to in togetherness, regardless of freedom? There is continual sex and yet she's never sated? She could be caught in a grand illusion though. What is love? Yet, perhaps a dozen erotic adventures are the present state of her life, just as she had dialled his physical number. 'Turn-on Babe', he called her from now on, her body, her physique were excellent. Her first half of her life have been lived already, she stated, as he found that only her one half, her torso without limbs seemed to him as being fit for a union. There was a lack of something higher, something spiritual that would one lift up and be part of a fulfilling of unifying bodies – the soul! At her first appearance her mind seemed alert, with a keen interest in communicating her state of being, he finds honest and direct. Yet he is rather keen on involving heart mind and soul for a satisfactory affaire du Coeur, not just the pure physical mechanics of getting sexual relief. Besides, it is not his thing to get drunk and become a victim of raw lust screwing about like animals.

She, Karin, stated that she was originally attracted to the rougher men in this part of the island, but if she had enough of their grunting grinding, she preferred to take the ferry boat to Athens. Meeting her halfway, she would enter the gentle and sensuous world of her girlfriend, seek her for her softness, tenderness, and romance. She was keen of finding a soulmate, engaging with different viewpoints, a different coast. But then it's reality on its own, taken as a serious existence, at times it's extreme, at other times, she comes on like an amazon, a sporting pussy, and a s a dangerous cocktail placed between her pretty boobs? Perhaps where her own feminine aspect had been left at one time?

He thinks of Myrta, where Karin is a complete contrast to her and Gudrun. How sophisticated and feminine does Myrta appear, a nymph in the gender-dance, a slender Greek woman to the harder Nordic sisters! Myrta is an elf amongst his Muses, number eleven. Her sheer cotton dress layers revealing a beautiful body, as she moves knowingly against the rays of the afternoon that encompasses her lean body turning her desirable to his voyeur-istic eyes that opened a gate of feelings as his eyes ca-ressed her bodylines, where desire started, as soon as he saw her and she approached him with her seductive stance. At an instant her presence melted into his. His heart stopped a beat in those seconds of union. Dis she feel the same as he did? There was an apparent attrac-tion, slight touches, coincidental smiles as they talked, expressing their wishes to be longer here; no, was he sure it would become intimate? Perhaps it could come to that if he stayed.

"It would be unfair to our spouses if you would make it": "Indeed?" He murmured. "I could not do that." He recalled the words of his past girlfriend, yet she received him in her condominium. "Make love to me in your house!" He said. Her place had a history of lovers, coming and going, he didn't mind, but she cautioned him. "Once I had a problem with this, so be considerate." With her cues and indications finished, he asked "who was it?" She replied "A woman next door, she shouted about my private life all over the building. My neighbour." She stated with an anxious look on her face. "Don't worry," he consoled her, "I'll be on cat-paws. Is she endowed with a sharp ear?" He paused. "She uses a stethoscope placing it against the common wall-divider." He rasped "No," he exclaimed, "never heard of that except once in the movies, as it showed a theme of unusual voyeurism."
"It's not that she's a voyeur, but she thrives on spread-ing stories about most tenants and owners of these units, claiming that they lead immoral lives."
"She's jealous of others, alone, disappointed, and bit-ter," he concluded. "Then we have to disappear into the underground," he carried-on with his thoughts.
"No," she said, "we are all right if we are just careful and do not express our feelings too loudly. No cries, no shouts, and no exuberant love-noises!" However, she closed the bathroom door and the bedroom door across the narrow passage studded with bookshelves that sup-posed to absorb noises, he thought. "It is like an ear that

provides an echo," she said, as she released the gilded door handle to the bedroom's white polished lacquer-door. Her peace of mind returned immediately and she turned visibly with ease. It usually took a bit of time to get her at ease.

Once she had released her tension in a first climactic height he could take her to quickly, she relaxed and he was able making love to her the way he would always remember her by.

Then, as she peaked for a second time, she started to be herself, free and unbridled she would straddle him, ride him, stroking him ever so gently, and moving up and down his cock to tease him into his first climax that then couldn't come so easy, but by the time she had succeeded, they tried to peak together in a wonderful orgasm. He loved that.

There were times they could reach their climaxes close together, but usually he came always later as she did. As time passed, they had synchronized their emotional beat and he was indeed sated as he left her. It lasted a long time for him. He could read her signs when she was sexually sated, from her radiance, her happy mood, her child-like attitude, and from her playfulness. She drifted into an adorable mood, teasing him, then genuflecting as he stepped from the shower, devouring him and arousing him again. As he became hard, she would pull him back into her bedroom and make love to him, and then being ferocious to him, offering herself in submission as he entered her from behind, encouraging him to live his lust with her. It was great lovemaking and even if he was near his height, she was allowing him only to touch her sphincter and never let him insert his small finger. Somebody had hurt her once and since rejected any penetration there. It had hurt her, she confessed later, but she liked stimulation of her bums.

Once he had finished chatting to Ina, who ran the café opposite Myrta's shop, he entered her shop through the glass door. He waited for Myrta, who talked to a couple, and passing time, he checked the display cabinets. He wondered where she kept her own creations, rings, amulets, bangles, she had shown the couple, who started leaving kissing Myrta on her cheeks. He gazed at a bangle with a theme from mythology.

"Hello," she said, "I have not done anything in here," she said approaching him fast and facing him closely, as if she wanted to kiss him too. "Come here," she said, "Your bracelet," she paused..."Let's do it together." She sat down on her bentwood chair at her small workbench. He sat there the day before, waiting for her patiently. He took a seat on the low stool next to her at the sales counter, facing her. He observed her way of working fascinated by her moving about. Having lit the acetylene torch, the silver started melting on the broken bracelet clasp. "There's a lot of copper in here," she said quietly, as if this bracelet was no silver at all. He had suspected this once, as green oxidation appeared on his skin and settled on the bracelet's clasps. He wore it doing garden work and the salt in his sweat had caused discolouration, but only at the clasps.

"Where did you buy this bangle?"

"In Athens," he said and recalled the day, he saw the three-piece bangle with intricate joints and a floral pattern of a repetitive palmetto motive, fascinating him immediately, in the window of a silversmith. The piece was unusual and had an oriental look about it, yet it had a Classical motive enhancing it. She smiled. "Well," he said after a pause, "I was had then, as it was sold to me as sterling silver." She looked serious and said nothing. "Then just solder an eye to the name tag, Myrta, and a catch on the opposite side. It'll be fine for a while." She just nodded and continued to choose a silver eye and a clasp from her parts-box at her workbench. As she worked, he saw her hands getting nervous, as his eyes were on her and he expressed desire. He had enveloped her into his being and she felt it. Having finished soldering, she got up and cooled the bracelet down emitting a swishing sound. Then she polished it. It looked fine to him, except that she had placed the eye on the right side of the clasp and the catch on the left, just the opposite to what he would have preferred, but he forgot to tell her.

"Thank you Myrta." He swallowed. "How much do I owe you?" She looked into his eyes for a while. Her left eye had a life on its own, moved slightly outward and was definitely connected to her calculating brain, while the warm glazed-over right eye remained fixed, looking at him tenderly. "It's fifteen Euro," she said. He took the bills from his wallet. Then he remembered.

"This is for you," he said, handing her an envelope.

"Oh," she said surprised "a letter?"

"It's a poem," he said. She opened the envelope and looked shortly at his poem. Then she noticed the drawing.

"OH!" She beamed, "for me? She studied the drawing.

"This is beautiful, thank you." She continued smiling. "I will read your poem quietly and study your drawing in detail." He prepared to go and looked at her for a last time.

"Good-bye Myrta, I will write to you."

"I like to receive your letters," she said. She stood quietly, her emotions played visibly in her face and her eyes. He walked up to her and placed his face close to hers and kissed her cheeks tenderly, something he wanted to do from the first time meeting her, but seeing only others doing it. Her skin was soft and it felt good to have her so close. He wished to be with her, undress her slowly and make love to her. She stirred slightly.

"I love to receive your letters," she said again softly "but I cannot write back."

"OK," he replied, "I'll see you Myrta." He turned at his heels and left without turning around. He couldn't. Certainly, to leave like this was suddenly painful for him. He hurried across the street in direction of his hotel and crossed the lobby – noticing his favourite receptionist talking to a guest – to take the lift.

The sisters had finished packing. Kim would stay another day, as she had a different flight schedule. She might still chat to the man who was interested in her, throwing his worry-beads whenever he saw her at the pool bar and terrace. He went downstairs to pay and arrange for a wake-up call.

He saw that the cute receptionist was on duty, as he had passed the lobby earlier. She smiled and asked for help with his luggage. When he had finished with the business, he said good-bye to her asking for her address, she responded in German and perhaps these two young women, Myrta and the cute receptionist were given to him as being pleasant company, as he felt to be out of love for some time. Most of his drive towards the airport it was like floating in these feelings of having met such wonderful women. His mind mirrored him the tale around Eurydice and he thought of composing a poem about his recently met Muses. Would he exchange them in a game of love? However, it was as if Myrta bore a look of sadness on her facial expression, if feeling unobserved. Since the death of his beloved Muse he had left a door to his heart open for someone new to enter. It was Myrta! How on earth was it possible that she had a lot in common, physically and mentally with his former Muse and instant lover? Sweet love – Myrta! Suddenly he understood what Anna, his dearest friend, had meant with her expression on love's bittersweet. While he was driving to the airport at Heraklion, a winding road in a continually changing landscape among a rocky coastal setting and intermittent hills, climbing mountain sides and extreme beautiful vistas of bays and holiday resorts at green-sea bays. The interplay of a soothing colour-varied sea and the mysterious dark shaded rock in a permanent dialogue repeated within the sound of traditional Greek music, streaming from his radio, he saw Myrto's sad facial side on her left profile, and as she turned, her other side beaming with joy, or so it seemed to him. Her face embedded with those twins – as he conceived it – perhaps she wasn't consciously presenting it that way. And this though, wasn't at all times, except for certain moments, when he sensed that she would open-up to him; whenever he gazed into her eyes, seeing her naked and unexpectedly her figure enveloped to a glow with the sun behind her. It took his breath away and he could hear the sound of his heartbeat aloud.

The winding road was linked into his thoughts. He loved this place and noticed that he was feeling uprooted again, just as he found the basic roots for a home. Since his last and greatest upheaval of his entire life, where would never be a permanent place for him to set roots again. That was almost a year behind him and was still vivid in his mind. Since he had met Myrta, a young Eurydice, embedded in her mystical presence, her eyes like dusky mirrors of her soul reflecting her being like a painting. In the dusk of its revelation, the pictures of all his Muses melted together into one dot of silver that flowed from the heat of the torch, Myrta was holding close to his heart, turning into a burst of fire that incinerated him at an instant.

But he felt alive and his mind wandered to her. He took her along for an extended walk on the beach and they bathed in the colours of the dissolving sun that melted into the horizon of the gentle sea, like his bracelet she had dunked into the cooling liquid hissing like a snake.

He had visions of her. Was this the return of a vengeful Eurydice who turned into parts of Myrta and wound around his tested heart, to squeeze the spirit of life from all its chambers? Or, was it her disappointment to find only ashes, foregoing a test she had wanted to approve of his new relationship?

As if he had met Anna's cousin in Myrta, from years back during his time in Athens, with similar tensions and habits that caused him to fall head over heels in love with her. And recently the dark and hot woman from a tavern in a small village with a glorious tree, having come across it through his travels through Crete. Damned! He sensed these women were related. She, an excellent cook of dishes she spiced-up with red peppers from a huge tree nearby, dominating the village square within a decked terrace. She had been flirting with him, some incidental touches and direct approaches quite soon afterwards, as she served him a hot stew, Cretan style. "This will spice-up your life," she murmured like Pythia reborn. He knew by instinct that she liked him the same way he liked her peppery food that set him on fire for her. He liked her co-incidental brushes and touches, the same way she liked his flirtatious banter. He called her A-2.

His thoughts turned from the three women he had met in Greece, again back to the road and an increased traffic, as soon as he turned onto the motorway that led to the capitol. Views along the way were spectacular: A calm blue sea that changed from an iridescent green to turquoise and blue shades. The boats looked like spots of leaves and debris floating on its liquid-metallic surface. On the horizon the cloud cover opened and let the sun have its fiery-bright interplay. The stage was set for a colourful good-bye. It hurt him and he cried inside. He suddenly felt the weight of his age pulling him down and push him around the snaking roads, to distract his concentration and toss him into the sea lying below, to join the debris-spots of boats and the solitary rock. He had a fight with his soul and part of it stayed behind, or was it still there, gazing into Myrta's eyes, diving into her soul. But only his carapace was here, driving and fulfilling the demands of contracts, and keeping to dates and transport agreements – A shell, knocked about by the waves, tossed onto a pebbled beach and giving-off a screeching sound? A knight, his armour confiscated and denied to him; he was made redundant turning to some other life.

He returned the Citroen to the parking lot, where he had started his trip. Walking across the square in front of the airport, passed the bus stations, and finally he arrived at the car rental office at the corner of arrivals. The woman-clerk present asked him to wait, while she walked back the same route he came, to check the car for damages. He was frozen. With every cluster of minutes spent, he felt that life had separated from him and was indeed ambivalent: Sad and happy at the same time. He had difficulty cheering

While his spouse, seated on a bench adjacent the car rental shop, waited patiently, he walked up and down the narrow elongated hall in search of a CD of Greek music, he had listened to on his car radio. Nobody understood what he wanted and there was nothing to buy.

As the DC 9 lifted itself off at the end of the runway, it slid across the blue-silvery sea, a slight shower rushed across his skull. For some time, as the plane banked and heaven and sea seemed to flow into one big blue, those moments belonged to his Muse A mingling with Myrta. 'Bye Myrta' he whispered, whishing he could kiss her. But as sudden as this image appeared, it disappeared again like the cumuli clouds, and marriage had suffocated love he once had. Repetitive waves breaking and white foam lapping the ivory sand at the shore. Within it and below it, he had found love, yet, however hard he pursued it he never had found permanence in love. And at present he found a matching woman and he hoped this love wouldn't be terminated through fate's strange incidents. Was it again to be temporary?

He had found Myrta on his last days of a holiday and he had lost her the same time as he had come across his sleeping spouse's back. She was alarmed as if something was wrong. Shit! He had suppressed to cry out.

"Yes," he said "it's life that's what's wrong."

"You have to get up early today, to do all your errands, and you are tired having worked hard. Don't punish yourself. Rest a bit and you'll be fine."

"Yes," he replied, "my life got-up too late and now it's upside down and it feels painful."

"Relax," she said. That's what he's done right now, hasn't she a clue? He thought, but didn't say. Gentle talking from his spouse didn't calm him down. The more she talked softly, the more he felt like shouting. He wanted to stand-up and start performing and he didn't mind the airplane went down to have a dip in the sea. Fate hadn't booked them for drowning. What a terrible death, he thought having discussed suicide with his friend before. She was occupied thinking about death since she was a child and her father had tragically died. She had dismissed various forms of suicide, only to reinforce her own mind that she couldn't do any of these choices to end her life. In the end, her diseased body's fighting capacity for life was lulled into sleep with morphine. It had been deceived and taken-out of her mind. Pain disappeared, but claimed her consciousness and she slid into a coma. He imagined it was like dying below water, a kind of drowning. Her beloved cousin spoke of a miracle that supposed to happen, if one believes in one. He, on the other hand, spoke about love as the best of healers. She let him touch her and then she felt on top of the world, dying and being loved felt as the best alternative to suicide.

Leaping from the top of the Acropolis, she also considered, as a couple did years before. But he did that feel to hit the bottom rocks holding hands? Of course one cannot, but are we getting punished? Imagine that you would be dead immediately, but what if not? If we do not succeed, we'll be punished. Is the law that stupid? But then one has been driven to come to this. One wishes to conquer death, slowly stealing one's life away. If there's a miracle then the win of life over death is the greatest one! We are fighting death with all powers we know, but many battles later we are getting tired. Not being the ones falling into the dust, get-up, brush off, and start all over again. How many people had come forward with a win over death and enjoying another life? Yet at one stage we have accepted our resignation, finally we come up with an acceptance of death. Besides, she mused: Life's unfair! He saw her fight, her final tiredness, her anger and sadness to leave him back in the land of the living. He felt a deep compassion for her, something he had never felt before at any death of a family member. He loved her and the bone man had won. "Beloved friend," he whispered, "I will write down our emotions and at least we held the shadows of death in check for as long as we could love and shy them away with our union." He murmured into her ear as he loved her for the last time.

"Life's short!" He still whispered as if she would be present. It had the same tone of sadness as the grey tarmac at E. Venizelos airport. He liked this airport above the other one he would land soon at the dark city that lay beyond the Dark Continent to the Cape. Beside he had to leave its jewel, the Acropolis, that held for him not only the gateway to the Western civilisation, but all the art that was unique in the world, albeit all the pilferage through history. It was his personal jewel that connected him forever to his Muse A, the one who had installed in him art and poetry through her teachings of heart and soul, body and mind.

You could see how an important gateway this unique place held for him, whenever he arrived from Africa of the South, for many years, but for his entire life starting from his childhood. Now, like a continental love affair, there was no friend arriving to fetch him and his spouse from the airport. He resorted to shop cultural remembrances through music, music, music, and remember her image through it.

He asked in a souvenir shop for a musical store. The young man directed him to the toy-shop. "They keep Greek music at the back," he smiled at him. As he entered the shop he asked the girl at the counter, who called someone else. He told her what kind of music he wanted. She showed him three CD's, but recommended him the popular one that mentioned: 35 Chronios, meaning 35 years of the performer Giannis Parios, who featured on the cover. It was a set of three CD's. He paid and left in better spirits. She was smiling as he read the Greek letters 'Coffees Iced' at the buffet next door. He bought two frappes for himself and his spouse, who still sat quietly at the bench. She was glad he was back and surprised her with a refreshing drink.

Then he sat next to her and made some notes into his journal. It was about olive trees and Minoan cultures and beautiful cities at the Med, mountains and winding roads; and he saw himself driving towards Makrigiallos. He saw Myrta's shop and she was just leaving. He stopped his car and she recognized him, stepping into his car like an old friend. She popped the door close and kissed him. They drove to a beach Myrta knew that was off the trodden track of tourists. She was the first stripping off her clothes and taking a run into the sea. He followed her example, and enjoying this free and sensual experience, swimming in the nude in the blue sea, touching now and then as he caught-up with her. He held her waist pulling her close and kissing her, and he had an exhilarating feeling of touching her, kissing her all over and making love to her for the first time. She was Lithe and Nubian, agile, fast, sensual, and the most passionate, just before she peaked, biting him into his shoulder. Then lying down on the soft sanded beach, drying from the water and feeling the body shrink until there wasn't anything left, soaked-up into warm ivory sand, like water into a soft towel. Two wet spots left behind that dried-up and were again wetted by a restless licking sea, leaving their footprints behind forever.

He fell into a snooze while the airplane climbed to its comfortable zone and the voice of the stewardess woke him to receive his food. His spouse was up while he slept, but fell asleep shortly afterwards. Was all just unreal and like a dream? It seemed to be real and when a dream happened, he didn't like to get back to reality.

Travelling that far was the end of a road of the heavens and nobody in his sane mind would burn to frazzles lying on the speckled sand, exposed to an attacking sun that was unfiltered. Due to carbon dioxide emissions, man had burnt holes into the protective ozone layers. He heard about the extreme conditions in Africa in the news.

He played the CD he had bought at E. Venizelos airport. "Who is that?" His wife wanted to know. "Gianni?" He said, being on first name terms since he adored his voice. "How nice," she commented. The music on the CD represented his own life, he mused, and he had played all of Gianni's CD's. "Only I'm not that famous." He looked into the distance. "He is as old as you are," his spouse said. "Indeed," he replied, "he's a great singer." He looked at the face on the CD-cover. "His music is soul-stirring." He said. He saw the eyes of Myrta, every time Pam played the set. She started with the first and listened until she had finished the set. "I'd rather be in Makrigiallos," she murmured, and then played the set again, until she was sated with the music. He was unaware that she love this kind of popular Greek music that much. It had obviously affected her differently to him. It gave her back some longing to an island she had liked too, but in a different way he liked. He was glad. He also knew that sooner or later they could catch a live concert with Giannis. What an experience that would be? They would certainly travel back for such an occasion.

*

The Enquiry

There it is again: This universal belonging to a woman. Why is it this particular woman? She had touched the pulse of my soul at an instant moment. There's not much time at the window of an enquiry counter, where people queue-up to be helped all the time. The thick separating glass brings faces closer, but divides them at the same time, almost mystically. I'm talking to a ghost, the voices are muffled, even if we'll turn on the volume of our voices and at the same time feel embarrassed about it. It's like the talk between persons hard of hearing. However, I place myself near enough to study her facial details and then stay hooked on her eyes that are the only windows through which there's still some personal talk. Hints of sympathy in the corners, where the warmth gathers like a tear to belie the formalities and the play of an impersonal look of business-eyes. In was drawn to her the first moment I laid eyes on her. I watched her the way she talked, kept her cool, but more than that, I was fascinated by her dusky appearance that had always fascinated me in women. Besides, her charcoal-hair falling like rich veins of shiny coal running along a granite groove, evokes in me a stream of consciousness at an instant. I study her well-shaped lips and her smile that's still indicative, but with the prospect of great radiation that'll burn into my being, once when I'll be close to her. The daily practicing of psychology is apparent in the way of her addressing people. The close touches with people on the other side of a sheet of glass, their emotions apart but deflected thus, is a double security measure for her safety. But then, why would I be touched by her personal vibes, or do I just imagine that I am? Perhaps she is putting me on, but I am not hurt in risking my emotions and then fail.

I don't place high expectations consciously any longer, but subconsciously I do that all the time. She helps, gives advice, and lets me have information on the state of my accounts. "Can I have your ID please?" I hand her my ID-book and she studies it, then looks at me again. I look straight into her eyes and she smiles back a business-type smile, yet cautiously and not easily obtained. The training she's been put through has left marks of indoctrinations on her face that changes her expressions all the time. I am finally identified as being the one who I claim to be in my green ID-Book. But then I'm still mesmerized by her eyes, the dark and mysterious mirror of her soul. It reveals to me love, pain, and all human emotions I have usually found in women I fall into love with. I have seen these eyes before. Somewhere I had transferred feelings to them to kiss them and love them, at the instant of a first visual contact. The first sparks of sympathy that ignites the heart for the other person. Then a chain of reaction starts, the flow of the spring of inspiration that has started with the first drop. It has since stayed as the start of a spring, but now it's gathering more drops and has become a trickle of water that meanders its way along the river bed of my feelings, often in narrow and fine cut grooves.

The spark of fondness has ignited the match that lit the candle, in whose light I'll see the outlines of her face. But the flame is cool and contained, flickering only occasionally, when I'm entering the banking hall on the first floor. The long access raises my expectation to find her here today. As I undertake to bank my deposit, I glance in the direction of the enquiry counter, to admire her smooth, long charcoal-hair, she wears with an unusual, asymmetrical placed centre partition upon her well-shaped head. Her slightly tanned skin appears almost white, but a shade darker than her shiny white teeth she'll show sometimes, when in the mood for a great smile.

"I know you," she says. I smile at her.

"Well," I tell her, "we used to discuss politics in the bank-branch I was meeting you before." Her eyes sparkle and her face lightens up. "I was staying in a nearby suburb with apartment buildings nearby."

"Yeah, I start to recall that." She replies.

"But now the bank is being revamped and it has moved temporarily to a place out of my way."

90

"I know," she says and strikes immediately that conciliatory tone I have missed long ago.

"I used to have a good relationship with the bank manageress, besides an excellent service, and most importantly she had always an ear for my troubles and did not shy helping me out. There was an intelligent dialogue and good communication. There are no more consultations possible with a direct access to a manager or manageress. The banks and institutions have written 'Ubuntu' on their banners, which is to be lauded, but that shouldn't mean to fend off someone with a problem that could otherwise be resolved. Collective responsibility still does need a leading person to be elected. The ivory tower thus created will let us have a blank paper form filled in and submitted as an application. Whatever answer we'll receive, we'll never know the reasons and the details of the voting. Even the loyalty of 30 years to a bank means nothing any longer. Certainly one could see the amount of contributions one has thus supported their institution with, or is that not discussed any longer? There is the hard-nose attitude of granite." I pause and she nods having listened to my narrative about banking relationships

"I know you," she says again. "Yes we have discussed politics way back and had a great time doing it." I smile at her again.

"I'm just kidding," I say to her, detecting the return of her initial joy into her shell of indifference. It seemed she is hurt by the sudden verbal floodlighting, her irises turn smaller locking in her soul, and the copper shine in her eyes recedes to a bland impersonal expression. I still detect that tinge of warmth left in the corners of her eyes, as she looks me over and my accompanying friend. Then her eyes come to rest on mine again, as she hands me back my ID-book through the small slot in the counter that supposed to be bullet-proof, like the multi-layered vertical partition glazing.

Here is no chance even to brush hands against each other, experience the thrill of a touch to express my fondness to her. Then I ask her for the printouts for the last six months on my current account. I wish to do this more often with her. There's still something left, unfinished. I cannot ask her for her private telephone number. I guess I could, but feel too restricted in front of all the people, my friend, and my spouse, who just joined me. It would be impolite, uncouth, and a show of bad manners. I have to come earlier in the morning and make sure I'll have a chance to get served by her window, when nobody is around and I could talk to her, get her name and the details of her personal contact domain. If I'm lucky, then I would invite her to an exotic Indian meal downstairs. Certainly, they would serve us well with her background. The restaurant praises itself to be the best North Indian cuisine. That's worth a test any day. But when will this happen? When? It has to be now! Usually I'm shy at the beginning, while all these thoughts cross my mind rapidly. I look at her and her smile warms my heart. She said that she knew me, but from where? I wonder, she made me curious indeed. Another branch? I might have mistaken her for somebody else.

Does she think I am in trouble with my usually large overdraft for an individual? She might have thought that he had made serious money once, to have such a generous extension of credit. Is he broke now? She certainly had thoughts about that looking at the bottom line, while she rubber stamps the print-outs. Would she though accept an invite for lunch? But would she in time accept an invite for a tryst? It had to be a tryst, the only workable relationship for married people. Is she married? I guess she would be as a woman in her early thirties. However, these details are interesting indeed, as anything in a tryst could be circumvented. Never interested much in purely historical facts, I cared only for what we could learn from them. If not, what are we then carrying all this junk in our heads around for? The moment counts, and who has not yet learned that?

Even my young Muse, D'Elle, tells me that and I agree with her wholeheartedly. Good-bye doesn't mean adieu. I hope to see her again. For now, I'll give her a name and incorporate her identity reference into my life. Her face

92

and her dusky appearance are imbibed like smooth red-wine. Now it's solely to make friends quickly and push without any strain to the stage of intimacy. There's not that much time left. There never is. I wish to return to the bank alone and take advantage of the opportunity, as I meet regularly with Gore, I work together with, who also has business with this bank.

That'll be the departure next time. What day? Probably Monday is best, as there are few people on a Monday morning at the bank. And what will I do then? As we have to deposit cash at all times, it'll be a good excuse to do it at this branch, without making it too obvious to see her. However, I have to choose the queue and have pretence to see her. I dislike to be called to another window, as there are three others.

This time I wanted to come alone, but my spouse had to go to see the dentist, so I had to take her to the surgery and we visited the bank afterwards. I stood there thinking about my chances I would be getting to be at the right time at her queue. Would she speed up her consulting to take me rather than let me go to one of the other women I do not fancy at all? I watched the TV screen that offered spectacular soccer with the Greek National Team against some English League team. From the corner of my left eye I could see that she was acting fast. I could hear her words sped-up. I was on! I watched her expecting me with a glow in her dusky eyes and the presence of a Southern woman, racy, and warm. "I'm here again," I said to start the conversation.

"What can I do for you?" I swallowed.

"I have forgotten the code for my account number, I carry for 30 years in my head, probably mixed up two digits. This is a bad day." I said to her and add: "Everything goes wrong today." She looks at me concerned.

"It will be better just now." She said and I gaze at her enigmatic smile that makes me weak and turns me soft. I wish I could be alone with her. Gazing into the dark corners of her eyes, as if she invites me to access her inner space, where fondness for me could be in store. How I like talking to her, besides, draw-out my time with her to watch her moves and actions to get this one month print-out for me. It's a joy to see her cat-like movements. Again I'm at a loss to ask her for her private phone number. If I would come alone next time, would that be too obvious? So what, she knows my soul's vibrations anyway, even through this bullet-proof window. It's just a formality to get the time and date fixed for meeting alone. Now, at the end of the year it's a date that I could set as a lunch for clients, the fashionable entertaining treat. But there is something more important. I'm interested in the depth of a personality rather than the pure surface skin sensations. In the pursuance of my existence, since my Muse had stepped into the 'Great Abyss', as she called it, I seek the warmth of another genuine human being, who could match with me in many ways. In the vacuum of my mature life thus created, I have been susceptible of growing sensors and feelers, to find people I really like. I am sure I will be successful in meeting her personally at one time.

*

THE MUSES

When he met her again, she was wearing a red sweater, opened up to let her generous breasts float between her thick arms, covered by a loose blue tee-shirt that was still at places pressed for tightness, as if she wished to let her soul press-out all the flesh she had accumulated over the years, since her husband's death. One day she opened up to him. You are full of life, she almost shouted pressing her top onto him. It surrounded him like a group of bodies in a Swingers club. He thought nothing much then and left it at that, understanding the exuberances of her feelings to be part of her motherly way of smothering her children with love. She had one son, intelligent, and bound to carve-out a living within the accounting department of a corporation that might swallow him up for life.

Over the years she sent him some photographs. They talked about many issues. She loved traveling. Being part of a world-wide charity organisation, she could see the world from a perspective of a volunteer helper, someone positioned in projects to further the life of millions of disadvantaged people. She never talked much about her life with such involvements, but handing him other data for a picture he painted of her: a voluptuous woman who lived alone, busying herself with many issues of helping others, never wanting anything for herself.

He mused: she was indeed a philantropin embedded in a luxuriant body, he observed through her webcam when she was up early in the morning, or going to bed late at night. She intended to have a man, but never would take the last step of acquaintance. He sensed that she desired love, but nobody would even think of it in her position being part of a traditionally repressed society of women. That was his mental concept she would appear in and now and then, as time went by, he would update this picture of her. She travelled to the desert at the Pakistani border with India, attending to the unfortunate and stranded, who were accommodated in temporary homes

95

at a tent-structured village. It always seemed that the people were victims of a war, brokered by men at the helm of governments and on higher orders. All he could see were the edited pictures on the mass-media of this unfortunate human entanglement in midst of two fronts.

He was alone in his world of seeking a Muse to whom he could relate to, but he was not in good luck since the death of his teacher and sponsor, who was a poetess in her youth and then turned to short-story writing as her means of expressing herself. They had a short relationship of exchanging poetry. She loved his poems and inspired by them, she answered him back with her own poems that were written in English, a foreign language to her, as it was to him. Yet, having lived for over 30 years in a mainly English-speaking country, he considered English as his first language. Their meeting happened at the spur of a moment, spontaneous and fast-track, like a Chick Corea interpretation on the piano.

He thrived under the spell of stimulating encouragement. She prompted him with ideas that turned into the best poems he ever wrote, or so he felt floating on a sudden emerging enthusiasm. Well, he did not know his depth of a writer yet. She took him on a journey to soaring heights, to some inky depth in the underworld, and to the dark edges of an abyss: 'The Great Void', as she referred to it. He had been previously there and he could tell her about his side of emotions and visual impressions. As she was pondering throughout her adult life the question about death, this was a topic they could discuss and broaden-up upon, stretch their minds across and explore their thoughts about.

He left her in the underworld and appeared as Orpheus to her. She disliked the mythological story, but in spite it stirred her deeply and already some sketches were thus laid down for his own Orpheus and Eurydice ballad, only he did not know yet.

He calls Vib his Earth-mother now. At one stage of their initial light banter she desired to see him in the nude. He had given up on video-communication since Artemis' death; he still considered as unreal and not a fact! Against his own wishes he had avoided seeing Artemis on her death bed, furthered by the woman who knew her best, who grew-up with her on a distant island in the Aegean Sea. He wished to visit the place one day, but had to put this thought off his mind for a long time now. Vib was like a mother to him and with her luxuriant presence, the right person to take him to her bosom, and one evening he was taken aflame with such longing and desire for his passed-on woman that he stripped for Vib, thinking of his first encounter with Artemis. Vib gasped and was extremely excited. He could hear her laboured breathing and her climactic cry as she peaked by his imaginary touches; his nude body enfolding on her as if he would magically stretch her bronze limbs and torso to the limit of their sexually imagined act. He was her first man in an intimate act, since the passing of her spouse, while Vib was his first woman since Artemis had stepped into the 'Big Void' of the universe, as he would call her tragic death forthwith. He wanted it to be a penultimate state of travel, rather than death. Death was ultimate and there was still something left over, lots of love still left in him he had not yet spurned on her. Maybe he could, through other loves, pour all on her, visit her in the underworld with Vib, and then through his presence and the help of Vib reawaken her to life again. Vib was good at reviving the unfortunate, care for the disadvantaged and listen to his needs, have compassion for his great love and bring her magically back to life.

Vib loved his lean body and she wanted him, but she didn't know much about enticement and sex, which he would teach her about now and then, slowly and in doses she could digest. She never even heard about oral sex, nor did she think about. He told her about his experiences. There were always aesthetical considerations involved in sex and eroticism. He avoided those issues, keeping Vib as an image for Earth mother, with her huge breasts overpowering her entire body. He had developed a need for a mother and Vib was healing his Oedipus complex entirely. He loved her as much as he disliked this side of his being, to use her for his healing, but she didn't mind at all.

Love has many shades. He could be wild with her and then philosophical, distant the next moment, and narcissistic as she accepted his varying moods of an artist. She loved his poetry and his ways expressing himself. Most of all she became obsessed with his body and desired him so much that he felt punishing her by not showing himself to her. She had by now met hundreds of people and then perhaps someone else who was having fun with her too. Yet, she always came back to him, a good friend. They kept their friendship going.

He thought of Sim and then his disappointment that she was into women more than she had even with the slightest feelings expressed for him, or shown on a continual basis, although she claimed she had feelings for him. This was the love that had been denied to him as unfulfilled, so he drifted between his Muses, Elle, and Vib, to carry-on living in the groove of a poet and to conduct a writer's life.

His self-realization depended on some of his poems to be published. He gave-up. He looked for another route. For some time he had subscribed to a newsletter from a writing company and when he mentioned this to Artemis, she said that she would run to such a course if offered in Greece. Yet, he was always afraid of influences, but then, there were books to read. Did selective reading not represent a possible influence? He wrestled with this question like ha had wrestled with his love, Sim. Finally the writers' workshop won over Sim, Vib, and Elle. He did not have to give them up, but further his own writing skills and then get additional motivation, preferably from a teacher, a woman he could relate to, a woman who could do that

He was entering a new phase in his writing life. He'll try anyway. Perhaps a way of entering a world he disliked: The bureaucracy of publication. He thought of self-publication for those books he considered as a work of art by his standards. And he'll stick to that at present. There must be possibilities of layers in us for the related genres of writing, like in love. There are many layers in us different with every other person one likes, for some or other part of their erotic make-up picture in one's mind.

Vib had told him that she had fallen and hit her styccox badly. Well, just now it's her turn to travel to the USA too for a course in building a village community. Elle is finishing her last year to become a professional nurse and Sim is looking for a new home to be comfortable in, with her newly acquired Borzoi hound.

He will write, learn and try to publish through his new Muse perhaps? He'll try any avenue, as it's the most tedious process there is: a real anti-climax on the long road of being recognized as a spirited writer.

*

The Sacrifice

When he intended to express himself in the past, he did that with a drawing. He once shared his longings with a fellow artist across the Atlantic. She was becoming impossible, suffocating him with innumerable demands. When she eventually turned pushy, he decided that this wasn't the relationship he really wanted. He recalled the word: 'Xanthippe', the Greek name for a woman impossible to bear. Besides, he felt threatened, but the drawing he had intended as a present for her, was in his new style he had forged. He liked it, but he would not give it to her.

Turning from drawing to write poetry, he focused on his new literary efforts, and he sensed that she was limited and that she was of no help to inspire him, but to satisfy her all-devouring appetite for new words she used to appear original, though plagiarising and copying other writers. He coined himself new words or had detected some new ones, but he wished to keep them as long as his poems weren't published. But she had found new friends and being disappointed in them, wished to return and have him in her large clutches, which he definitely refused. She had found again friends beside friends and made herself seen on the Internet poetry café as a sought after member of the poet's circle situated in San Francisco. He didn't mind, as he was getting tired of her antics and when he started seriously to write, she faded completely from his life. Ever since he was falling into a creative groove recalling an aunt who had given him some crayons for his sixth birthday. One of his first noticeable artwork was a depiction of three colourful clowns, he submitted to his art teacher. He received top marks.

He read about various programs to communicate on the Internet. He chose one new program, then he added two others that had different features one could make use of and he had a good time making new acquaintances. Soon he had found more company that he was able to handle. Yet, once the novelty wore off he stayed with a few friends he enjoyed talking to, but time restrictions limited his progress. When Myrna came along, he couldn't believe that she had the personality he was looking for. Indeed, she had found him, but as soon as she sensed his interest in her, she stopped communication, but messaged him: "I am leaving on holidays. I will travel to a Greek island. One can see the coast of Turkey from there." That was it. Period. Her line went dead and she disappeared, a ghost swooshing into the hull of an enormous ferryboat. The white phantom of the Internet. He had to give-up on her, but instinctively he had left his door ajar. Games – he thought, stupid games! In spite, he wrote her a few freely composed letters. After sending them to her mailbox, he left the initial incidental meeting stand on its own in the corner of his monitor.

The time she had mentioned to stay away had passed and she still hadn't answered his mail. Bitch! He thought. In midst of his writing exercises she burst into his door he had left ajar. "Hello! Are you there? "

"Yes, I am," he replied waiting she'd explain herself.

"Thank you for your letters, I was happy, I could write."

"Hello Myrna," he said. "I thought you might have someone else to write to." He sighed.

"No," she said in a serious tone, "I have not looked at all. When I write, I write. There's no time for anything else." His thoughts about her changed like day and night. Suddenly he would see that she was a writer. She had never told him. He started to send her his poems, as she encouraged him. At times she corrected a line, or suggested a better punch-line, and better subtleties. Sometimes she just suggested, but left all open for him to decide. Then she made a forceful gesture to influence his style. "I agree that rhythm is important. Try not to be too narrative." Slowly she would introduce him to her world of poetry. She was a poet from her teens, like he was, with the exception that she was coming up the ranks in competitions and she was becoming an icon for him.

She sent him photographs of herself from the age of eleven. Then she asked for pictures of him from a similar age onward. Their photographs exchanged depicted their lives they now relived together. They had become good friends, met since childhood and grew up together. Now they felt romance and the sensation of falling in love. She became his world now: "Myrna I love you," he mumbled and kissed her for the first time. Then their ways parted for a while.

The middle chunk of their adventurous life made them seek different continents. They tested their professions and life's first knocks left their indelible marks. She intended to join the bluestocking sorority, while he studied art and design of buildings and their construction. But he wasn't satisfied. Within him raged at times a violent creative need, the need to love a woman the same way he created art. He knew that once he had satisfied one, then others would closely follow, just like in creating his work.

For now his wings in creativity were cut continually, like those of a parrot; a hindrance to fly freely and to thrive as nature had intended it. He suffered, fell in love numerous times, as it wasn't the love he imagined to turn-out as he wished it would. Something was always amiss. His art suffered. He started developing a neurosis of being a failure, became serious, and tended to be withdrawn. Solely being happiest when he handed himself over to the stream of creative consciousness, locked-up in a fortress of his mother's home. He would withdraw into the loft, where he could fall unrestrained into his groove of creativity. It was painting. He created new and good art, and even his teacher and mentor praised his work. He sat still in front of his work and looked at it, sheet for sheet, and he seemed to be mesmerized, not saying a single word.

To stage the group-exhibition of five artists never would happen. It had been dependant on financial support and finally as time went-bye someone else had a similar art-idea, with similar styles of work and even the use of similar colours. The financially better positioned artist had beaten them. Especially he was defeated by an artist, whose name he still remembers, who had kicked him off the cultural scene of an important exhibition. He cried in anger: Same colours, same theme, and same expression. He was devastated and from that moment he had set foot into the Gallery at the Dome, he was never to touch paint again.

Myrna liked him and they found that they had many interests they shared. The more they met the more they fell in love. They became intimate. He experienced great moments of his creative spirit when he was with her, and the words would flow from his pen.

"Be prolific," she had as a saying whenever they parted. And he was. His creativity a butterfly, like she was. He flew after her and stepped into the air of lightness. His mind could fly instantly. She had opened the rusty door to his innermost and set his fantasy free. After all these years of searching and suffering she became his lover and Muse. They carried on exchanging their lives, carrying on where they had left off. There were many stories, many happenings. Above all, with her daily prompts she motivated him, taught him tolerance and patience, the use of his senses and the sharpening of his mind's concentration. One thing he couldn't though conquer: Jealousy. He was jealous about her former lovers, but not more than she was about his. Above all, he couldn't show her all the hot intensity he had for her, being a great distance away. How could he ever meet her? He was jealous about her free spirit and her fleeting mind. He was caught in it like the parrot with clipped wings. Perhaps in time he could be out of it. And indeed, as more he learned about her, the more he wanted her. But he also knew that he could never possess her. He had to adjust his position constantly, throwing all else aside: Tradition, marriage, and friendships. He wanted to be free as she was and fly unbridled, love without restraint, and be happy like a child, as she had said.

"We love for love, like l'art pour l'art." She spoke from his heart. It sounded like a revolutionary slogan from the heart, reawakening his corner of an avant-garde artist, he thought of being on the way to become one.

"I don't want to hurt anybody," she told him one day, having harboured serious thoughts about their relationship. She thought about the society she lived-in, about her relatives and dependants, and about her own marriage. The more they turned free from all trivial matters, as they had originally stated, away from a hackneyed life, the more they became conscious of their surroundings and duties: He, through his drawings and she, through musing and writing.

He pushed for love. Had she not promised him happiness? He couldn't function without her. In a way he was married to her in a fulfilling sexual way. Both had partners who were much older and had succumbed due to a lack of libidos from sexual love. This was the propellant to their life now, the lustful emphasis that enabled them to develop into the artists they strived to become. He was in the heaven of his last third of life, or so he conceived his exhilarations, she could induce in him, every time they met. Or was he perhaps living in a fool's paradise?

He didn't analyse his life with her as she did. He felt that would destroy his feelings, as he wanted to be instant, true, and free. She adored him and then agreed to meet him. "We say here, in flesh and blood," she was smiling as she spoke. Further discussions turned into instructions for him: No drama, no sacrifices, and no sign of affection in public."

"Agreed," he confirmed.

He was frightened the moment he stepped off the steep stair from the all-night flight that landed at Heraklion airport. It was warm for early March. Must be the early spring days, he thought, she had mentioned. All has to be stealthy and discreet. The tension mounted in him: It will kill me, a voice said inside. But his curious mind drove him on. He wanted to express his life and he had to meet her. Thoughts of doubt crossed his mind while he took a cab at the exit. The driver spoke English.

"Where do you stay?"

"I wish to go to the Artemis Resort Hotel."

"Oh, it's quite a distance." The driver explained, while he handed him the address and directions.

"I got it," the driver said, before he could respond. He saw the man's eyes were forming pools of water from tiredness. "It's excellent. I have a friend there, tell him Nikos sent you. His name is Takis Konstantinos."

"Thank you," he murmured. The driver carried on. "See? We have clear weather coming-up. Crete is all mountains and the sea. It will be warm and a fine weather, you've brought along." His laugh felt like friendly slaps on his back.

He thought of Myrna. Was she ready to see him? Was she as pretty as on the photographs? He recalled the last one and a half-year of correspondence, all the talks, her endless queries, and a multitude of questions she put forward to test his genuine personality. She was convinced he was, yet she was still querying it all.

"This is my character-in love," she said. "Take no notice." But how couldn't he? At first he didn't mind, as love makes blind. All he did was cast the reality aside that was projected through the daily slog to him. Now the time had arrived to place a milestone here in the heart of ancient cities that served as the cradle to the Western world once: The Minoan Culture. "They dig-up the whole island," the driver carried on pointing to an excavation site.

He could not recover from his thoughts and views as quickly, as the driver pointed already to another site, when suddenly a small village emerged behind a multitude of small hills, along a snaking road along a mountainous drive close to the sea. Driving toward the spread-out village he saw the hotel. "Nice," he said "they have finally started to build beautiful hotels, like the Artemis. There's good progress. They drove downhill to the hotel sign and the driver stopped at the entrance. The view was already spectacular from here. Indeed! All-turquoise sea with a gentle bay in iridescent blue colours. He paid and the driver handed him his business card. "Don't forget to get up to the terrace, the view over the bay is breathtakingly beautiful.

"Thank you," he mumbled. The cab drove off. He felt exhausted and he longed for a shower and a soft bed with fresh white linen. He was awaited at reception. He apologized being tired and the friendly lass handed him a key. "Welcome," she said, "please fill me the forms in later."

Once he had set the alarm, he pulled off his clothes, fell into bed, his face sank into the soft cushions and he fell asleep. He dreamt about the Classical times, participating in a bull ceremony at Knossos, and saw her coming towards him, having sprung from the shadows of the dark-red columns, her beautiful breasts exposed in her tight blue dress, in the traditional Knossos hourglass-fashion with a long skirt.

He was happy. They had made love. First, she took him to the most famous sites of Knossos. They were early for the masses and could enjoy their walk through the excavations of this ancient site. At the charming Queens chamber he kissed her. The tall wall beside them covered-up their intimate embraces. Step for step she allowed him touching her. She enjoyed being touched by him, as she wanted him to search for her wetness, feel it, stroke her, and taste her. Then she touched him too, desiring to hold his arousal between the fingers of her cupping hand. Suddenly it started to drizzle and he pulled her hand to follow him to a niche in the passage. His left hand slipped between her slacks and her skin. For the first time his mid finger could reach down to her vulva's moistness. He could feel that she had cut her pubic hair. Wow! He sighed, for eighteen months he wanted to her like this. It felt like the heaven he had with her virtually, only that it was undoubtedly a superior feeling. She gasped, he retrieved his hand and licked his finger, tasting her for the first time: cinnamon with a touch of almonds and the musty smell of rain, adding the salty spice from his body to it. Some drops running down his face mingling with this delicious cocktail of her life, melting into the palms of his hand and onto his bruised lips from kissing her continually. He licked his fingers and inserted them into her pants. As he pushed his hand passed her slackened belly button, he wished to be in her. She buckled as soon as he inserted his finger into her pussy and then moved it slowly in and out of her gently, as the rain fell and whispered a tune above their heads, on the rocks and on the roof above their heads. She gasped more as he touched her hardened clitoris and began rubbing it to come to her first height with him. The moment she threw her head back, he sensed her climax to be close. She peaked and spread her juices across his fingers, hands, and her thighs, excited him. He was hard for a long time. She clasped her fingers tightly around his cock as she climaxed. He kissed her deeply and she moaned in his kiss down her throat. He kept kissing her. Too many tourists were passing at present close to the spot, near the path to the lower chambers, but nobody came close to their spot, the only spot they could find, being impatient to touch immediately. Her pussy was flowing with the juices of her life and he wanted to take her pants off.

"Not here!" she said aghast, "there are too many people."

"I want you," he gasped with a dry voice. "I want to make love to you."

"I want it too," she agreed, "but where?"

"Let's go to a hotel," he continued to convince her that it was important to him.

"I don't like hotels," she said with an even tone.

"Perhaps tomorrow then?" He eased up the tension, releasing her from his tight embrace.

"Yes," she said, "perhaps tomorrow." She paused. "I have to sit down, my knees are feeling weak." He sat down next to her on a low marble wall. The drizzle had stopped. They rested. Two lovers on the verge of committing to their first intimate meeting and in search for a venue to complete their physical fusion.

"I have not done this since I was at university," she said to him.

"I love you," he said.

"I know," she replied, "I could feel your cock in me through this stroking of your fingers."

"I have placed the seeds of my desire into you, Myrna!" This petting had brought to him the ways of her arousal: quick, instant, and intense. He could feel his excitement in the throbbing of his penis that was still erect in the bulge of his jeans. But he had held back. He knew that he wanted to satisfy her first. They were in a unified rhythm that had, due to their virtual relationship, grown into mutual harmony, though tested continually many times.

He was exhausted, tired, and in a tense and irritated mood. But there were minutes he wanted her strongly as she bent down. In a sudden mood he turned her around and devoured her. Then she lifted one leg up over his shoulders in her heat that he could take her easier. This play went on for some time. He thought that he was finished and his libido had given up, and whatever they tried, he couldn't climax. She started fellating him, then had to give up eventually, having been like two wild animals .He collapsed finally.

He could not sleep and paced up and down his room like a caged animal. When she contacted him on his mobile phone, they started to exchange their common moments of great arousals, and he almost went mad wanting her. Even in communicating over the phone their desires flooded them with want. She told him she was in pain. His penis had grown hard and was hurting him.

The following day she came in the early evening. She was late as usual. He waited for her leaning against a lamppost, writing some sketches he intended to use for a poem. She had chosen a public square in Heraklion. He wondered why. She appeared with quick steps, kissed him fleetingly, and took his hand and pulled him around the corner. The square was deserted at this late time of the day and during the early wintry season. A slight mist had settled over the square and the lights shone as if below water. He felt quite hot and did not mind the early evening's cloak that had started to cover up everything, besides it added to aid unobserved intimacy. Passed the corner, she walked with him to a clear area, down a few steps, an ancient church appeared with a sense of place and history. Its ancient level extended to him immediately an aura of sacred intimacy, the whole atmosphere reflected. She liked the northern wall of the church and the spot next to the ancient brass studded entrance doors. He leaned her against the warm wall and kissed her, while he moved slowly down her neck, eating her. His hands slid below her soft top, she had no bra on. His hand on her left breast, he exposed her right one, closing his lips over her hardening nipple, and enjoyed sucking it pricking his lips like a needle. Then he slid down on her body opening the waist button of her pants. He loved this triangular exposed skin of her belly that opened her styled pubic hair to him. She head forfeited to wear her thong tonight. He took her pants down and his finger dipped into her wetted vulva, he adored stroking gently. She threw her arms up against the weathered limestone wall, he could hear her sighs and gasps while he seduced her. Excitement, mixed with the fear of being detected while making love at the ancient church, brought her to her climactic edge. The moment he had her clit between his lips, she came in one fast and soft-elongated cry. He moved up from his cowering position and kissed her nipples with soft bites, and then as she shuddered again, he licked them one by one, until she was feeling relaxed.

"Now show me how you do it, she said, having pulled-up her pants to cover her bums, leaving her fly and well-sculpted waist exposed for him. He opened his pants sliding his hard cock up and down her wetted thighs. He placed his crown against her clit and she became aroused again. Then rubbing her clit with his red crown faster against it now, she gasped again: "I will come," she sucked air in noisily, then placed her right leg across his waist, as he began pressing her against the wall, speeding-up his thrusting movements, penetrating her slippery flesh, just that bit. Her feet tiring, she stood in front of him, leaning against the soft stone wall, as he pressed his cock all over her thighs and passing from one side to the other, he touched her clit sliding along. Then he began to love her clit again and she became aroused again. He eased off and then pressed his penis against her soft skin between her belly and her thighs. As they were calming down, he used his hands to show her his strokes he took to entice himself. He still couldn't come. Finally, he found a way of rubbing against her that enticed him with spiralling lusting feelings. "Ah!" He said.

"Close your eyes," she said, whispering the way she always had whispered to him making love. Remembering their telephone-sex, she began nudging his earlobes. Showers of excitement ran down his spine. "Keep it up!" He said.

"Ah! You are coming," she whispered, "I feel you inside me stirring my pussy." He sighed. "Come now my love, come!" And for the first time he could let go, as he closed his eyes, concentrating more, and it was the only way. "Ahh! Ohh!" He could feel the point of no return approaching. "Come my sweet!" She played her tongue tip in his ear. "Ahhh! Ohhh!" She kissed him as he moaned, muffling his cries. Finally, he would feel his semen spurting from his cock, most of them passing her right thigh as she kissed him, meeting the wintry moisture on the glistening ground. "I'm glad you could come at last," she said. They adjusted their clothes, just in time, as a priest appeared on the opposite side of their spot. Myrna was afraid to be detected, but he shielded her, kissing her softly. When she looked up again, the priest had disappeared.

She took her lover's hand and asked him to come with her. At the corner of the ancient Byzantine church, where the square opened-up, she pointed to a light at the upper floors of a building. "What's where?" He enquired. "A voyeur?" She looked at him. "Well," she said and paused, "a friend of mine works there." He was surprised.

"At this time of night?" He frowned.

"She is a mural artist decorating a bar for gays."

"How interesting," he said quietly, but it wasn't affecting him the slightest. He wanted Myrna every day. She had praised their meetings as one in a million. "Like a lottery ticket," was her repeated way of expressing her once-in-a-lifetime chance, as she called this unique experience. He wanted to live with her and work on developing his art. She wanted no sacrifices, neither separations from her family, nor any great waves in her social circles. She wanted distance to all through secrecy. "We could live to-

110

gether and work," he carried on. "Yes, we could," she replied. "Everybody has to have their own floor, their own domain," he continued his projection. She said nothing.

"I have detected the perfect place," he told her with an enthusiastic voice.

"I am curious," she said with concern in her voice. He described her the house he had seen the first day they had passed opposite the 'Tower of the winds'.

"No sacrifices, "she said repeatedly. It had to be stealthy love all the way." It suited him now in more than one way. He feared the enormous tension building-up with the fact of their possible detection one day, any day now.

She loves the thrill of possibly being detected, but it made her highly vulnerable and insecure. She smiles, she had done it before. These moments of fornication in stealthy love have in real life been even sweeter than virtual, with the inert danger of detection hanging like the sword of Damocles over it. For him it was the sweetest love ever and she knew it. He queried her history of unfaithful adventures and she stirred again. "Perhaps twice," she said and smiled. He'll find out later more, he thought.

"I have never loved this much before," she said and he is glad that she loves him as much as he loves her. She lives in a condominium, in a sought after suburb, she told him on the first day they met. "You have to take the second internal passage that'll lead you to my door. You have to tread on cat paws past my neighbour' door. She is a curious elderly woman, her entrance door perpendicular to mine, in the same short passage. She developed a nosy attitude." He listened to her carefully. A successful meeting with her depended on avoiding any noisy access by him. He nodded. This additional stumbling block only added more spice to his adventure, he hardly could wait to tackle and enjoy his first tete-a-tete with Myrna.

He rang her doorbell at the street entrance. He said his first name and he entered as soon as she pressed the buzzer. Inside the entrance hall he walked up the stairs on cat-paws as agreed. He could hear a needle drop.

When he arrived at the first floor, he took care to sneak past the nosy neighbour's door, and as he noticed that Myrna had already opened her door quietly, he sneaked in delaying to talk or embracing her. Myrna closed her door quietly and locked it. He could feel his heartbeats in his temples. She took a long time to release the door handle and then turned the key to lock the door. Then she turned and rushed into his arms. They kissed and embraced. He saw Klimt's 'Kiss' as they embraced and he kissed her again passionately. She was ready for him, passionate and all-demanding taking him through to her bedroom, placing her finger across her lips, reminding him to still being quiet. He suppresses his urge to fall over her. Once she closed her bedroom door, they feel free to make love. He opens her top and caresses her breasts, pulls her pants from her well-shaped midriff, touches her slender legs and touches her thighs, feeling her aroused state, he goes down on her, stroking her pussy-lips. She tastes sweet and he is loveable. He kisses her pussy and starts licking her gently, his one hand touches her breast and plays with her nipple. He loves everything about her great physique she kept in good shape. He devours her more and more with his tongue playing her clit. He loves her pussy. "You are most beautiful," he whispers. Myrna starts to sigh and twist slightly as he places a finger into her pussy and takes her to her first climax. She enjoys this first part of his lovemaking ceremony. She rises from her supine lie and she pulls him close, taking his pants down. He steps from his jeans and Myrna touches his arousal. She kneels in front of him and pulling his underpants down, she plays with his penis, placing it between her gorgeous breasts, pulling and stroking it, exposing his crown, placing her lips on it. He has to hold back and let her devour him to the tilt, her hand cupping his balls, her other hand at his bums, playing around his sacral bone. Suddenly she gets up, letting his sit on her bentwood chair and she kisses him. "I love your body," she said, not yet using a lover's jargon. "I want you know," he utters with his increased breathing that makes them horny for each other. She pauses. Taking his cock into her mouth catapults him into the forecourts of paradise. He moans, but she holds her forefinger to his lips. He must be quiet. It means no excessive cries or any love-noises. He is about to explode. Then she saddles him in the chair, facing him with her pin-pointed nipples chafing his chest as she rides him, gently at first. "You do it so beautifully," he whispers, "please don't stop now." She smiles. "No, of course I won't," she whispers back. He tries to counter-move into her riding strides. "It's heaven," he sighs. She agrees with heavier breathing. He tastes himself as she kisses him. Suddenly she leans back, her breasts touch his face and his tongue is over her nipples as she moves. "My favourite position," she gasps as she rides him harder, feeling great in her dominant role today, and he enjoys her joie de vivre in sex. Her eyes are two coals firing in heat, her dark hair a lioness' mane. Her full blushing breasts feel wonderful in his palms, rubbing within his clasps. It all entices him further. "Pinch my nipples," she calls-out suddenly to him, as she breathes faster, ready to climax. He still is able to hold back until she is reasonably sated. Then as she has thrown her head back and cried her soft cries in love, she comes back along like a dancer and faces him smiling. Disengaging from her straddling position she bends down for him.

"Fuck me," she says and he moves into her almost instantly, pounding against her firm buttocks. He moves closer and she buckles under his forceful pounding, his hands seeking her swaying breasts greedily, and she follows his fast rhythm, giving-in to his possessive act. He is breathing short, gasping that he is close to his height. He cries out finally with a muffled cry, as she had asked him to do. In his anti-climax he recalls that her neighbour has her ears at the partitioning wall. He imagines a woman who looks like a man, holding a stethoscope against the wall, having thrills listening to their passionate lovemaking.

The days pass and his time of visiting is up. He muses about this unexpected feast of love. Indeed. There are tense moments on the day before the last time he sees her. She cries warm tears of love spreading upon his chest. It makes him emotionally attached to her like to no other woman before. It's unusual for them, both proponents of free love and the purity of a free spirit, now feeling the sacrifice of partition, separation: The Worst! He cannot live without her. Not now. Not ever.

It's a turmoil! Everything happened inside, nothing showed of their love-struggle outside of their daily lives. He senses this life - and - death struggle of their beings: An earthquake of a great love that had to end. She had told him that the day she had cried on his chest, in their gentle embrace after they had made love. With the ending of it, and its innate drama, he flees the taboo of the mountainous stealth he shared with her. He rushes out the door and stumbles, falling to the warm marble floor where he lies still with his arousal.

He has lost her. It was though as if programmed by fate, by powers that are stronger than men. And while he ponders about love, deceit, and death, he meets his friend, sombre looking and of pale complexion. He is walking with him along his weekly exercising routine. It has become an invigorating exercise for both, body and mind, and serious talks about life and love. "The mind is a wonderful machine indeed, but it could also deceive one," he says to his friend.

"Mine was deceived indeed!" His friend returns his side of thoughts. He senses that his friend has paid a sacrifice for the life he leads, having fallen in love with a woman, he was unable to read into her completely. What is his friend's sacrifice? An ailing heart, high blood-pressure, and loss of sexual love. The loss, one is finally feeling it'll tear one's heart out. How many seek great sexual love? How many have found a partner they are happy with on all counts of living?

He'll turn to the innocent pages of white sheets of paper and place his words on them about this thing called love. He will write about his Muse and the sacrifice of his

Health, and the pain of coping with his feelings. He's communicating with her and observing his friend, in the country and tell her that she's a distant Muse.

*

Veena

It's one pm and I think I'm late. Just one thought crosses my mind: It's Thursday and at lunch break she usually walks down the pedestrian promenade, between the shops and the two big banking institutions that line the outer pedestrian ring of Rosebank's shopping core. I stand behind a petite blond woman, slim, young, with tight blue jeans, and a black voile top where one cannot see the tee-shirt below. With silver bangles on her left wrist, she stands with her back to me and I think of her face as one of my subplot's heroines, I had called Sue.

She is the blond sultry goddess beckoning everyone for sex, when Zsolt comes across her, in *The Informer*. I love it, and I'm afraid of it, as I nearly touched her cute behind. She must have sensed something of my intentions, as she turns her head slightly to the left. I can see her fine-cut profile that had turned a bit pink due to some inner stirring. Will I ask her for an interview? As I intend to, she steps forward to the cubicle, where a black clerk extends his help with a gesture of polite words, one could hear only muffled.

I am next. I see Veena in one of the serving cubicles through the corner of my left eye and I pray that she'll not abandon me now to take me on, finishing her present customer quickly. The tension kills me. I take my notebook from my pocket and overhear the high-pitched voice of the petite blond. Immediately I decide not to take her as a model for the sultry Sue in my novel. I am disappointed, she's not what I originally imaged she could be. Her good figure is not enough. Thinking of my work, I near the deadline for finishing my novel this month. I'll need more speed, with shorter sentences and more scenes with lively dialogues. Besides, I'll need two action scenes. Wow! I suddenly visualize one, it's like a movie scene rolling in front of my eyes. No! I don't wish to see the end. People have to die and spill their blood for the villain, before he's going down from the bullet of a sharp-shooter, taking with him some victims. I feel a shower of Goose-bumps along my spine. It's impossible if she calls me as her next customer. I'm going to die.

What's the speed I require to find not only my own voice in writing novels, but also the right pacing? What's the art of novel writing all about? Indeed, I write like Ste-phen King writes. I read his book *Stephen King about Writing*. I have to tell Melanie, my writing guide, about it, not Amara? Well, with Amara I have to turn the forbidden into beautiful acts of love, but she is avoiding the issues, as she sidesteps erotica. Melanie doesn't. I see her face in front of me: pale and balanced, dark coals for eyes that stare at me, while I look aside to see if she still wished to unnerve me, or still has an interest to be with me, swal-lowing me up. I see her face morphing into Veena's face and my fingers stroke her face; she bites my finger, her lips sucking on it, while I unbutton her blouse. She lowers herself, letting me slide between her generous breasts she squeezes around my erection, pushing me up and down between two balloons.

Great god, I feel the vibes of a lonely poet bouncing to and fro, even through this security glazing. I feel the urge to have her in a way she'd permit me to: face, lips, mouth, neck, breasts, under her arms, and in her back –

I get aroused from this scenario and I cannot talk, as Veena takes me finally. I am speechless and I don't mind being at her mercy, as she has all controls firmly between the palms of her delicate hands. I must look excited to her and I sense her holding my erection, playing my balls, move them back and forth, and in a pleasure of close-by pain she'll bring me to a height.

I'll die and she smiles, as if she senses my pain of be-ing cut-off from fornication forever with her, masturbating this side of town, while she strokes herself into a sweet frenzy on the other side. Shit! Life's unfair. I would not hurt her, stroke her and complete her happiness. That's all, isn't it? Why make such big waves about a handshake of intimacy?

She smiles a hidden smile today. Lost taste and desire have fucked all night, while I just adore her, does that not count for anything? I used to excite her, include her into the world of my lewd and erotic thoughts, affecting her with a natural glow. All's dead now, all's finished for years now with us, as she is getting pregnant and will bear children.

Given up on closeness with me? Traveling by car, she says to me, one hour every day to here and back. That is a lot, I comment and I cannot even smile, my longing slides below the glazing slot into the waste paper basket. I live on the other side, she moves her head in a disappointing gesture, followed by her sadness that makes her talk slowly and he eyes losing their shine. I feel like hit by I'll write her a letter, pour my heart's cockles out to her. What is the use? She'll be under the thumb of some bureaucrat or male chauvinist, who'll kill if he would catch us in flagranti, in my car.

We were close at one stage, getting closer before she closed the shop. I did not get it first why she was in such a hurry to meet and then with a snap of her fingers she was gone. Now, back again here, she tells me she's married and I don't mind that at all. But her spouse will mind that. No use for our wild chemistries to match, at least it would be worth a try. It's a shame to be close and apart by one cut like that. I see it in her eyes, she gave up for now. There's only one answer. We don't dare to take it yet. It'll kill everything. It will be too much of an effort for a slow and painful death of sex performed in a car or in a nearby hotel.

All's nonsensical and absurd.

That's why it's having a magical effect on me and it pulsates through my body. Thoughts turn from an abstraction into palpable skin and flesh. Tangible nearness prevails. This is a rare physical experience that I feel in my chest. My nipples are on fire, especially the left one. I behave like a teenager in heat. Is a secondary puberty emerging? I feel hot in my skin and I see myself sink into a hot bath with Veena, a bubble bath in a Jacuzzi, where our legs meet, entangle, and slithery bodies cannot mingle with ease, but slide off like water from a duck's back. I have to lift her up, let her slide upon my face in love's fellating inferno. Then she lets me straddle her breasts, adore her lips, and slide between her bruised lips. Her mouth swallows me up completely. Ahh! My God! It feels good! So bad, perverted, and thoroughly lewd. I expire completely.

Erotic thoughts, primordial lust, and forbidden frontiers are still an exhilaration of transgressing taboos and will raise my heartbeats, I have to control with white pills, slow down and chill-out before toppling prematurely over the edge. But it was worthwhile bursting for terse moments through forbidden barriers. I'll die for sure, for Veena, for Symi, for all dusky-eyed women I could have and have never been allowed to have. It's a great effort to be in love, sustain the momentum, but never for me, never, never?

Must I stay away and flee the places of erotic interaction that present themselves in such delicate and sensual waves? Why is it then impossible, why then?

Anger is of no help and the situation becomes quite desperate. She – married and physically engaged to relax – I, alone and thinking of her, enticed, and calling up similar nudes on my monitor, to find enough sexual stimulation to reach an autoerotic climax.

Fine. Nobody's hurt. It's not the ideal scene as we know from experience. It's after all a reality. I live with it. All day and night. I write.

I live close to her breasts, her lips, the imagined coitus mammilla, and the fellating act. Nothing new, you said to me. It is exciting though. I cry and take my clothes off for you again.

Fin.

BOOK IV

Orion's Love Nest

A Walk Rising Expectations

Walking alongside Val through the streets of Gly-fada is a new experience. Her youthful gait is further-ing my own. Keeping up with her pace is still achiev-able for me, although I find stressing in the muscles of my hips, especially the left side. Due to an acci-dent, falling from a retired racehorse, is an experi-ence I wished for being without. My fall onto hard rocky ground has been painful at my mature age. I am still cursing myself having fallen prey to a silly challenge, I accepted from a hardnosed business orientated and ruthless character, with a streak for malicious pleasure. Of course, that dawned on me much later. Flashes of mosaic thoughts began to re-assemble to a greater picture.

"This wind blows all my hair," Val said suddenly as strands of her hair veered across her face. I enjoy looking at Val's profile, her cherubic lips she purses when she senses my gaze.

"Your hair looks great," I said, "the colour suits you." She looked at me and smiled. At that moment a gust of wind blew my hair into my face. I had to laugh and she joined me. Evident that we had the same thoughts, even the same habits, and just now sharing the act of waving the blown hair from our faces. One could assume we were brother and sis-ter, yet we were more like father and daughter, but I wouldn't entertain a thought of grandpa and grand-daughter.

"How old are you?" The question took me by sur-prise. "Well, I'm over 65," I replied, not to give away my age, as I still have a streak of vanity about being younger, and most of the time I'll get away with it. So what? "OK," she said, "you look younger."

"Thanks for the compliment." Well, she carried on talking and we started comparing our physical attributes. Strange, usually it's done with same gender friends, however.

"I'm not happy with my hips," Val frowned, clapping her hips.

"To me they look good," I asserted her.

"Look, it's my bone, there' no fat here." She stood in front of me pulling her coat aside and hitting her hip with her flat hand.

"Let me see." I felt her hips for the first time, she felt good in my hands. "It's great Val," I said and smiled.

"Yes it's my skeletal frame, but I like to have a slim waist."

"OK, I think that's super, like an hourglass figure?" She gave him a big five. "Well, you'll get there if you want to." We carried on taking up the pace of walking again, talking about where we wanted to go in the first place.

"Let's try the herbal shop first," she said and I reminded her of the Starbuck's Café, she wanted to go to. "No, I meant I don't know which road it is from there."

"OK, leave it to me, I know." Val shook her head thinking I'm bluffing her, but I had suddenly an intuition. "It's not about Starbucks," Val said, "but about what street?" She could be stubborn.

"OK," I replied, "I'll find it if you let me."

"Sure." She simmered down. I like Val a lot, besides I have dreams about her, as she's my youngest Muse in years. She laughs as if I would have misunderstood her, pulling her lips to that ironic curl, one of her characteristics, when she wishes to get a resolving discussion about some matters that have been laboured her too much.

I take the road familiar to me, where I have walked along many times and where H. has once taken me to buy some green Chinese tea, which I like. Once we reached the spot of Starbucks, I continue straight ahead as I recognize some familiar buildings. My gut-feel tells me I am on the right road. Val stops. "Hello," she winks back at a woman standing in a shop's entrance door. I waited for Val to finisher dialogue and looked up meanwhile the herbal tea I wanted to ask for. She said finally good-bye to the woman. "A former school mate of mine. I haven't seen her for years." I nodded. "I have the name of the herb, do you have a pen?" I jotted the name into my notebook.

"Where to now?" Val wanted to know. "Why do you smile?"

"I had a gut-feel that it's the right street we are in. I can smell it." I laughed and walked ahead. "Here it is." I pointed at the shop, looking at the buildings on the opposite side to find a plaque with a street name.

"Oh, it's B. Georgiou," Val read the slightly obliterated sign, my bad vision couldn't pick on exactly. She waited outside the herbal shop smoking one of her self-rolled cigarettes, while I entered and talked to the shop assistant. She didn't understand me and went to ask Val to speak to her in Greek. "Well, they do not have the tea you want, besides she does not know the type, as it was not in Greek." Val translated. We took our leave and the woman gave me a stamp with her shop's address into my note book.

"And now let's walk to Vodafone," Val said falling into the paced rhythmic stride, she takes to when aiming to walk to another place. The phone shop was filled with many customers. "Fuck!" Val swore, as she uses the word regularly, if annoyed.

"Val, these are my written down verbs," I showed her my notes, I'm carrying around with me at all times, to learn the Greek language to her method of teaching. She's a wonderful teacher and I like her a lot. Val and I go on well with each other and perhaps we might even become best of friends. Where do we stand? Teacher and student, doctor and patient, artist and model. Well, I have many scenarios tucked away in my head with her as my protagonist. However, Val is presently in a serious relationship and yet she flirts with the possibilities love offers at so many levels. I enjoy exchanging opinions with her about any topic.

We queue at Starbucks Café ordering for her a mocha with fresh cream, while I stick to filter coffee. The barman wants to know where I am from and we joke about nationalities. Finally settled down, we relax with Val's famous self-rolled cigarettes.

"What is love?" She asks starting a conversation about an abstract theme.

"There are many aspects of love," I replied. "I want to draw you," I said, but Val murmurs something about a portrait of her granny, I supposed to do for her as a priority.

"Let's see," she opens her smart phone and just a few seconds later she has a definition about love on her screen. However, there are many forms of love, from compassion to erotomania, self-love. Of course the Greek words are from agape to gamo, from idealistic love to physical love, and I am all for fee-love, pure and not bound by any rule, not predetermined by scheming thought, or any tainting influences whatsoever!

Val reads me the definitions from the Internet's encyclopaedia, while I think about the passionate lovers Tristan and Izault; I've been fascinated with all my life, until I have experienced a similar situation myself. But then that's embedded into my brain and chiselled into the granite memory tablets of my soul. Granite is unchangeable through the millennia of time, the message will never be eroded. Is LOVE embodied in the granite blocks of Giza? Have the gods left the imprint of their souls back for us humans to understand most important messages about their lives on this on this planet?

"Ah, here you are!" Val greets her lady friend, a young, blond, and good-looking woman with an explicit joie du vivre.

"Hi," she extends her hand and it feels soft and firm in mine. Her exuberant style of talking takes over. She's fluent in English. "Excuse me for comparing you, and I don't mean it as an insult, but as a compliment." Oh, here it comes, I think, some grandpa-thing. "Not at all, carry on I'm curious."

"You remind me of Anthony Hopkins," she smiles and I think aloud: "The silence of the lambs?" She has not noticed my take on eating a part of her up, but she carries on in her overflowing mode, "No, not at all, but rather 'Howard's end." Oh, I have suddenly some strange connotations of love and death, thoughts that follow me since Ana's death. She is interested to know my relationship with such questions and I tell her my position. I observe her talking, gesticulating, and imagine her being nude with her reactions to a man making love to her. She would be a great model. Before I have a chance to ask her, she suddenly excuses herself for visiting the ladies' room. Val dons a pair of sunglasses and said: "What do you think?" I look at her shades. "You know, you look like Lolita with them." She is shocked.

"I'm not a whore."

"Well, I do not mean that. I mean the shape of your glasses looks like hers in the movie." I wonder why she has such a disgust for sex-workers. "Listen, just don't rush to judgements that fast." I don't have to explain to her aspects of society, but it seems I have to lecture her about all aspects of love. However, it'll be another time, but I have an immediate thought.

"One aspect of love isn't mentioned."

"Which one," she reacted fast.

"One aspect of a poet's love that's necessary creating great poems."

"What's that?"

"Longing!" I said and watch her face. Val said nothing pursing her cherubic lips and remaining silent until her friend returned. The girls talked about shopping and presents for X-mas. I smoke a cigarette Val has rolled for me. I wish to linger on my thoughts. Her friend seems restless and wished to go. "Let him finish his cigarette," Val said.

Finally we break up and walk toward the shops along Metaxa Avenue. The girls bade me good-bye and we kiss in friendship. I walk to the close-by station and take the tram for one stop, wondering what will become of such a friendship and why Val introduced me to her friend, who acted superficially. Maybe we'll meet again in the near future and the two girls will model for me together. The painting *Demoiselles d'Athenes*, that'll be a homage to Picasso, hovers still at the back of my artistic mind.

*

Love in the Mistral

A sudden fall in temperature stifled the senses and I felt my limbs turning numb. The ongoing storm that had started during the night, made everybody restless, stirred dogs and men. The shutters creaked in their rusted hinges. One shutter had loosened itself from its keep and banged rhythmically against the window, as if an outraged voice demanded something in Spanish, I have heard all evening yesterday in a nearby restaurant, famous for paella.

I felt pressure building-up in my temples, as I slipped from the bed sheets and tiptoed to the bathroom in search for an aspirin. Unzipping my toiletry bag, I retrieved the blister package and popped two tablets from the silver foil swallowing them straight away. The second pill refused to pass my gullet and started dissolving in my throat. I swallowed some water and had to cough. I noticed that Bee did not stir as usual. When I recalled that she complained about her chronic headaches that became a migraine as soon as the storm had announced itself.

I headed to the open kitchen that stretched along from the entrance lobby and thought I'd prepare a sumptuous breakfast. The wind howled its eerie music around the three sides of this unit No: 29, the end unit of block B of arranged holiday apartments that were situated close to the Mediterranean Sea, the people here called: The Med. I checked on Bee, who still rested in a deep slumber.

Yesterday the news of Heather's tour cancelled, had reached us in the restaurant next door. We had booked a table for three, expecting her for dinner, but her voice expressed disappointment on the phone, her voice raised like the storm. I had to calm her down. She still could catch another plane, once the storm had died down and the airport at Malaga would be opened for regular flights again. I told her that I had rented a spacious unit that could sleep four people. "Bring your boyfriend," I teased her. She would contact me later. The space next door, I could rent advantageously, was suitable for an artist's studio with the intention to paint Bee, Heather, and her partner as a composition of three figures. Heather was looking forward to this painting, she had already named as *Demoiselles do Sol*, referring to Picassos famous painting that heralded the start of Cubism. "Yours will herald the age of free eroticism," she quipped looking at my sketches I've sent her by E-mail. Heather, the wild one of Bee's sisters, always searching for a new adventure, always open for a new perspective, as long as nudity was involved. I painted her and Bee as lovers, as nymphs and as entangled Amazons in a fight. "As long as nobody recognizes us," Bee said. "I want the world to recognize me!" Heather said and laughed aloud, "think how jealous my girlfriends will be." So, I painted Bee with an alien face and Heather as she appeared to me. "You painted me with an ugly face," she frowned.

"It's how I see you," I protested my artistic license. "I thought of taking a photograph of you," I told her "and place it on an object in the painting, like a lover's present to her beau. She agreed at last.

This kitchen is marvellous, I thought, enticing anyone who likes cooking to create some deliciously tasting food. Every gadget had been installed and I mused about Heather, who had promised to show us her culinary talents with a menu, she had especially drawn-up with a theme for lovers, inspired from Isabelle's cook book. For now I relied on my own cooking skills that were at best experimental. Then I realized I had neither flour nor milk. I searched for eggs, but I couldn't find one basic ingredient for pancakes. I also didn't know that Heather had such problems to travel here, stranded in Paris. By now she might have met a man she fancied, and other plans would emerge that became a more viable alternative, than to spend her time in a mistral-blown Costa da Sol with an aging couple. But Heather's ego had been tickled by the prospect of being immortalized through art on a life-size canvas.

But now, Bee is sick with a migraine and I'm pacing about like a feral cat on a hot tin roof, nursing my right foot, where I developed suddenly pain through an inflammation. "Damned!" I burned my finger on the pan, having switched the stove on daydreaming, intending to cook a meal? I doubted my sanity.

Meanwhile the wind increased to a permanent howling, I compared to a wolf pack's. The sound of breaking glass woke me from my thoughts. At the same time there was a knock at our apartment door. I could see the outlines of a grey figure through the obscure glazing. I opened the door. A gust of wind burst the door into my face and I fell. Somebody else fell on top of me and my face was covered with hair; I felt a woman's breast bouncing on my chest. Her cheeks on my cheeks felt smooth and I smelt vanilla and cardamom. A woman!

She rolled to the side and I struggled up, closing the entrance door between more gusts of an ill wind. Then I gave her a hand pulling her up. A barrage of Spanish greeted me while she straightened her pyjamas, tightly knit trousers and top showing her curvaceous body.

"I'm sorry," I said "I don't speak Spanish."

"I do speak little English," she pronounced 'Inglis'.

"Please have a seat," I pointed to the French-blue leather settee and picked-up my Spanish phrase book from the nearby shelf. With basic communication sorted, she apologized again. "He is drunk again" She sighed, her breasts were heaving.

"Oh, you have domestic trouble?"

"No, I have this man follow me – I am sorry my Inglis…"

"A strange man following you?" I had to smile.

"Well, he not from this complex," she said enticed "now he is fallen into the door…"

"I will look," I said. She jumped-up. "NO!" Don't go," she held me back. I came close to her. The scent of vanilla and cardamom filled my nostrils and I enjoyed the alternative odours. She pulled a nose, sniffed, and flared her nostrils. "Oh, I'm sorry," I said rushing to the open kitchen, where butter in the glass pan had turned brown meanwhile. She rushed behind me taking the pan's handle and shifting it to the side. "Do not put water!" She shouted into the howling wind that seemed to come through gaps around the windows and below the door and rushed through the room. I gazed at her athletic body as she moved about and helped me to control the mess I had made, perhaps feeling herself somewhat responsible for it. She turned. "What you cook?" She rolled her eyes switching the vent on above the kitchen hood to rid the air of the burned smell.

"I intended to make pancakes," I whispered.

"But you have no prepare the mixture." She looked into the kitchen cupboards, stretching and showing me her perfectly rounded bums. Her top slid up exposing her dusky skin.

"I have forgotten the ingredients," I looked at her and felt opening the window, flying away on the wings of the storm to shop all ingredients I would need.

"Ah!" She said, "wait, open door for me please." She rushed out and the gust of wind blew her top tightly around her body. Her nipples stuck through the soft fabric of her top. "Uh," she gasped as I caught up with her and held the door of her apartment open for her.

"Come in," she said and I noticed the smashed glass in the door to the bathroom. There was no sign of a drunken man. The storm had increased and a heavy rain set in. She packed the ingredients in a hurry talking Spanish all the time.

"I did not notice that we are neighbours," I said as we had settled back into the elongated kitchen at our unit. She smiled.

"My name is Zen," I said.

"I am Samantha, but call me Sam," she laughed softly. "You are nice. I want call my daughter." She looked at me intently.

"Yes, sure," I said, "use my phone." I pointed to the phone on my desk.

"No," she replied "cellfon please."

"OK," I said and fetched my mobile phone from the bedroom. Bee was still asleep. I handed Sam my phone and her fingers touched mine. A spark ignited in me a chain reaction of fires that began in my belly and spread upwards. Lines of a poem shaped in me:

She came like a cloud
Blown into me like a leaf
That hung on for dear life
She wouldn't feel the
Touches/ the strokes of
Unruly hair and her body's
Bounce all over me.

The verses came to me like her scent of warm moist air with overtones of cinnamon, while outside a main storm bellowed like a horde of wild cats. "Sit next to me," she said pressing close to me. She typed her daughter's number in and sighed as I moved my hand over her legs, trying to grab my notebook to jot down the stanzas I heard inside my head. She spread her legs slightly.

The moment she had connected with her daughter, a strange convulsion took hold of her. Sam's Spanish became faster and suddenly she reached for my crotch. Immediately m hand moved her soft top up, stroking her skin, belly, and breasts. She became bolder, stroking my erection, while I slid my fingers into her pants. She felt moist and her vulva opened for my finger. "Uh!" She gasped in between a barrage of words. "Uh!!" As I touched her and stroked her pussy.

I pushed up her top entirely and cupped her breasts. "Uhh!" she gasped again between her fast talking that increased in intensity with my stroking of her. I kissed her brown nipples, and when they turned into hardened knobs, I slid down to my knees. She lifted her bums and I pulled her panties off. "UH. UH!" I stroked her breast with one hand, while I used the other on her vulva, ready for my face to dunk into her wet and most wanted rose. As my tongue flicked into her vulva, she cried "UH" again louder. "UH darling," in between her conversation that sounded by now a cacophony of words to me. She opened her legs wider and moved down the couch for me to enter her. Verses from an erotic, Far eastern adventure came to mind:

Let me see your cock she said

I have no webcam
No microphone either
So it was like making love
To a veiled woman
Who sent me her picture
And played on the thrill
Of dying for sharing pure
Body pleasures
In the eye of this
Blinding night.

I have not loved before at an instant and the excitement
mounted to my crescendo I held forcefully back
"More," she moaned, "more darling, uh, give it to me."
Sam moaned and writhed, she threw her head back in
this copulating heat of my sudden crushing into her.
"UH.UH...I come. I come. I come..."
"You are the best I had for – "I couldn't speak for my
breathing choked my words. I could not stop this animalistic pushing that evolved in me. The phone slipped from
er fingers, and in the heat of our fornication she must
have pushed the loudspeaker button. I could hear the
gasping of another woman, and shards of Spanish words
sounding like love words, interrupting her heavy breathing. Then her "Ah, Ah, Ahhh," as if she had a climax, cry-
ing and breathing the same way as the woman between
my thighs. "Now – please come now – she uttered and I
had to close my eyes to concentrate. "Now!" I gasped,
"now my pretty Spanish woman...now!"
"Yes," she cried, "yes, yes, now – as a wild flame shot
through me and I couldn't stop my gyrations into her, as
the rhythm of my movements echoed the barrage of her
talk before. Then, I realized we were online to her daughter, sounding like a threesome-gasping affair, the air filled
with our lewd talk in heat, in utter excitement, and in pure
lust. "UH..." and pause, and "UH..." again.
"I fuck you both," I cried from my gasping mouth, the
mistral howling and a pot of water was still boiling on the
stove, but had already been switched off by the time
switch. I fell on top of her, the cushions of her breasts

crushing my chest, as she drew me even closer. A giant or god had entered her body, she moaned and moving up she let me lie down and stretch-out as she began fellating me and I rose up again in her heated mouth in a spiralling sensation, satisfying her with another erection. She straddled me immediately and started riding me, while she continued her Spanish conversation in a softer tone. "Maria," she sighed and I opened my eyes to see tears running down her cheeks. I froze and couldn't progress to another climax.

"Sam, turn around," I said and she pivoted around my erect cock. A sudden clasping fiction held my pushing and I enjoyed the new-found stimulation that made me move below her in a frenzy.

"NOW," she cried out, "now! UH!" And more gasps in short breath followed.

"Oh God, I feel it coming – I increased my pushing efforts and shouted: "With my stake, my avenging sword, my cock" – She threw her head back and the tips of her long hair fell on my chest, tickling my skin, my face, and my hard nipples. My body started to burn as I climaxed again.

I sat next to her and stroked her thighs. She straddled me with one leg and kissed me. Having exchanged all our energies, I felt charged-up in my reborn state, better than I had felt in years.

"I am sorry," Sam said.

"Why?"

"I used much time for my daughter."

"No, not at all," I whispered, "I hope she could enjoy it too." I looked Sam into her eyes that had a magical shine.

"You know?" She gasped, stroking loose strands of hair back.

"Well, it sounded as if we were together here," I said and her face turned to a sullen expression, as she pursed her lips and her dark eyes radiated with a deep glow. A dusky Madonna, I thought. "For her I did," she whispered.

"Is she alone?" A sad expression came over Sam's exotic face and tears welled in her eyes. She started to sob and leaned against my shoulder. "I do it – for her!" She cried. "Oh OK," I stroked her soft black hair, "you are not only pretty, but compassionate too."

Samantha looked at me in a pool of tears and I kissed her. Her tears wetted my face. I became fond of her in such a wild-wind-howling way, in my mistral affair, as I tagged the video I had taken. Sam became aware of the digital camera, placed on top of the TV. "You taped?" Her eyes widened in astonishment, then calmed down. "Yes," I said, "and I am glad I did."

"Uh, I like a copy," she smiled again.

"OH Sam, I will make one for you." She chuckled. "Write your address into my notebook." I handed her my crimson covered 'Cink' edition, whose style and paper quality I fancied.

"UH," she exclaimed leafing through it and looking at my erotic drawings.

"Nice this one, like we together," she gave a throaty laugh and then started writing. I stretched out feeling a wholesome tiredness and snoozed off.

When I woke, I heard tinkering sounds from the open kitchen. Sam stood naked and cooked, humming a song. There was no sign of Bee and I wondered that she still slept. She must have taken a strong sleeping pill, as she couldn't stand the storm. She once described to me the feeling of pain from a constant battering inside her skull. I stood up strolling over to Sam who smiled at me: "You had good sleep?" She laughed.

"And you?" I said, embracing her without waiting for an answer, and she pressed her back against me.

"I want you," she said, as I started to grow hard against her sensual skin. She bent down for me, next to her pan-cakes. The scent of olive oil and cinnamon mixed in my nostrils with the smell of her body to a powerful aphrodisiac. Sam had a beautiful body and she used it to entice me, performing a love dance with her "UH"-cries and her passionate moaning.

"Enough now," she said as I cried-out and released my regrouped energy into her warm vulva. Life's juices cooked in me like her breakfast and I could only stop as she moved away from me. "I feed you," she stated, serving pancakes with a filling of chocolate, nuts, and honey and a dash of her spices.

"It's delicious, like you are Sam," I said as she placed her thigh across my leg and fed me, while I stroked her gently, enjoying her moist vulva, and she infused sweet-spicy food into my mouth, kissing me in-between spoons.

"I feel high, as if I had taken a drug," I murmured, swallowing gorgeous food.

"Yes, love like food," she smiled kissing me.

"What is it?"

"Moroccan," she said, "it make you hard" She laughed. I shivered. The cold wind had turned the lounge into a fridge. "We go to hot tub," she said as I finished eating. Even in my track suit I felt the icy air blowing in through the gaps of the main entrance door.

The steam room was private and Sam had the keys. It felt great to stretch out on the tiled seats for some time. "Let me love you now," she said and fellated me. I never experienced such a hot sensation, and I thought I'll burst and die, but Sam held all the tricks to pleasure a man, without killing him in the process. "You healing like me," she came up, kissed me, and carried on curing me from depression. In between she rested and used her hands, telling me about her life. I closed my eyes enjoying the heightened heat inside and out that would burn me to frazzles. She rose, took my hand and led me to the Jacuzzi. "Ah," it was my turn to gasp, as she did before, when she straddled me tightly. There was no letting-up with her. She was indeed a master of healing with a process of loving, she drew me into relentlessly. I had forgotten pain and worries, but I felt sorry for Bee, who had to flee into sleep to have relief from a reality of chronic headaches and a nervous condition, as I had explained to Samantha.

"My daughter has a handicap too," she murmured.

"No," I said, "not her too!"

"Yes, tragically, she cannot marry."

"Why is that?" Sam paused and took time to answer.

"She had accident." A tear appeared in her eye.

"I'm sorry," I sighed, but then understood the telephonic participation of her with me and her Mom, who wanted her to partake with us together and become excited when we made love.

*

Magic Resurrection
(Thirteen Songs of Eros)

I went to bed pondering about Aleta's words: "What if our libidos stop?" She had looked at me concerned. "I don't think they'll stop. Right now mine works nicely," I replied.

"How do you know?"

"Because I'm aroused now as I talk to you! IT's in the mind after all, you told me. My mind is connected to the erotic world of Zed, which is hot-lined to me. Thank Goodness it's intact and alive!" I sensed a slight disappointed tone in Aleta's voice.

"You chose the road called Eros, we both wanted to walk, and I followed you," she stated like a lawyer states facts. As I was still upset about her, not showing yesterday evening, and her explanations were too casual – she even sounded aloof and distant, with her mind somewhere else – we still tried discussing matters of regular and repetitive time together as stressful, forced, and the death of all passionate relationships.

I felt tired and emotionally exhausted, and it affected my psychic condition. Having carried the sweet burden of Eros in my rucksack at all times, steering the boat of our lascivious togetherness through the milky stream of the web-world. Our e-love life has been endangered getting into a repetitive rut. How intensive our meetings piled upon meetings to this mountain of high-level lust, as I sense Aleta slipping back and in dire need of rest, maybe this could be the end of our erotic life. She's quieter as before, she cannot come to her height for a few times now. Routine kills most relationships, just like good instant sex.

Have we not created a symphonic poem in fucking that had been conceived and lived in all its fine moments of titillating stirrings, eager stroking and tight caresses, with the build-up of sexual tensions to our well synchronized climaxes, well intonated and exceptionally highlighted with our gasps and screams of relief? The emotions we feel for each other and with the final giving of our bodies totally to each other, has fires soaring wildly through my veins.

But in a dream all dies, even lust and love, pleasure and its colours. All went black like the screen on my trusted laptop that crashed the moment I stripped naked and came to your bed, the moment for our merging. In this darkness I couldn't find you. I felt like being cut-off the living, joining the ghosts of the dead bodies that float around like frozen in the eternal space of the web-cocoon. There's no light, no sun, but maybe the upcoming moon and the clustered starlight will help to find my way back to your room that exists for the moment only in this e-world of zooming icons, flashing signals, streaming music and sounds that shape words and intelligence, so we can feel, touch, and exchange emotions and function as friends and lovers.

I take this lyre of my heart and compose and sing these words of love to you. Maybe you'll pick up my vibes, maybe you could catch my voice recognizing me. Could you find me? But to no avail, tonight is a cloudy night, the light from the Milky Way is missing, the web's illumination source is interrupted once again. I will not see you now. Only the sister of love has attended to my sorrow, 'Hope'. She holds my hand and has this compassion with stranded souls and lonely poets.

I intonate a song of the child's wonder cup, entailing all the wishes that should come alive: Closing my eyes, singing my heart out, believing in the pureness of love. I do:
Oh rose but red
Dewdrops like tears
Running down the soft
Petals of your cheeks/
I lie in my greatest anguish
I lie in my greatest pain!
Much rather would I be in
Azza's pleasure-filled
Heavenly domain.

Then I strolled upon
A wide green path
An angel came/ lifting hands
Stopping me/ wanting to
Dismiss me.
Ah! No! I would not budge
Never be dismissed/
Not now!
I am from Azza/ Heaven of
Gods/ whereto I would return/
Return to Azza I would –
I'll need your help oh Gods!

Give me a light/ yes one light
Aleta will give me a light/
Embodiment of Aphrodite/
Will light me to a blissful
Everlasting life in pleasure!

There was a stirring in me, as if I would have received
my calling. Coming back from a darkness like death, I re-
called the 'Resurrection' ode, and placed it on top of my
own. Loved this chorus song, as much as Mahler did.
Sang:
Rise again/ rise again
You will my dust/
After such a short repose
Immortal life.
Will she/ who called you
Bestow upon you/
To bloom again?
You are sown
Lady of the Harvest
Who gathers the sheaves
Like souls/ like us/
Who died.

Oh believe my heart/
Oh believe
Nothing of you will be

Lost!
What you longed for is
Yours/
Yours what you've loved
What you strived for.
Oh believe
You were not born in
Vain!
You have not vainly
Lived/
And suffered!

I can feel you Aleta, close to me, know, as if this was not an imagined ghost, it's you, really you! Now! Give me your hand let me sing to you, let this choir of our souls rise in pureness together, sing with me, and let our souls sing with us.
Die we shall/ as to live!
Rise again/ we will
Your heart and mine
In an instant!
While our pulses rush
And in the throbbing beat
Our bodies merge in this
Eternal flight
That carry us to the
Gods
Above Azza island.
This music encompasses the essence of our beings. We float together, in this realm of pure beauty. There is a continual change of scenes, following in a kaleidoscope of colours:

'Aleta naked, Virgin Mother with Child'
An intense glow of gold and ivory solidifying from my toes to the amber covers of a rich folded waistcloth. Circling amber cloth like cloud formations turning to shaped pieces of limbs and penis-like horns, legs and arms that challenge my stretched-out body, hanging from the cross

of your thighs and womb. Motion-like freewheeling creates the gilded turbulence that roars against the iridescent skies, features your saint-like portrait and of your Virgin Mother's nude.

'Andante Moderato'- In peaceful flowing movements as Mahler writes for the second set.

I see your face that changes through the motions of an early age, as a kid to this young woman I admire. I fall in love with her continuously.

A herd of golden sperm oozes out of my erection as I am flying through the motions and the painful climax of a crucifixion.

My love, my mother, my beloved Aleta, my all, my love in pain I suffer, my love in love I am in you.

From the pale blue spherical globe around us I see you as *'Galatea of the Spheres'*.

In a myriad of planets that disappear like toys and further into microbe cells in their mutations from ivory to white and yellow-amber to dark tarred tiger-eyes. Shapes of a hologram from across the blue of heavens, a beautiful face, as I know you, created out of cosmic dust, molecules that rotate with effortless speed. Turbo-charged in the centre of your heart, your soul, your being that radiates deep into my innermost, my own being.

'Corpus Hypercubus' appears in a crucifixion scenario, upon an assembly of equal cubes in perspective from the artist's view. Like a metamorphosis of crystals into this cubistic cross, whose centre cube projects and attaches itself to my spine, lifting my body up into this naked stretch, smooth, weightless and endless. When do I reach the limits of physical endurance that will let me snap like tensioned cables into two curling ends? A chessboard patterned earth that forms into an array of building blocks, and into cubes that disappear into the horizon of a wine-red sea.

Gold and amber, liquefied against the darkness of a universal void. Your love lifts me out of the dots of magnetic clips that let me slide down toward your naked feet.

You let me lie supine. In agony and pain I see your rich draped clothes that slide down your shoulders as you bend down to kiss me and then they drop, forming a bed of softness that'll receive my strained body to become light and open for your gentle caresses. Your heated body slides onto me waking me from a dream of impossible cruelties, and while we make this inflaming contact skin to skin and chest to bosom. Belly to belly. Cock to belly and cock to cunt, and slide, and while we feel oncoming climactic sounds like nails that are hammered violently into the wooden cross.

And then as in the last moments, where desire is mixed with pain and lust, the lance of driving into flesh and splintering bone pierces my heart. Pierces your soul. We cry out into this flash-flaring piece of eternity that glows in our cries. This – a depiction of a glowing landscape of eyes and faces. In endless stretches of burned-out lands, charcoal peninsulas, rocky islands in dryness and dust – your fondness of my body that arches into your honeyed wetland's warmth.

'Aleta Bends over Balcony Naked with only Nylons'

I knee in my nakedness in contemplation of this universe that changed into the endless chains of blown-up molecular structures of all sizes, balls of multiple colours, out of which your body forms like golden mist that condensates as it rotates, holding the data I desire with my mesmerized eyes. Now an array of bands cling to cylindrical phallic parts that move and toss, rocking in the magic scenery of a bland, misty curtain of fog and streaky stripes of light.

You lean across a thin-lined tubular balcony, wired titanium formed from sperm emanating from my body's elongations that penetrate your behind.

Mahler's Urlicht depicted in lights flashing across the endless Blue. I see your buttocks flare, your pussy opens and spends that honeyed jizz to spread across my thighs, and it runs across my body while I listen to your moans, watch your bobbing head, and feel your rocking flaring thighs jerking together deep inside each other.

Your legs rise, as you are standing on your toes like a ballet dancer, and you cry-out: "I come, I come! Ahhh!" Into a pink shell of sensuous beauty, spent semen like pearls take-off and drop from a chain of twist s and curls.

'Aleta's Celestial Ride'

On a celestial ride, your naked body lies relaxed, stretched-out with one arm supporting your head on the grey wrinkles of a rhino, whose legs stretch endlessly into the clouds upon the skies, a king size bed in his belly, where I lie in my post-coital slumber now, while you control this soft-rocking ride across the swamps of time.

Again I ride in a stormy cloud of horse-shaped thundering sounds, racing me like Pegasus' white flaring nostrils and fiery hooves sparkling across the blue-white air. In the cupola of the blue heavens, shaper of great faces, holy men and virtue-faced women search for the absolute match of hearts. I see that you are just perfect for me and my mind. We seek to merge into the twin-shaped body of fused souls and minds, observing all the couples that have merged and thus found each other since time began: White translucent shadows that take on ivory shapes of beautiful sculptures from beginning of civilisation to now.

'Painting Aleta's Nude'

I love you like a Vestal Priestess of the heavens, Virgin Mary of us all, 'Gorgoepikoon' of our secret wishes, with her naked child that depicts most tender love, giving and taking. In the flowing coat of her regal vestures, the roses turn from gold to pink and carmine red, taking on shapes of beautiful women. The great depicting of all stages of her past life follows. The sacred Vestal Goddess that created Venus, Aphrodite, has created you, Aleta!

Assembled in her rich regal corona, earth's history and the wealth of our desires and longings are highlighted above the fruit of never ending love. The pleasures and lust thus glow.

From the endless barren lands of earth below a grand white lily flower, a pure maiden climbs from the delicate glass bowl, its ranking supported in the breathed-out air.

I paint you in the nude: A virgin mother of my feelings, a delicate Muse of all my most intimate thoughts, a lascivious harlot of my secret desires, beautiful Venus of my lust.

Your dark amber hair flows like silky strands curled around your nape and right shoulder as you turn your head towards me, dusky eyed with blowing lips. We make love within a bed of wide-open flowering roses in golden yellow, deep burnt-orange, and dark wine flooded reds.

I see you vested in ivory-white robes, rich and soft, your top sliding off, revealing your right breast and its pink areola with its pointed nipple. Your right hand holds a wooden cross carved from an olive tree for the Easter celebrations. Your left leg steps forward, as you are seated on a cloud. Your left hand holds an open book that is weighted on your hand and your right arm lowers to your marbled thighs.

Your face is elated, shadowed slightly on the right side, highlighting your profile's noble face. Your hair surrounds your oval shaped face. The millions of worshippers to life and the arts, achievements of the gifted, resurrected lovers that come to pay homage at *Eros'* altar, make him come alive in a golden cage of a niche embellished with Renaissance art. Women in love touch their breasts, enticing their lovers to join them in life's eternal celebration, with the oncoming collective climax in this erotic assembly in the clouds.

The poet observes and touched by his Muse will report. Further along the way the sharp-eyed artist positioned in concentration at his easel, paints the stirring movements of bodies that tumble between the clouds in the ever-changing light from the heavens that dissolves some shapes and highlights others. Colours fluctuate with all the sizes, like we all fluctuate when we make love.

Your shape that emerges from the yellow glaring heat, fuzzy at the edges, floats toward me. I could make out a Venus-like shape. The Venus of Milo? The face is yours with the draped sarong around your hips, your facial expression with lightning glances emerges from your dusky eyes, and wakes me from my trance. You reflect your thoughts about beauty, love, and desire; about your lover's last kiss that had this fire demanding an instant fuck. Your lips remained slightly open, as if you still revel in his request you granted, but it hadn't yet been fulfilled. The fire of his possessive nature is flooding you with the longing of your body, you wished to surrender to him. He stalks around your nakedness and you sense the intensity in his eyes desiring your body. You feel this sweetness emerging from your thighs as he views your fine lines along your spine and back, meeting at the top of your ravine between your well-shaped buttocks. Admiring your body with his gentle fingertips, he is afraid of startling you by touching your most precious spot of your fleshly sculpture.

Your pose invites me to join you. I see you in midst of a field of soft greens. The sun has started to lay its tired head into the cushion of a wine red sea. We swim in the red wines of our lust. Your body's ruby-red glow causes spiced-up throbs throughout my boiling blood.

'The Multiplications of Aleta'

I see millions of Classical statues along the arches of the heavenly arena. Its dark-red niches flow around our close-up faces. Your face that floats into mine, kisses that bare instant lust: A merging of all our molecules, all our earthly particles.

The red roses glow in white burning highlights, twisting and rotating their curling petals into millions of Aphrodite sculptures. I see myself, a little boy who stands and gazes mesmerized at your beauty, Aphrodite with my mother's face, Aphrodite with my aunt's face, Aphrodite with your face – and my whole being absorbed into these beautiful women.

I ride a dark grey horse, with a white highlighted mane, into the deep dark dungeons, where his mane glows like liquid light. I can make out your body, twisted, angled, and with your arms tied high above your head that is sagging back. Your hair like a flowing river gushes in front of me. Your tight soft dress has been ripped off your shoulders, revealing your tormented body that tries to wriggle out from the closing poisonous grasp of a blood-red monster that gnaws at the base of your feet, eroding the safety of your stand. Like Saint George and the dragon, now is my time to act and free you from the frightening ordeal and certain death.

'Aleta, Mistress of the Dome of Winds'

My face is wide-eyed, flushed and in the eyes reflects pictures of your writhing body. Your stately torso stuck partly in your embroidered wine-red robe that falls with your slight moves finally down to your thighs, revealing all your regal beauty I always seek. And now that I am about to touch you, I expose my own body to rub upon yours at an instant.

In this Dome of the Winds, where the blue skies meet with the gleaming rays of sunlight, the pink and purple clouds that carry the gilded veils of gossamer cloth from the gods, we meet below the full-blown sails that throw the covers of their shadow onto our bed. We rise and fly and I will come closer to you. Your body rises up ahead of me, passing my body with your legs that open up and spread for me, enticing me to slide into you. My head nestles in between your thighs, rests in your belly's cup, while my lips seek the pistil of your clit. My tongue-tip that tastes you, sending shivers of excitement through your body. My heated tongue that digs into your pussy's pink, darts along its moistened slit, unfolding your rose in a diving lust that baths in your vulva's sweet petals.

Your arms that express your high, pull me up and I slide from oral pleasures to brushing of hips and your salty tasting skin, my mouth filled with the softness of your copious breasts, its swollen discs with their prick-hard nipples stabbing my lips, cheeks, and tongue, my chest

148

and my belly. My cock and my balls rest now in the warm lagoon of your mouth that sucks my cock deeply into its warm fleshly lagoon. We die. Let's die together, having travelled the long road to this most enthralling height in freedom love's expression.

Then you kiss me and I see your vulva glow and your clit become that huge, as if it would be my cock that I suck and lick. I gasp as it fills-up my mouth and suffocates me in this Soixente-neuf. Your nipples graze my thighs pricking me to ecstasy. Your lips kiss my cock that turned into an enlarged clit you enjoy. Then in midst of these metamorphic enlarged fantasies we find our heights of come, with spasms, clasping, and enjoyment of our spent energies that fill us up with honeyed jizz and lakes of free flowing body juices that become the stream of sweet, fortified wine that transverses the landscape of the garden of lust.

Wines of Aleta and golden bodies mingle entwined and twisting, wriggling, rubbing into knots, and into a Bacchanal of sensual flowing bodies, juices and wine flowing into the cold sea, like hot lava that sends water sizzling with steamy clouds into the scented air, as fire meets water, as red-hot body bows into glowing red body.

'Aleta my lustful fuck'

I meet Aleta in a morning of her desire being on edge and in our subsequent temperamental conversation, our words turn into touches and strokes, we extend on each other lovingly. Our juices have begun to flow and I notice Aleta is ready to let herself fly into her climax.

I am still aroused.

She was excited about my invitation to sit in my lap and she started to take her clothes off. I feel her high state of arousal, my slightest touches will get her off. She desires to fellate me and as she does, she wraps her lips around my crown. I stretch and kiss her clit, she rubs in her gyrating moves around my finger and my mouth. She gasps and I feel her contractions. My other finger slides along her buttock's fold.

She gasps in shorter breaths and I increase my sucking of her clit. She becomes fully orgasmic and I desire

149

her so badly that I tell her I wish to penetrate her in this instant fuck, she desired to be a fast one: "I want you on the floor and thump you in this back position," Telling her about my wild feelings, my violently throbbing cock, screwing her between my subjugating thumping. On the floor, thanks to the flokati-rug, we only burn inside and not on our skins in our hefty slides.

I roll over to find a position allowing more friction for my shaft. She uses her moving pelvis to counteract my strides.

Pushing myself in total lust into her now, closing my eyes: "Into you, Aleta, I want to come into you!" Continuously repeating these words as in a trance. "I abuse your pussy, Aleta, I want to rub you into another high. I want you now, deep! I merge my white blood into your wetland's warmth that has embraced me in its totality, ahhh! I cum! I come!"

Aleta is in desire of such fast and quick fucks. I follow her since some time, but more so now, as her life does not allow more time and often we have an intense burn in us for such intense quickies that turn us into cannibals of lust.

I follow her often, as her climaxes turn on mine so close in an instant. But then, I also wish to come with her close together. *As often as I possibly can.*

When she comes close to her climax, I become at ease and wish her cry and her burst to carry mine, wishing to let go and join her upturned flight and prolong her pleasure that multiplies with mine. Our orgasmic curves complement each other, matching and extending all the time. Never ceasing lust pervades our pores. Aleta has freed me from all inhibitions in a way that makes me transgressing the age-old taboos with such vigour and pleasure that our copulations are sweeter still.

I love to show myself at times to her. She loves to see me naked and observe my body's reactions to her emotional world, she shows me with her body movements. She lifts her knitwear top up, exposes her beautiful breasts, her excitement shows on her pointed nipples that sit on perfectly round, dark-pink coloured aureoles. I desire to kiss them, suck them, a most arousing act for me and for her to start up our lovemaking. I desire to suck them up totally, bury her breasts in my mouth and let my heated mouth spread this fire into her.

"I lick you Aleta, hmm, …your most desirable breasts. I love to devour them for a while. Ah, so good, so good." I talk to Aleta all the time. Love talk she enjoys and it makes her feel high. Often I desire to get Aleta off just talking to her all these acts of love I describe in detail, what I wish to do to her and with her. In this active and passive flow of our words, our emotions will be highlighted along similar routes, and we crave for fulfilment of all our wishes in our naked exposure to each other.

'Our Narcissistic Body Show'

Aleta thrives on my lustful expressions and in return, as she is turned-on, she does inflict more lust in me to the point that we become narcissistically inclined, and having lost our inhibitions we throw off our clothes. This morning she wasn't able to show me more than her breasts and she wanted to see me. "Stand up," she demanded. I did with my trousers off, and as I became aware of her eyes watching me in my nakedness, I became aroused again. I had such a hard-on that I showed her my cock in all its appearances, from every angle and all sides. She gasped.

"I love your cock," she said and after her good view of it, it made her aroused again. She closed her eyes. "I want to lick it." She whispered.

Then, following her exclamation of a fellatio, she loves to give me now every time, when she is extremely aroused and horny. I want to see her too. Aleta is very conscious of her body; she thinks though that it is not yet honed to the shape she would love me to see. I still love her body, even if she cannot lose some of her weight she wanted to. I love her full breasts and her gorgeous areolas, her fine nipples that remind me of my first love, her face with her dusky-eyed expressions, and her legs and thighs. Aleta is a wonderful lover and when she has her privacy she shows me her body. After we made love I observe her pussy for the first time on a web-transmission. I want to see more and she shows me her vulva-lips, her pubic bone, and her beautiful appointed thighs. How much I delve into her and lust for her, even if I just climaxed, it'll give me another high. We are after all together, intimately, sliding on each other, performing together for each other in continuous lust and desire to satisfy each other.

Together. Liaison. Little Death. Kind of e-lovers we are, who are beyond the restrictions of the old century that has gone and passed like the dodos.

E-love, e-togetherness in an intensive e-come.

These days of reflection at Easter, when the theme of Jesus' resurrection is made aware in the mind of pious folk, I ponder about my own resurrection in love with Aleta: Our incidental meeting online, our friendship that formed then and subsequently turned into e-love, followed by the desire that drove us into heights of pleasure, we have not known for such a long time.

Desire formed in us suddenly to meet also in reality, as we matched well. The first meeting in the street, the caress, the touches, the love that flourished and sprouted even in wintry surroundings of a city that has its roots back 3500 years and that transferred inspiration from its Classical art into my innerness through its goddess-like messenger and Muse : Aleta!

'Five Days of Love, Death, and Resurrection'

Five days of intense passionate exchanges in word, voice, and physical togetherness have enhanced our lustful lives to another level. We feel lustfulness we never imagined and we have buried these in the inner vaults of our reawakened libidos.

Yesterday she told me she will be off to church and now I have problems comprehending her attitudes.

Does she just pretend, or does she enjoy to perform a sensuous act?

She told me that she's not religious, yet she attends church services. Is she keeping up an image? How dreadful that must be just to conform to the larger part of society, in a mass belonging and a collective support of the major religion. For something one has lost faith in?

I guess I'm an outcast and care little about a society that has left me badly in the lurch, due to the ruling political views. I'm thrown into the pot, together with all who supported the apartheid government, yet I had very little to do with it. Besides I am categorised as a second-class citizen, be it in the former or the present government. You can check it out!

She comes online, as I look at my past history and I am still trying to find out how this darned message system works, she seems to know so much about. I am surprised that she takes delight to be messaged continuously by strangers. Of course she gets a thrill out of being desired, otherwise she would customize this system to suit her privacy. Called collective sexuality, for the sake of a personal experience? So be it.

This nearness to sexuality must excite her. Immediately she is at me with her curiosity that drives her libido.

"Are you talking to others?" These questions are lined up towards me, as if she wishes to justify her own desires and her being that constantly seeks to be loved. A search for love she has missed out as a child?

She tells me she is concerned, but she has that craving for continuous communication, day and night, and I guess that she knows quite a few friends. Where does that place me? She admits one, just to tell me soon afterwards of another. And so I am even careful not to ask anymore. She would just wipe it off with her smile, her cute act of exposing her breasts, so, as to turn me on for her. Seldom would she go any further. But on some occasions she did and I loved it.

Reminds me of 'Thirteen Steps' in the hills of P.R., her summer retreat, where we became intimate. There, at the very delicate moment, just as I we settled down for a languid lovemaking, her cell phone rang. Why didn't she switch it off? Was she doing this on purpose to put me off penetrating her? Masochistic tendencies I guess. To me they appear sadistic and I refute them wholeheartedly.

Now, she tells me of interruptions that are of similar nature, while we were together online. I question the way she is careless about etiquette, especially in matters of love. I think I have been had badly.

"Is your aim to be loved by many?"

"It's only messages I get," she quips, playing the astonished and surprised woman, who might just crave this. And my question relates to the assembly of men interested in her. There must be a reason besides hobbies and literature. I wish she wouldn't tell me all of this, then I would be less jealous. She tells me she isn't jealous, does not even know about that. Hah! I wonder. Even a blind man can sense that she's popular with men. Her sentence from the start comes back to me now: "Are you violent? I hope you are not angry with me."

In a way she was emptying some conflict that might arise out of her selfish behaviour. "I don't think that I'm extremely selfish," she stated. Hah!

Am I tending to violence if I'm duped? I didn't understand this question back then.

She plays on, acting at all times.

"I freeze if you get angry," she tells me in a way to induce guilt feelings in me. In the same breath she does not want me to change my character or the way I behave. This is becoming impossible. Does she want me to become mad? I think that there was an element of great fear attached to our intimacy. So now, as it has developed into a life, it becomes threatening to our existing ways of living: The unavoidable usurper in an intimate relationship.

I'm not the only person she's in contact with, but she insists that I do believe that it's the case, even if I see her late night being online. Well? Not talking to anyone else? Do I believe it? I know by now that one cannot possess one's love, but my innerness is in revolt about her in a giant wrestling match.

"My mind has turned around full circle and has become that of a child, with blind beliefs in matters of love. Hm, do I? However Aleta, you might be different that way," I muse. "You may have your girlfriends and still be with me. But I don't have boyfriends, while I'm solely with you."

However, I have some loose girlfriends around the globe, but only one is more playful with me and she sends me her photographs. Well, would she become jealous if I'll send her photographs of them? I better shouldn't rev her up yet and I will not send her my reactions to her needling of me. She talks about being equal partners. Now, are we equal partners?

I admit, I love certain nudes that are artistic. With Aleta I love also pornographic ones, but that is between us only. She loves mine and I know secretly she demands more of them. Now and then I send her some, when I'm in the mood and she has turned me on with her beautiful breasts, her body-wriggling, and our web-cam lovemaking. If I'm in a sensual euphoric state, I love to expose my body to her. She assures me that she is not jealous. But the other day she put me through a rigorous questioning, querying about my free time online and my other friends. Do I ever query her friends? Who aims to be possessive now? It's ridiculous, I must say.

But she insinuates to me the nature of her instant messages she is getting from strangers with their hackneyed lewd content.

These are the small needle pricks, life online is so generous with, and what all sexual meddling does, is ruining a good friendship, a wonderful sensual love. But at the same token it had helped to meet Aleta and so it also has its own destructive mechanism built-in. I have to successfully counteract this by being alert to it, the same way Aleta is; she had taught me. In one moment life's sweet and loving, in the next it crumbles just as speedily. The fast and fickle character of personal relationships challenges one to be alert enough trying to keep the one that is appreciated the most!

It's now Aleta's turn to worry about me a bit. I see that it had affected her with a measure of guilt. I had my share before, when she told me about her friends who adore her: Mostly women. So, I am here on a losing ground, especially on woman's day, women's year, and this century of women's rights for absolute equality. Maybe Amazon-like squadrons already rally to a war against men as their equals. Achilles bending over the slain body of the queen of the Amazons, having slain her, admires her beauty and laments about the unfortunate end of her. It might be now the opposite scenario.

'Do You Love Me?'

Aleta loves cats and she has herself cat-like associations, while I love dogs and have those related associations in my moods and character straits. Maybe men are easier duped, the cat teasing the dog and having brought him to the annoyance's edge, escapes unscathed of the dog's brawn onto the nearby roof, ridiculing his ineffective powers in a posed scoffing.

Then she is with cat-like charms rolling up in my arms, against my chest and extracting fatherly feelings of tenderness in me, I have to be alert. The next moment she is making me my favourite green tea, in the strength I prefer, and feeding me also some health-cookies. She is going all the way to possess me now!

In principle of course, this dualism will never change. How much we desire each other and how much we do love, as against a competitive edge in the sexes.

"Do you love me?" She asks me suddenly, even if it is self-evident at present – I wonder why, as we have just made love this afternoon, with desire, with an inflamed passion, and all of this before she went to church.>Why does she bring this up? Because I stayed home and did not intend to move out of my study? Did she suspect me to have somebody else to talk to?

Well, it sounded like I had planned manoeuvres to outdo her with avoidance tactics. Our relationship had a certain swing to changes, especially when Aleta is so taken by one of her lady friends she praises continuously, in bits and pieces, mostly indicative, never saying anything about her status of closeness or intimacy. She even wanted to travel away with her, the one she loves and of one she had shared photographs with me a year back.

I always love Aleta, even if she admires younger women and craves for their intimate touches. I realized

156

how difficult it is to keep an online relationship, whose inert intenseness in any direction may lead at times to a dampening of the mood for lovemaking. A dullness of one's feelings will set intimacies between high roads and down to the valley of blunt emotions, feelings of loss and sadness that are overpowering. This is then the sign for a pause in the excitement of the musical chores of love and lust, and a short break will re-establish ones strength to face another round of the web-life roller coaster ride, if one has indeed fallen in love.

Yet, every pause, holiday, or sabbatical from the communicative window, will be interpreted as a loss of one's love to somebody else. A loss of interest. A painful period of frightful messages. An anticipation of love's end.

I love Aleta, even with her contradictory ways. She's a wonderful person with a warm compassion for humanitarian issues. She is the most responsive of all women I have ever known. She has found a magical access to my soul. I support her battle to keep her literary interests fresh and her attempts in writing vivid, her desire she has towards me to transfer my mind into her wondrous world of narration that's her other passion. Yet, family life mostly polarizes literary ambitions.

Aleta is a special person to me, naturally also to all her friends. She must be. Giving persons are always special to their demanding friends. I am testing neither her loyalty, nor her love towards me. We are after all free persons to have friends of our choices. I wondered why she has shown suddenly such an affront toward me possibly talking to other persons confidentially. I cannot imagine Aleta wanting to clip my wings, but sometimes I need to fly free. That will neither belittle my intense feelings, I harbour deep in my heart for her, nor will it dim my emotional love life with her.

'A kiss like an instant fuck'

She has told me these last days of our intense lovemaking during the Easter week, dying together on the symbolic cross of our lustfulness, and then in a glorious celebration of a resurrection, in this feeling of an instant burn, we exert from our mutual e-fuck – she us afraid of the door opening to her room suddenly and without any warning. Then she might be caught by her teenage daughter, exposing her body to me, with a picture of my body spread over her laptop monitor: heathy breathing conversation in the middle of a come. It's Aleta's nightmare. But now, suddenly she tells me she was delayed by some pop-up messages from a stranger in the middle of her oncoming climax.

Really? What does this mean now? Weakening of my own messages and efforts of transferring my genuine feelings? Aleta has a secret thrill of men contacting her, the openness of a possible seduction, as much as I might have perhaps. The detection by others, like by her family members, works as a strong aphrodisiac in her and drives her to a heightened climactic response.

Like back in the five days we had our secret meetings, when a possible detection of our intimacy heightened our want of each other, as all obstacles that cause it seem impossible to be mastered. Public places, semi-deserted, churches, parks and clusters of trees, which give a semi-protective barrier towards the unforeseen detection by others: The nearness of spouses and the close vicinity of a moment in instant lust. The thrill of being at all times ready for the other lover to give all in that instant.

"You must be always ready," she said.

The stolen kisses, the close-up caress in an adjoining room. The intenseness of the moment creates an adrenalin flow. The drum-beat of our hearts, with a kiss loaded with the heat of want on the tip of the tongue.

We both haven't taken off our respective profiles from the Internet's white pages. Do we thrive on this thrill to be contacted by others secretly, randomly, and in a chance of serendipity?

*

ORION'S LOVE NEST

There's a small street around the apartments set-out around a square, where I stay with my spouse. It is an unimportant street, a new building being constructed for some years on the opposite side, a concrete skeleton, which stares at me like a beggar in tatty clothes looking for a handout. Next to it an empty plot overgrown with thistle. Some stray cats roam it for mice. At the incline to the east the street rises to the hills scattered with the homes of well-to-do Greeks. To the west, the road falls toward the sea in a gentle manner inviting me down to the acacia lined part, where a terracotta painted two storey building nestles in between, like a private mansion. It's unassuming with its simple façade, but reminds one of a villa from years back, when the quaint suburb of Voula has been developed. It followed in the footprints of Onassis, who established another suburb further north. I like this building. It's simple from the outside, yet as soon as one enters the plate glass doors into the lobby, a cosy atmosphere wraps around one immediately. I called it Orion for a code name.

I met her here for the first time, as we agreed to have a couple of hours together for a start, nurturing first mutual stirrings. The key shows 113, first floor corner room. A cool atmosphere is enhanced by the head wall painted in light-blue. She switches the AC-unit to a slight cooling mode, but for me it's too cold. She deactivates the unit again and instead opens the French windows slightly, placing the voile curtain over them, making sure that we have privacy. I am less afraid of being eyed by somebody. Besides, who would follow me around? She responds to my concern and indicates a nosy neighbour, she has experienced in the block of apartments she's living in this area, who makes it his business to spy on his flat neighbours. This petty bourgeoisie attitude amazes me. I smile.

We sit next to each other at the end of the wide bed and talk about us. She unscrews a bottle of tsikoudia and fills two glasses with a decent tot. "Cheers! To your health." We toast each other and she says the words in Greek.

"To Orion," I said.

"Oh, it reminds me of a star."

"Yes, it's somewhat related," I replied. She has activated the TV set with a remote control. A special program is announced for guests. It's a pornographic clip. "Well," she mumbles and switches it off again. I don't mind to see it, but as we intend making love, we'll not even look at it. I say nothing.

The drink has loosened us up and we kiss. This time with more comfort than in the lift. I feel stirred by her touches and experience myself growing toward the ceiling. Bit by bit we take our clothes off together. She visits the bathroom first. I follow-up on hygiene, as soon as she's finished and clean myself thoroughly, although I have cleaned myself before, but that was hours ago. Just to make sure. As soon as I return to the bedroom, she is already covered with a plain white sheet. Moving close to her I notice that she is snoozing. It's good, she has started to relax; tense domestic environments have an immediate release when one is away from it.

Making love is a process and it comes naturally, given time and avoiding any stress bay hurrying. We have long forgotten to let things happen naturally and to tone our sensual awareness. I feel good enjoying a skin to skin contact, as it's wanted in this first intimacy and it entices me. I touch her and she loves it. In time we relax completely and fall asleep. When I wake, she is already up returning from the bathroom. "That was quick," I remark.

"Thanks for relaxing me," she replies.

"But – I'm …not sure, if we…" I stutter.

"Did it?" She cuts in. "Never mind, it was nice to cuddle with you below the sheets. Perhaps next time we'll be less tired."

"Aha," I said and sit up in bed. She comes close and denudes me from the sheet. "Stay like that," she said and kisses me. Her hands slide down my body and her head follows. "You are in for a surprise!" She said and smiles concentrating to pleasure me. "OH, my god!" Indeed, I have lots of pleasure, as let her fellating waves flow onto me like the water that laps me stepping into a warm bath and slowly sinking into the full tub.

The sensation of lustful compliments like having this fellatio bestowed on me, is not only extremely desirable, but one usually doesn't get it at home, a friend once remarked. So, it's the main ingredient in making sexual love – complete love – oral, straight and anal. Now then, I'm glad that I've found a partner who is enjoying it as much as I do, as we reciprocate and are on equal terms. We had a good session and finally had completed our tete-a-tete with a successful outcome. We had sated each other.

"Bravo! Great! Super! "I praised our time together.

"Kaliallo – next time," she said, which meant an encore. And being of mature age it would also have meant that another sleep of an hour would be needed to be ready and if one is virile. However, available time had run out for us.

The intimacy of the Villa-hotel is amazing. I have not seen one couple during our check-in, nor when I paid and we left.

"Kalinixta," she said and kissed me, moving into her car seat.

"Good night and sleep tight," I replied.

"I love Orion's love nest," she smiled as she drove off.

*

162

Paraglia Marathonas: Marie

As I wrote to her a short story about a morning's walk along the beach of Marathon, called in Greek 'paraglia marathonas, the beach at Marathon, which to find as a newcomer has not been the easiest for me. My driving skills have been tested through dense traffic, my eyes peeled on the winding road ahead, whereby missing signs. I couldn't decipher the Greek letters in that speed, but I tried picking out familiar signs as a clue. I circled around the area where I guessed the beach to be, like an old makeshift sign said in Greek, like an old buzzard missing out on his catch. Stopping finally at a café I received vague directions, with arms waving in a staccato of words that meant nothing to me.

Finally I found the alley with the sign facing onto the opposite side. I parked my car and walked towards the reception cubicle, which stood at the entrance of another boom and suddenly the world stood still. The lined-up pine trees along the boundary bowed their crowns in the evening breeze.

She stood there. I only noticed as I came closer, in the shadows, dressed in black garb, looking like an athlete. Dark hair and eyes, slim and reminding me of Anne, stirring in me comparisons for being her cousin, or perhaps she might be related to her. A look-alike Greek woman, she tricked my mind in the descending twilight.

I approached her with a trivial question and she communicated well with me. Then she started telling me about her life and not the usual sales talk. Her pretty face had lines engraved on her forehead, I assumed it was from suffering. She asked me if I minded her smoking. Not at all, I replied, just go ahead. I wouldn't give her away if the job didn't allow her to smoke during her shift. She pulled a packet of fine snow white paper from her jacket and I noticed she didn't have a bra. Then she pulled a pouch with fine cut tobacco from her other pocket. She distributed the tobacco evenly on the paper and I watched her fine fingers rolling the cigarette. She darted her tongue across the end of the rolled paper's glue-strip. She enjoyed watching me and she tried perfecting her joint. There was a certain sexual underlining in her ritual. Her tongue licking constantly the edges and then as she inserted the filter tip and she looked at me, I felt a stirring in my loins. I wondered if she read my mind having seen my eyes fixed at the tip of her breast as she moved to search for her matches. I shifted a leg as I felt her tongue moving down my face and neck simultaneously with her movements. She must have noticed my growing bulge in my pants. She smiled as she looked at my crotch. She couldn't find her matches at first. Then suddenly she produced them. "May I?" I said and lit a match. I felt a spark in my hand as I touched her fingers. She sucked greedily and blew the sweet smoke into my body. I gasped as if she had blown upon my penis. I stopped to gather myself. There was no point to regroup now. At that moment a group of people passed and edged me towards her. I came closer to her face as she exhaled. She sat down on the wooden step to the reception. The warmth of her exhaling went through my jeans as her lips touched my pants. I felt her hot breath on my erection and her fingers opened my fly. –

"Are you all right?" She said as I was lost for words.

"I am sor…ry," I mumbled, stirring from my thoughts, "Yes I am," – She smiled, finishing the sentence for me – "Aroused?" Her dark eyes pierced me. I looked into her shining eyes, as she placed her cigarette to her lips.

"Yes," I said somewhat collected again, "you have …"

"Let's go in here," she took my hand and pulled me into her cubby-hole of an office. "Sit on the desk," she whispered loosening my belt and pulling my shoes and trousers off.

"Uhh," I said as she moved her lips close to my cock. I felt as if I would burst at the moment she blew another puff of smoke against my cock. Then she wanted me to cool down, but I felt strange and impatient for rather be in the warm cavity of her mouth. Then she kissed my crown and her tongue played on me, and I thought to rise through the ceiling. My heart pounded and pearls of sweat formed on my temples. She stopped her fellating act and pulled her soft leotard down, bending down on the table. "Take me, take me," she whispered. I positioned myself in the tight confines as she pushed against me, taking my time teasing her. My crown, most sensitive for entering a woman for the first time, is a sensation I wanted to savour as long as possible. I entered her slowly and closed my eyes to the oncoming dusk that created an eerie atmosphere, with some blue light through the high-level window. I felt like being with Anne, holding her breasts and tossing against her well-shaped bums. I could hear her voice murmuring between her breathing: "A final time, come Zoi, a final time, come –

I met Marie every day at the beach, as I walked the few kilometres along the promenade that stretched out to a soft curve of a beautiful bay, then narrowed to a pedestrian path. I mused about historic events: The Persian ships of Darius, which had landed in the bay at 490 BC; and about the Athenians who were positioned to the west. Miltiades, whose strategy of a weaker centre, but strong wings worked out well, and joined by the Plataians in the valley of Vrana, just a few kilometres to the west, the combined Greek forces, although outnumbered three to one, won their battle and chased the Persians into the bay, conquering half a dozen of enemy ships. The birth of the Classical Marathon run started from here, as the young soldier Phaedippas was sent by Miltiades to hurry to Athens to give warn the population for their immediate preparation to defend their city. He ran the whole distance of 42 km, uttering the words "we have won, prepare…"collapsed and died. However the Persians changed their minds attacking Athens, when they saw the population had prepared for defending their city, licked their wounds and decided to sail rather home.

Arriving at the point where the pedestrian road narrows down to a path, a small building emerged from the morning's mist. The emerging red of the sun highlighted the flowering oleander shrubs to glow. The fisherman's hut began to reflect the sun and the simple dwelling came alive with the gold as on the helmet of the general in midst of cries at the heroic battle, the place was lit up in a blaze of fire and battle cries the sun had suddenly ignited, "Vrana Valley," I murmured gazing at the blue door that opened and the steeled frame of a fisherman – like a general – emerged into the early morning. I saw the general lifting his sword high that reflected the sunrays piercing into my eyes. His helmet's reflection lit up the scene of the many fallen and the jubilant Greek soldiers in this pure and brilliant light. Marathonas, a sense of place.

Marie waved at me from the sea. I placed my clothes next to her wicker basket and ran into the calm sea that appeared like a lake. The instant the water hit my naked body, I gasped, it felt like Marie fellating me the first time. I dived in to swim towards her.

"Zoi you are nuts," she gasped, "they will arrest you," she breathed out. "This is not a nudist beach." I laughed.

"No," I said, "this is Greece," and kissed her. We dived and wrestled. I clasped her thighs and removed her panties. "Sit on me," I said and stood firm. Marie braced my waist and I held her, until she let herself down on me like a bird perching on a rock. I made love to her.

"You are like in a fever," she whispered.

"Yes," I replied, "you have woken in me a gigantic life."

"Yes," she laughed, "I can feel it right through my body. I joined her laughing. I felt wonderful with Marie, as I hugged her and tried this impulsive act of lovemaking in the sea.

From the first moment I knew I would fall in love with Marie, even if she used me as a conductor for her pent-up anger, frustration, and pain; as if I had been chosen by her to help creating a black-sheep, she'll load with her heavy inner burden of an unwanted pregnancy, she had carried with her around. She had been loading this black sheep with her sorrow and her hurt of being demeaned by a vulgar person, and she chased this black sheep into the thistle-valley of Vrana and its dehydrated exposure from the heat of the barren mountains to certain death. Once the vultures had cleaned all edible flesh from the bones, the relentless bleaching of ant's acid would render a grim skeleton that appeared ghost-like in the moonlight.

"How do you like it?" Marie whispered as she slid her bikini off. Her small breasts stood-out firm with every breath she took and my hands touched them gently, my palms cupping them and my fingers caressed her nipples, turning hard between them. "Kiss them!" She gasped. I kissed her knob-hard tits pursing my lips around them sucking. "AH." She bowed like a willow. "I'm getting so wet. AH." Once more on the breast of my mother, I felt like a kid. Her fingers circled my cock. I remembered how Anne had touched me the last time, and it felt like the most wanted touch since.

The sun burned my bums through the open door of the fisherman's hut and we made love without a care in the world. The old man who let us into his domain said a few words in Greek and then went out to fish in the bay. For a whole morning we could be as intimate as we wished, Marie commented. "Lie down on the couch," she said, "slide your bums down to the edge." I wondered if she has a new way of heightening my pleasure, as she continued. I followed her command and she straddled me and moved up and down my penis that felt like stretching into her, even as she removed her vulva in this game of a teasing Amazon. I desired her madly, stretching like a bow into her, bury my cock to its tilt into her. She continued the tease. I closed my eyes and felt her G-spot at my base, my body responded with more bowing into each other at each of her stroking moves that brought me closer to a height. My awkward lie pained me, my spine fully stretched, it felt as if it would snap at the moment of a climax, or if love would stop before my deliberate peaking. Marie, the cold and calculating Amazon with her artful lovemaking made me die another 'little death'.

I lied at her feet. I was at her cunt's mercy. I am dead I thought.

"Another round?" She asked with a natural cheek. I nodded, unable to speak, my breathing laboured, heavy with gasps. She pulled my hand helping me to get up. My spine had stiffened in a cramp and I could hardly move.

"I want you Marie," I said and waited for her reaction. She bent down in front of me. I grabbed her behind. Her pert bums inspired me with a spark. In a sudden urge fires licked my body with an eruption of innate primordial desires that oscillated between anger and desire to pierce her for good and let her die this pleasurable way as she had wished. The sun had heated her back like freshly baked bread and as I entered her in repeated and varied tossing, my own bums burned in this early morning fornication. "I love it," I moaned.

"Tell me," she gasped and I let off a chain of four-letter-words from my mind's library.

"I fuck you," had become the sweetest sentence of love I've ever repeated, since years of sabbatical. Its sound matched the swishing sounds of our unification in this fusion of lust that I didn't want to ever end.

I had no scruples in trying to delay my climax, as Marie had artfully tuned my sensuality to match her own timing of an orgasm that announced itself with vibrations and spasms of her vulva, clasping my expanding dick so much that I never wanted to stop pounding into her. My sexuality took over and I had no control over my body any longer with reflex-like pushes and pulls, long after climaxing. Marie gasped with a suffocated cry as I shouted my peaking joy, and even as she collapsed along the couch and I fell over her in my ecstasy. She paused and then asked me to lie down supine for her to stretch upon me. Her wet pussy squashed upon my half-hard cock that became alive again. It felt like a sweet hangover feeling, my heart pounding in a strong rhythmic beat. I closed my eyes and let Marie have her post-climaxing game. As she rubbed herself on my hips and chest and she had made me wet all over, she slowed down having exhausted herself and she slid off me. "Let's clean up," she announced and stepped over to the stone bowl that served as a washbasin, on a blue painted wooden stand, in front of the small, misted-up window that opened the view to the beach.

I watched her from my lying position. Her body became an expressive diagonal line in a dynamic perspective, with her movements of washing and cleaning that recalled our lovemaking ritual. I rose to join her and cleaned myself while she towelled off, taking care to wash my penis. She looked at my movements and knelt down in front of me and started kissing my glans. Her mouth, warm and moist, made me hard again. "Come," she said, "take a seat," and I placed myself on an armless bentwood chair. Straddling me, she slid on top of my erection. She felt soft and warm. The contrast of a cold water cleansing and her body heat aroused me completely. She danced in my lap and hummed a song, as if she'd summon all her loves to huddle around and celebrate her new love, at this glorious morning of the tenth of September, the date that related to my favourite number. I told her and she let out a deep laugh, happy as a lark.

"I am happy to have you here," she announced, "you came out of the blue like a boat from the sea." I sighed.

"You Marie, you are the wondrous woman born from the foam of the sea," I whispered. She laughed again and mumbled lover's talk. Being the lover she dreamed of a sweet sexual union, and never thought of experiencing any longer such a fierce and passionate lovemaking. "Neither did I, Marie," I replied, but she carried on with her monologue, praising me to have just now, been always ready and hard for her. I whispered to her love words, about her charm and beautiful body she absorbed and used for fuel, to burn a lasting memento of a lover she idolized in me. I felt that this praise would entice me trying to be better each time I met her, but rather kill my relationship with her than enhance it. "But you praise me too much, I have my off-days too," I tried to smother her overflowing praise of me as a lover.

"You don't understand," she replied, "this is a godsend meeting for us, as we are a perfectly matching couple." I sighed and thought of nothing short about matching, but could we keep this passionate madness alive? "It's not an accident," she continued, "just as my late husband told me to stop mourning him."

Marie's passion made me want to come, but I couldn't climax any longer. I asked her to come for me, wet me, flood me with her body juices, so I could swim in the sea of her desire and love, the most pleasurable sea of all. She started to climb to her height and at the top of her climax it sounded like a tune she hummed again: "Thalassa, Thalassa," she threw her head back and cried, followed by names she gave me in her lust. I kissed her breast and her hardened nipples she thrust into my face. Then she clasped me tightly like nobody had ever held me this close before.

I've found the woman I always wanted to be with, my voice sounded inside me and I held her tightly. The waves from the bay started rising in high tide and changed colours from dark grey to inky blue and turquoise at their height, just as waves of passion did: The rhythmic lapping of the sea against the sandy beach recalled in me pictures of pounding myself into Marie, her straddling me, perching on me like a seagull on a pointed rock and riding me with most delicate slides.

She loosened herself and kissed me. I kissed her back for as long as my lips would enjoy her sensuality I felt everywhere present. Her whole body became one lip I wanted to suck and lick and darting my tongue into. And this time she loved me with her bruised lips, her hot lancing tongue that let me suddenly explode like the rising sea with a sound of its breaking waves.

"You came in my mouth," she laughed and kissed me. I inhaled her animalistic scent of wild flowers with the taste of love's mingled juices, vanilla and asparagus, impossible to define as I drifted into the beckoning sea of endless warmth.

When I woke, I felt like fallen from the clouds having landed on soft and warm sand. My eyes were gummed-up and my throat in need of a refreshment. I kissed Marie. She stirred. "Let's clean-up," I said.

"Oh, I slept like an angel," she replied.

"Yes, me too," I smiled, "but it's time to go." Marie rose and stroked me. "It's enough for one morning," she said and walked over to the washbasin. I washed as she put on her pants and top.

The fisherman appeared with his boat, the harvest of his living made from the sea. The restaurant next door took his catch. Marie had called out aloud "Thalassa!" As if praising the source of his catch. It sounded like her peaking cry, in my ears, I heard before. He conversed with the woman, who came to see him as his next door neighbour. His face radiated for he was looking forward to another round of relaxation. I greeted him with a Greek word I had learned: "Iassu."

"Iassas," he returned my greeting and then addressed Marie in Greek. "Could you help him with his boat?" Marie turned to me. I nodded and accompanied him to the water's edge. I pushed the prow in order for him to prepare it for the next day, digging my foot into the soft sand, while he pulled the boat's towing string. Finally we secured his boat 'Alexandros' to his liking. "Efharisto!" He sighed. "Endaxi," I replied and sighed. Then he patted me on the shoulder. He smiled, shook my hand and then told me something in Greek, I didn't entirely comprehend. Marie came over to kiss me. I kissed her back. "Let's eat," she whispered and turned her head towards the fisherman. "I invite you both," I said She spoke to the old man, who shook his head, but Marie convinced him, as he had offered us his small but comfortable habitat for our tete-a-tete.,

The fish tasted delicate, the octopus grilled to perfection, sweet and tangy with slight dashes of lemon on it, converging with olives to a taste that recalled the morning's celebration with a melting of tastes in love's merging. It recalled Marie's love to me as I touched her legs, gazing at her as she opened her lips slightly. My hands wandered to her thighs, my amorous game hidden by the blue-white chequered table cloth. She opened her legs and her thighs clasped the palm of my hand for a while, opening again and clasping, until I felt her warm pussy through the thin fabric of her panties. I rubbed it with gentle strides and she responded with her hand on me. The fisherman rose, bade us good-bye and told Marie that he'd catch-up on sleep. "Iassu Alexandros," Marie said and I repeated the same greeting. He waved us.

Marie wanted to go for a stroll along the promenade, but changed suddenly direction at the next alley. As soon as I followed her around a bend, she kissed me.

"I want you, Zoi," she whispered and my eyes scanned a copse of nearby olive trees, ideal for intimacy. "Just a quickie," she said and bent down for me below the trees, holding on to the gnarled bole of an ancient olive tree.

For days on end now, Marie had been away. She sent me a note through the receptionist of the resort where I stayed, waiting for her. She had to attend a funeral of her stepmother on the island of Santorini. She had written at the bottom of the message her address, and "I am longing for you. Come A.S.A.P - Come!" Marie thinking of a good time with me. I packed my belongings in a hurry. Notebooks, books to read, Greek poetry, pens, sketching block and crayons, and my mobile CD-player.

The French girl at reception smiled at me and organized me a trip to the island. "It's less expensive after the season," she said, but she understood the magical powers, Marie held over me in love. "I'll go there anytime," I replied absentmindedly, "for me love has no seasons," she looked at me with large brown eyes. "Oh la la," she exclaimed stretching the last syllable, "your girlfriend is a lucky woman, monsieur."

"No my dear," I hastened to reply looking past her hazel eyes through the open door and along the beach of Marathonas, swung gently along the bay like the lips of a woman, "I'm the lucky person, chasing the love of my life." I turned my head and looked into her hazel eyes.

"I wish," she paused, "I would have found a man like you found a woman." She mumbled and blushed.

"You'll find him," I said.

"Where?" Her eyes flared up.

"On a walk along the beach of destiny," I said slowly as she frowned.

"Where is that monsieur?" I asked her to come for a moment to the terrace door.

"Along here," I said and pointed to the stretch of the long, gentle swung beach.

"Oh, the Paraglia Marathonas…" she said as if disappointed.

"Yes."

"How?"

"Just walk every morning at the crack of dawn to the fisherman's hut, with the light-blue painted door and windows." I smiled.

"Ah!" She said gazing at me as I left. I smiled and winked at her. "Just try it," I said, lifted my holdall at the door and hurried to catch the next bus.

*

Vienna Revisited

I haven't seen the city of coffee-houses and deliciously baked cakes, Art-Noveau- and modern buildings in exciting contrast, for a very long time. I had promised Dani, my friend from the outposts of the North of America, to write her about my experiences. What better place to write up a concept than in a pleasant seat of *Café Central,* where its great decorative wall paintings remind the visitor of Eastern cultures. However, I would complete editing of the first immediate impressions, once I had arrived again back in the Africa of the South.

"Yes Dani, of course I will write you a long letter, after all we are very good pals indeed, and I have missed your wisecracks and your temperament too. How could I have survived in a dry land in midst of my sea of longings without your kindness and hugs?" I heard my voice inside calling.

I am glad I feel better today, however the altitude of 6000 feet in this City of Gold gives me a headache now and then. I recommend rather the cold weather I enjoyed in Austria. However, it takes time for the body to adjust to the European cold. But there are also many advantages there with better security and a generally well established order accepted by most people concerned with these issues. Sometimes though, too much red tape and order could kill the artist like me – HA! But I'll try finding a category into which I might place myself and therefore still stay the individual I really am.

Now what came out of the many doings during a revisit of my favourite city, Vienna? The museums – I met two American girls in the Jewish museum – I thought that they were rather pleasant, visiting as well the exhibition about the poet Paul Celan, also a favourite of mine. So then, poets and persons interested in poets, will meet therefore. Perhaps, having been influenced by his poetry at one stage in my life, I bought a book of his poems as well.

I had numerous visits to various coffee houses in Vienna and enjoyed the local fare and the fine cakes, even if I knew that the additional calories will hit me. I found that out as I became aware that it was always more and more difficult to get my shoelaces tied. Ha-ha, it has arrived – the bigger belly – growing day by day. I had to think of you, but you do not have to tie shoelaces.

When I met them with a bang – as you know I am an observer, a port, a writer, or my friends also think I am crazy, as the Greek ones do – the so-called better society here. Now, here I was in the heart of Vienna, in a coffee house at the 'Graben', the chatter of odd dialects hit my ear, stirring-up memories of my student days. Wow! At this moment this love-hate relationship with a city and its people hit me, as they had comments about me smoking a cigar, I had bought at Tenerife airport. I was showing off, I wrote into my tiny notebook, perhaps being mistaken for a spy or a police informer. Apparently as a citizen, you could go to the local police and report someone anonymously. This gave me the creeps. From then on I would always ask if I was allowed to smoke a cigar. The friendly woman serving me must have thought that I was nuts to ask, after all there were ashtrays everywhere, hm? I felt like a fool and I explained to her between bites of delicious apple strudel that I had been reprimanded in this upmarket coffee house, where Patricians once enjoyed their coffees and flirts, not to smoke a cigar, as it is forbidden. She just laughed and murmured "that one", and with a low voice "the new proletariat."

OH wow! Times have changed since those literati and writers had left or died, who transformed the city into a thriving intellectual melting pot, I thought aloud. "Quite so," an elderly man, with long hair like mine, said to me, "but don't talk aloud, it could be dangerous!" So, where is the right of free talk, the unhindered human right of self-expression? My world crumbled through my experiences in the cafes. I have to wake up to a new reality here, I was thinking for myself. This wasn't so different then to Africa in a way. As every café has its specific clientele, I was sitting further southeast from the tourist-trapped centre of town, in a café oriented towards the human individual. So I began a tour of cafes. It was interesting, educating, and often hilarious what I observed. Sometimes I saw faces I will not forget. They stuck with me for a long time, even now as I write, I see them in front of me: The young and wild, the adventurous, the smart, the educated, some looking like villains, the hungry and self-centred, the fat and ugly, the bored and the treacherous looking, all the characters out of Arthur Schnitzler's plays. Fascinating. I could sit here for months, live here just to observe. Mind you, also the poet Peter Altenberg comes to mind, who had a reserved table at Café Central.

Meanwhile I had ran out of cash to pay for the huge sums my appetite was costing me and I remembered I was sitting here already for four hours. It turns dark early in winter and I always try to outsmart other people by stepping ahead of them to secure a window seat. Ha! I got one, so I may see the people walking by. Sometimes the same types walk in a circle, spotting a customer ready to go, to secure one of the window seats. They usually stare as they walk passed one. I had to chuckle inside and soon had to laugh out loud, tears running down my cheeks. It was too funny as this one guy with wide open eyes stared blatantly at me, as if I was in the process of leaving, or as if he would quietly push out waves of instigations for me to leave. He was inside perhaps a comic figure and he would be a great choice for a part in a Spielberg movie. The waitress came, alerted by my raucous laugh, checking if something had happened to me.

"Someone died?" She asked.

"No," I replied, "I ran out of money," I chuckled, "do you take credit cards?"

"Yes," she said, "but American Express is not taken here," as she had spotted my card. I took out another card. "Yes!" She beamed, "Visa we take!" I wondered.

"That's the best card here?" I murmured, "it's the worst in Africa," but then left it at that.

Buildings, museums – The *Stiftung Rudolph* – that's an excellent one. Recently constructed, it has lots of outstanding paintings, a galore for art-connoisseurs, but also for simple artists, like me. You travel by lift to the fourth floor. I had two housewives following me, self-appointed

176

art critiques, who permanently commented on the paintings I choose to view in quaint contemplation. The one with a round face and cheeks like a red apple had always the first word, educating her female friend, short and stubby, she always nodded and agreed with the know-it-all-girlfriend, who commented aloud and always turned her head to see if I also agreed. I chose to leave the two to their loudly conducted art-enjoyment, seeking my quiet contemplating one at a distance. Finally I was rid of them. NO! On the next floor it was them again, and due to the curation of the exhibition, I couldn't get away from their nervous talking, so I fled and we circled around each other in a chase for something, as if seeking some hidden treasure. But the treasure wasn't hidden, it was there on the walls, beauty, elegance, modern, and lyrical, only these two couldn't see it. I guess they just wanted to show off to their friends how well educated they were, having seen all there was to see in modern art, but in reality they had seen nothing.

The paintings of Egon Schiele were magnificent in their stark expressions of love and pain. He was a famous Austrian expressionist painter of the 20th century and commanded a whole floor for himself. Well, not all pretty in the aesthetic sense, but worthwhile looking at and experiencing the strong directness in his powerful, nervous, and jagged lines, also admired by Gustav Klimt, who, being a darling of society, supported him.

Driver behaviour on the roads is civilized in the dense traffic, with the oddball in between, racing for honours of the road, speeding like everywhere in the world, Mr. Roadhog himself.

The weather is cold and moist, but when it turned sunny and dry, it refreshed one's senses. Of course this was an easy excuse to try a glass of red wine or a cognac. But not that often, as prices were princely. Yet the atmosphere in general was pleasant. I was told that there were fewer foreigners this year, less travel enthusiasts had taken to the roads.

The churches, places of art and contemplation: I am not religious, but I treasure artistic Madonna statuess, they seem to exude tranquillity that soothes one's weary mind – a break from the hustle and bustle. Sometimes it serves as a refuge reflecting about loved ones who cannot share one's excitements any more.

The goods in the stores are much too expensive for the average pocket, but one could find good shops that offer a sale at this time of the year.

So much for my impressions I have still to digest to write them down in time, I guess as you are my friend, you'll be the first reader of my sketchy report I see your eyes take on that wicked smile when I write about the theme of women's liberation. Here there are more women than men, so there's no lack of a flirt, or should I say it's rather easy to make a contact, find acquaintances and sample the sleek offerings the young ones display. It's the age of see-through fashion and even under the winter coats the ladies show their female assets to appreciative eyes. My wife was fascinated by the fashion and so I had a good look at it too-ha-ha-well it was great fun.

The city hasn't lost its character, with many nice shops, bookshops filled with many readers, and casual ambling along tiny streets. The atmosphere of its past will meet one at every corner in the city's heart. But its heartbeat could only be sampled and felt in the many eateries, bars, and coffee shops, where one overhears conversations, as tables are close together, even hands and feet may touch and one wouldn't know if this is the way one is to get to know somebody fast.

I'm getting tired. The steam of scribbling has dissipated today, but this draft will give you a first class impression how I spent my days: Some with art, some with revisiting known places and noticing the changes, sometimes making mental notes about small anecdotes and sketches of a sped-up visit."

*

At Botticelli's

At Botticelli's one settles down quite quickly, once the twelve entrance steps are mastered and one steps through the double door whose leaves are widely opened. It feels as if one arrive immediately into a bit of Italy. A dash of Florence, where the famous Renaissance artist lived and painted. We all know the painting *Birth of Venus,* the master artist became famous with. It's an uplifting spiritual feeling to view the painting and absorb its beauty.

The colours of the restaurant resemble special areas of Tuscany: The fresh lemon strip across the top of the beam and windows, a precursor of the spring in Florence. While the light watercolours of the rainbow represent Renaissance thinking, the rebirth of the greatest movement since Hellenistic times. Overflowing with joyful exuberance and yet earthbound through the terracotta colour of the ceiling paint that reflects wall tiles within its larger squares and on the columns in monochrome fashion, a playful interaction with well-integrated lights. The face brick-red of the counter and the wine-red painted entrance door are engaged in a lively dialogue about the love life of the Florentines, who celebrate in high spirits the 'Rites of Spring'. The lightness of living and the taste for colour that filters down into the glorious food, which takes off with your sniffing of scents and raises the wings of your taste buds, letting you fly above the maddening crowds of Gauteng. Wham! In an instant.

There's charming Tonino, who immediately greets us as we enter, if he happens to be at the front desk. There's the sinewy pizza man and the third partner, Adolfo, the Don, all playing their contributory role to make you feel at home and enjoy the immaculately served delicacies. But it does not have to be specials, the ordinary pasta dishes taste just as exceptional and I'm looking forward to a glass of Italian beer or wine, depending on the chosen dish and the mood. For me, most important are the ambience with its soothing atmosphere that takes one away from the rat race.

I'll sit here forever, forgetting the maddening rush, having fled to 'Botticelli' with my spouse, a friend or a client, wedging breathing space like an invisible wall against the world outside; to enjoy the unusual and genuine retreat I wish to help preserving with our patronage.

Every time we step through the double entrance door that leads to another world, either Tonino or Giuseppe, the friendly Zulu waiter is present to guide us to our favourite place. Once settled at our preferred table covered with a fresh table cloth, in matching colours to the interior, the unique character of the space merges to the colours of Tuscany with the food offered. It's cooked to tradition in an extraordinary environment.

We always settle down immediately enjoying some fresh baked bread or rolls and a sip from our well-cooled drinks. Soon the scent and the taste of the well-cooked food calls up the colours of the seasons: Lime and pink hues of spring, which the artist Botticelli depicted in mythological scenes that transfer the spirit of lightness, the float above the undulated fresh greens in the wonder of rebirth, we both feel to share with.

Venus, born from the crest of waves at the nearby seashore, merges in the colour range with the skies and provides the background to rich foliage of vines that shape reefs around the heads of Muses. They dance to the tunes of a flute played by a shepherd. Nymphs from a groove sing the bard's lyrics to praise the rebirth of a young nubile woman, symbolizing spring, the forerunner of summer's ripened woman, in midst of corn and flowers, cherries in red and white, the emerald green of the picnic scene, and the green and black of fine skinned olives for a necklace of the frolicking dancers. Outside the world races past, but we don't notice that any longer.

The wealthy Northern suburbs suffer as well under the dust and grime of the dry high ground of Gauteng, especially in wintertime. Crazed men chase each other with fast sports cars in dense traffic, being rude like road hogs are, speed-cutting across lanes and endanger less punchy drivers and the middle class, who rely on their economy styled vehicles, driving defensively. The pushy taxi cabs, declared as the best transport system in the world, flex their intolerant metallic muscles to rush without a care for other road users. By now most road users make way for them. Their battered motor vehicles show their hard-bashing attitudes and disrespect for other people's properties. By now everybody stays clear of the Toyota-phalanx, except for the huge bodied drivers of Hi-tech trucks fitted with bull-bars, ready to strike when challenged by the aggressive hordes, poised like angry animals. 'Catch as catch can' rules.

I had my review of actions sitting back and consciously trying to relax, while in front of me a silent movie plays scenes of road-rage and frustration by alienated youngsters and mature men. With the meal consumed, I feel a gradual and pleasant semi-sleepiness engulfing my whole body, where immediate reality merges with past leftover memories.

It's desert time and the 'Italian kisses' are a welcome conclusion to a wonderful meal of 'Prawns Mafia' and 'Veal Cacciatore'. Yes, the macchiato! Giuseppe remembers and smiles, having recalled our liking for that special espresso.

Soon I have to leave and face the hordes of road users again, the cunning builders who are scheming, the clients who know all about building, and who, if their ideas turn out to be wrong, blame the architect and his professional team for it. I think about my client and prepare myself mentally for the next meeting. I will drive home slowly, I say to myself and enjoy the aftertaste of the food to linger on my palate. It would be crazy to spoil such a wondrous palate-clinging taste of a perfect meal with some cheap, rough talk at the building's site office.

I wish I could come back to 'Botticelli' more often. A sport car passes outside with the throaty roar of a thoroughbred. The man drove off in his Ferrari like a pistol shot," the chubby man, a witness, said. He was interviewed by the insurance agent, who blocks the door with his huge frame. He must have been a rugby player in his younger years.

"Well, tell me what happened," he says in a slow talking mode, "start at the beginning." The voices blur into the afternoon atmosphere with a murmuring chat, while new meal orders are called out. Giuseppe brings me second helping of ice cream and for my spouse another macchiato.

In the middle of the entrance area the interview by the insurance agent appears like a scene of a local play. I hear shreds of their conversation and overhear a story of guilt, love and hate, jealousy and self-destruction. If I would be in the guilty guy's shoes, I would have bought myself an art gallery and a huge plot with an architect-designed house and atelier, instead of a red mean machine, but we all have different priorities. But if you talk to Italians, the name of Ferrari has them shudder with the sound of high-revving engines and squeaking racing tyres, it's the crescendo for the motor enthusiast. It's beating up their boiling blood. The accident story carries on for a long time to unfold: By now it became clear that the wife of another man was dining here with her boyfriend who drank excessively. When the husband of his girlfriend arrived, both took off in a hurry and were involved in an accident further down the road.

OK, it's enough. Basta! I mumble to myself and I pay the bill Giuseppe brings me. Tonino and Adolfo bade us good-bye. 'Arrividerci'. We shake hands and depart. Botticelli's unique dining experience will stay with us for a long time to come, if not forever. After all, it's a genuine island of Italy in South Africa.

*

My Favourite Journey

Down the Nile is one of my favourite journeys and it happened once in my lifetime. Since then it happened many times in my mind, as any journey that brands deep impressions into one's mind and leaves its trailing fingerprints on the soul.

Immediately after the journey the conscious flow within the mind recalls vistas and aspects of details that vary each time reflecting about it. It's the trip I wake up with and go to sleep with. My mind feels at ease with it and it rises like a balloon into the night air at dusk. This magical hour of twilight propels me high and takes me on a different trip each time. It's always a surprise and I cannot get enough of it.

The trip happens within the rhythm of day and night. Midnight hour soothes my mind like the gentle lapping waves in a bay of iridescent waters: The smell of salt on a warmed-up skin by a relentless sun, baking one's body like bread. I smell another body next to me, dunked in suntan cream, giving off scented odours and I sense an enticement caused in me. She lies still and touches my body length in a lazy stretched-out snooze. Time elapses and I am woken by the rising tide of the sea. That's when my journey begins:

It's a single winding road of five kilometres. I have never been able to read the speedometer on my hired car. At these moments of intuition the mind leaps-up and dons wings of imagination, with love's sister – expectation. It has all the powers of a beautiful, seductive woman; it rules my heartbeat and the stream of my blood that pumps into all the branches of my arterial body roots In its heat it assumes all shapes of wondrous trees: Flame-lily, baobab, tamarind, and fine feather-leafed acacia. The landscape changes to the rhythm of my heartbeat that desires constant changes. The vistas during the roads rising above the beach, along this narrow and winding road, appear as breath-taking and disappear with irregularity. Driving through the bends with left and right body squeezes, power shifts in speed and break manoeuvres, we slide through this bold and barren land. The blue extent of the sea recesses more and more as I drive towards the high saddle of mountains. Along the giant mountain's legs I ride the Citroen C3. Its temperament has moulded with mine, fitting like a glove.

I expected a tree that grows as an exotic stranger in midst of rocks and ravines that rose once from the ancient sea amidst thunder and lightning. Hisses of glowing rock and the scent of phosphor burning on this new earth that rose and calcified, changing from red-hot fire, in a cooling down phase, to grey and blackened ash. All turned many thousands of years ago to rock, I now drive upon.

The sun has burned out the day and the colours of creation cool down to darker shades of crimson-red and turmeric-yellow. The sky has faded to a bluish illumination, meeting the sea at the horizon. Her ink-blue sister of an Aegean Sea has spilled this deep-blue dye to douse Helios' flames and his fiery horses leave behind a widely spread trail. The fired-up red-hot carriage once burned Icarus' feathers and he plunged to his death into the deep blue.

I dislike masses of any kind and opt for an early morning, or later in the day, when all visitors, bound to a tour guide, will be herded to their coffees and kulouraki-biscuits. I have arrived at the small parking lot at the entrance to the main street of the village; my lady-friend has told me about. Information held sacred to an elusive critical guide, I have not come across in my known bookshops. Like a secret shared, it entices my expectations and raises my adrenalin in this unusual adventure.

The stone-paved street to the village of Pefki is exciting to walk upon, with its rich history through rural legends, steeped into a stubborn tradition that lasted through centuries. The place is at the rear side of main trodden paths, where eco-tourists swarm across the land in search for a glimpse of the subterranean place, where the Minotaur had been kept prisoner. Pefki's legends come alive without the sound of voices, murmuring like a procession of locusts that hit the rich historic fields of the Island of Crete.

The warm air at dusk is laden with glow worms flying about, signalling a midsummer night. My heart pounding increases with my longing to be at the top of the ascending road. Scents of fennel and oregano waft from the kitchens along the road. Moist air rises from the valley and clouds the village into veils of mist.

I rush to see the name of the street: Odos Pepperi, the sign depicts in Greek. I'm glad I had mastered the Greek alphabet during my various visits to Greece. The natural slasto steps are low and rising a bit with every second step as I rush towards the bend.

There, in the dusky evening, the huge crown of a tree covers the entire square. Its leaves look like acacia, but the red dots remind me of a Renoir painting with their glow worm intensity. I rub one red corn that dangles low, between my fingers. The warm burn of red pepper singes my skin as I smell the spicy powder. It spreads across my upper lip and I start to glow like the magical tree.

"You are eating something, *oxi?* The dark voice of a woman brings me back from the magenta dots spread in rich clusters, like small red grapes across the green feathery crown I lay happily upon for a moment. Her eyes glow like shadows of the night amongst the tree, whose branches hang low down to head-height.

"Yes," I said, "show me what I may choose from."

"You can have this," she points to the menu and I read about a dish I have never tasted before.

"Who is cooking?" I ask.

"I cook," she said, "I'm Maria," she adds and shifts her leg.

"OK, I have the dish," I said and the dusky-eyed woman darts from my table below the continuous wafts of spicy perfume from the tree. Its strong scent makes me drunk. I feel a rising itch. She had disappeared into the lit-up stone framed entrance of the tavern: *Taverna Pepperia.* The sign above the entrance says in bold black letters.

I ask Maria about the tree, when she returns, serving hot rolls and butter. She explains in rudimentary English about a local adventurer, who left the village after the Peloponnesian wars and travelled the world. He brought back seeds of a pepper tree he found on the tropical islands in the Southern Seas. He planted the seeds as his gift to the villagers, founding a great symbol for the main square of his home-village.

I sip my ouzo, having watered it to a milky consistency and enjoy the atmosphere of a slow descending night. Some locals play backgammon and card games. There's laughter and joyous camaraderie. The dark blue sky, against which the red and green of the pepper tree were lit up by a myriad of dangling chain lights creates a magical feeling of harmony and romance. This scene dominates the night spot of the village. Maria and her partner argue matters with hot-tempered outbursts, as she has donned her jersey top and appears in her tee shirt. She has been spiced-up by all this peppery cooking and so am I spiced-up quite a bit.

I walk to the shop. Maria has big dark brown eyes that judge immediately, when confronted with a potential sale. I ask her for some local honey and home-made bread. She returns with quick steps from behind the shop's counter and as she passes she brushes against me.

"This is a present," she says and hands me a postcard. I thank her. "I need to take some red pepper," I said, but it's not for sale. "Pity," I muse and ask Maria where I could stay overnight in Pefki, as I wish to relax for some time.

She takes my hand and rushes out the back, up some steps, I can hardly follow her energetic strides. She leans against the wall and places her arm around my neck, offering me her open lips. I taste fire and pepper, turmeric and chillies. "I burn," I said and she laughs.

"Wait and see when love really burns," she said and rushes back down the steps into her shop, where the next customers have arrived.

I walk down the road, the descending Pepper Street, and turn to see the tree growing into the night sky, lit-up like a X-mas tree in September. The air is warm and a fresh breeze takes the scent to somewhere else. I drive the winding road down to the sea with caution. Too many memory-shrines mark the bends, where people have driven to their death. I have never encountered barrier rails on small winding roads across the island.

I empty my pockets. A small jar in my outside pocket bulges my linen jacket. Maria, I think. There's a piece of paper on top of the tiny red pepper corns: Are you coming again?

*

Sites of Love

This afternoon on a quiet day that appears like a great reflection of my soul, and as a fledgling young man in love, it has challenged the endlessness of the heavens. My fingers have touched you and reshaped the lines of your body in palimpsest movements, as if my soul had seen you as a young girl and fallen in love with you back then, losing you to the woods of custom and a boisterous living, which has shied it away to push me into the arms of a passionate woman of the arts. She has kept me prisoner on an island of snow and ice, where she froze my heart and subjugated me as her slave for many years. I have struggled with the idea to get myself freed from the sexy mistress and find my muse I had lost to the scissors of Atropos, who cut her life's thread with her long bony fingers. Like daggers they finish off anybody with a stab to the heart, a penetration of the jugular, a long cut across the pelvis to finish off a life that demanded too many hours of pleasure.

In midst of a maiden flight of a mature love I behaved like Icarus, who took Daedalus not serious enough and tumbled from the carriage of Helios. It hurt me nethertheless, being too arrogant to think that I have detected the secrets of lovemaking at my mature age of travelling for 70 years across the blue globe in the layers of love's shade that I had inherited from my forefathers. No warning other than a laugh and the depiction of Eros in the nude leading us to our other halves. Wonderfully shaped women in the nude, my uncle adored and shared their images with me. I wanted to be like him, strong, confident in matters of love, never having to say: I had enough. His untimely death should have been a warning to me. He died on the threshold of his love-nest, emerging after a tete-a-tete, cut off from his beloved with one big stroke of fate's dagger. He never regained consciousness, but died as a happy man.

I have his smile engraved in my mind. Every time I go to NAM, the greatest museum of antiquities in Athens, the archaic smile of Classical Greek sculptures reminds me of his smile. He had discovered the secret of life. I wonder if he ever has been to Greece, as he always talked Hungary, the country he loved.

I am not ready yet to die, but who is ever? I hope that Atropos is influenced by my past Muse, who promised me a compatible woman who would love me the way I wished and who, in time, I would also love. How strange are thoughts on a quiet day like this, preparing for a Holy Night? Whatever our beliefs are, it's not about religion, it's about friendship and love, the nurturing of precious people we feel to have an intimate bonding with. At times it's difficult and it seems to be a mountain of an effort, which is necessary to keep a relationship going, we were initially madly affected with. Is it love's ups and downs that turn us into beasts of possession, burying our fangs of sexual love deep into the flesh of our soulmates?

I think of her – H, eighth letter of the alphabet, against Z, the 36th. Adding them up and reducing it, I get eight. Well it's H, the eighth letter of the alphabet. And the name of my Muses seem to have their relationship with same or similar names. It might be coincidental, but then the mind always questions the chance of serendipities.

She is voluptuous like a dancer from the French revue at Montparnasse, a small intimate joint, where I met her for the first time. H for Hanna, heroine, harlot, hetaerae, hearsay, hallucination, and heritage: This is what the doctor ordered, the one who wouldn't cut the skin below my tongue, as my mother wished that it would improve my diction. I still wonder why. An old fart he was. I disliked him, as he shouted at his soulful looking wife. Mrs Ianus the double faced? No, she wasn't double faced, but he was: A man afraid of his feelings, a man who wasn't a man at all. Later in life I met his son, Ossa, who was genuine and honest, with a mission to bring me the lessons of some Saints. I listened and mused, but found more stimulation with my own Muses.

I like H, yet I don't know why I'm attracted to her. Well, there's the generous abundance of her breasts, the firmness of her thighs, and the juicy offering of her coral pink pussy. I have my finger in it, experiencing its velvet feel, the soft warmth of a hiding place, where love has materialised its pleasurable home. And it's X-mas eve. I cook dinner to please my spouse, my long term friend and mate. I found this Italian recipe on the Internet. It sounded to me, the amateur cook, just like a possible hit in the kitchen. Wow! And how the smell of the casserole wafted through the air, along the passage and into the dining room, it watered my taste buds.

She said "I cannot come to eat, there's a documentary about Ives St. Laurent on TV." Shit! How could my amateur cooking compare with the image of fashion's greatest creator in the 21st century?

I have to switch the prepared meal off and warm-up later then. But as soon as I go to the lounge to have a peek of the TV show, the movie has been finished. So, back into the kitchen and warm-up the cooked food.

I serve the food and my spouse likes it also just warm, so I just kept the plates warmed up as well. During summer we don't mind the food not being piping hot, as external temperatures soar into their late 30 degrees Celsius. Of course we have regular debates about nothing. I wonder how we could have, as such controversial characters, stayed together a whole life and not split. But now at an advancing mature age there remains a speck of respect, I hope is not one-sided.

"It tastes good," she said. "Thanks for cooking." With that said she stands up and departs back to her bedroom, she claims as her sacred domain. OK, I'm glad we have two bedrooms at present, so we could stay separate whenever we want to. I wish though she would show a bit more communal spirit and help with washing the dishes at times. I do it quickly, as I wish to avoid another lengthy debate.

"I have lived a solitary life for most of my life," I told an artist friend who comes past at times.

"As a writer you must know that," my friend remarked.

"Yes, you mean a poet's *Site of Love.*"

*

190

The Black Dog

The black Labrador-mix nears cautiously. A dog that has been kicked, beaten by man, who supposed to be a human being, by a coward who took his anger on a dog, an easy object for a coward who is incapable of raising his voice against his suppressors out of fear being hit himself, so he lets it out on a dog. The black dog comes closer. Is he begging for food? No, he begs for some love and attention to believe in the goodness of man, as he senses a different man against the one who had beaten him. He is intelligent and his eyes reflect his inner need for love. As I share with him a piece of koulouria bread, he chews happily on the piece settling down at my feet. I sit with 'Mavro', as I called him, and when I get up from the bench he wags his tail and accompanies me to the gate of my habitat. The next day he is back. I talk in English to Mavro, and place some learned Greek words into our conversation. He seems to be content accompanying me anywhere.

During the summer months I partake in an artist's seminar and workshop at the Art Gallery Café and paint his face into my compositions. Mavro is grateful, returning love a thousand fold. A loveable dog, his wounds healed by human kindness and company, just as I have been healed inside by the power of the written word, which I translate into pieces of visual art. The symposium director is an academic painter, who has worked at his specific art for 30 years. Tall and dark haired, his moving about in tennis shoes, faded green shorts and a terracotta coloured top with short sleeves, serves the purpose of commenting on our work in progress and listen to our personal philosophies about art. We originate from different backgrounds, a group of ten artists, three men and seven women, who'll express their respective world view of art on varied sizes of white grounded canvases.

"Is this your dog?" Mavro sticks his nose into the door, I call him and he approaches me across the thrashing floor of the art teacher. Slobo smiles, he reminds me of

Josic, a friend from Croatia whom I met in South Africa. Maria fancies dogs, and mavro wags his tail as she talks to him. She pats his head and a stain of blood remains on her finger. "This is not paint," she calls out with Greek exuberance, "this is blood."

"I will go and fetch some medication," I said and stood up. "No, wait, I have some in the first aid kit in my car," she said. I leave it to Maria; she's immediately prepared to help. Mavro settles down at my feet. When Maria returns, she applies some antibiotic cream on Mavro's wound. "He's been in a fight," she said.

"I think he was hit with a blunt instrument," I replied. Maria checks his swollen head and agrees. There are many parties around here with people getting high and drunk has become a weekly event. Some crazy heads take it out on stray dogs. Mavro is grateful and licks Maria's fingers. She pats him reassuringly that he is in a safe environment and Mavro nods off. I study him as my model who is absolutely quiet without the slightest movement, taking as many sketches as I'll need to depict his well-shaped head.

"Great sketches, you should do Graphic art," Slobo said. I smiled, as I have other ideas in my head right now. Slobo means good trying to move one permanently towards traditional painting styles that'll sell to the general public, but I resist tenaciously. I am developing my own unique style, with its hidden source in my innermost. Slobo wouldn't accept it and fight me, an artist against another one, a teacher he could be to others, but where I come from there's a great striving for being an individualist. "No copies from this 'Okie, my baas'," I mumble some Afrikaans words into my breath and wonder if he had heard it. He turns and walks to the bar counter in the opposite corner to fetch another tankard of draft beer. "Psuff," I mumble in a Viennese dialect, he certainly wouldn't grasp even if he would hear it. Besides, he had woken Mavro, not that it matters anymore.

"What's that?" Maria asks and I explain to her, with my head down drawing something interesting with Mavro's head, and expanding on it with different constellations and groupings. Then I apply acrylic colours to it, layer by layer. It's fun and suddenly the grouping of lines turns into a woman, as I have, quite intuitively included Maria with her expressive body language, then another layer of myself tops it, then again some faces around me, like colleagues and Maria's sexy girlfriend Eva.

"I thought you drew Mavro's head," Maria expressed astonishment and despair.

"I have."

"But where is it?" I show it to Maria, outlining it with my pencil. "Aha! I see." She carries on having a trip around my painting. Starting with the ears, she speaks of a circus clown that jumps from his ears into the drum of an orchestral drummer, with a trapeze artist flying about. She compares my pair to Chagall's lovers and moves her hips close to mine. It seems that Maria is stimulated by my painting and she carries-on with suggestions. Her black dog is beaten up by a gang of young rappers. The dog flees into an artist's workshop to seek refuge. The rappers appear, but are only welcome if they pay a contribution for the medication of the dog and spend a round of beer to the thirsty artists. The leader agrees as a policeman shows up and enquires. All's well now and a party may begin. "I am here with Eva in an embrace," Maria carried on, "and here comes Slobo who shouts at us that we are tribadists, pouring black paint over Eva's unfinished painting, which shows two women in love. Oh no, here you are sweet Zoitan, aroused by our lovemaking, painting a man who masturbates. "

"Well, what's wrong with that?"

"Nothing, we all do it, even if the men are ashamed of it here to admit it."

"I'm not."

"We know that, that's why we love you," and she kisses me. She takes a bottle of scotch and welcomes her friend with his girlfriend. He greets me and starts his journey around my painting: "Ha! That's Klimt!" He talks of flowers and gardens, olives and oranges and golden meanders around the seam of translucent garments fitted tightly to bodies of women dancers, the emblems of décor painted on their skins like tattoos. This is the 21st Century art; he calls out finishing his tot and placing a glass in my hand. "Carry on my friend! It's good." He paces around mumbling. Slobo arrives and is immediately drawn to our group of rebels, as he calls us, hoping for being invited to a glass of rye, but nobody offers him any, as he is the only one who enjoys a free run of German draught beer.

He places his tankard next to Eva's staff, takes a brush from her holder and carries on shamelessly destroying her Eva's esoteric painting. I asked him if he is pissed, but he didn't reply. Fuck him, I think and carried on painting another set of faces with gleeful stares thinking of George Grosz, but I doubt anybody knows of him in this art workshop of the summer 2011. It's of now use explaining him, anyway. We all defend our painting styles and I take a break to see Maria, who paints landscapes. She wishes to paint flowers, she mentions to me. I say to her that irises would suit to her painting style. She takes to it immediately selecting another canvas. After some time I check on her and by Jove, she's good at it, having some of Van Gogh's fire on her canvas. We toast with scotch and are a happy crowd indeed. Long live the freedom of artistic expression, long live Maria and Mavro who had adopted her the moment he came into the sanctuary of this artist's workshop. "You should paint him," I suggest to her. "I will," she replies and prepares to leave.

"Viva Maria kai Mavro," her friends salute and down the last drops of her rye. "Salud," I toast her and she smiles.

*

The Pen

When I moved my shoulder bag from a side position to my chest, I felt a pinprick. I opened the top flap where I keep my ink pens, pencils, and other writing paraphernalia and I saw that my black parker pen was missing. I remembered having placed the delicate ink pen next to the stainless steel ballpoint pen in the morning. I felt the pinprick again as the bag strap moved on my shoulders. I always keep the strap of my bag around my neck to secure it from misplacing it while I think of other tasks, or from leaving it behind in one of the print shops I frequent lately. My fingers searched the pocket and found the pen, but I couldn't find its cap. It must have been slipping off while I retrieved the ballpoint pen in a hurry to write something down. Blast! I've tried to retrace my steps pf today, but then there were many places I've visited, the hardware shop at first and the last one, the photographic shop came immediately to mind, where I was for passport photographs. But then, I would not have taken the pen out there, as I keep my wallet separated from the top pocket of my bag. It must have been at a place where I wrote down an address, or noted down a Greek word I wished to study later.

I felt bad, with age creeping up slowly on me, drained of energy and irritated by my lack of alertness, not having noticed the cap of the ink pen falling to the floor. It must have been at a place where the ground was soft, perhaps the grassed area between the tram stations, or possibly a shop with a carpeted floor. No, there are hardly any soft floor coverings in shops, as all of them have stone or ceramic floor tiles. My eyelids felt like lead. I took my glasses off rubbing them, feeling frustrated. You should not do this, my inner voice reprimanded me, it's bad for your eyes. I stopped and removed my fingers from my eyelids. As I opened my eyes, my vision was blurred. I felt dehydrated, rushed to the kitchen and placed a glass below the water dispenser on the fridge. The cool water rushed down my throat like free flowing water from a natural spring. Immediately I felt refreshed and the first bout of anger about losing Anna's ink pen cap subsided. Memories about losing her travel ink pen reminded me of losing her as a lover, with her body slipping from my grip. It still feels devastating having lost her. I recall that at one time I had lost her first pen she gave me as a present and I told her. "Don't cry," she said and handed me immediately another one. I thanked her and she smiled acknowledging my efforts to write while I was riding on a bus for an hour to see her. I kept this pen in my travel bag. These gadgets were cute ink pens using cartridges, compact and ideal for writing while traveling.

Unfortunately I fell asleep while writing my journal on a bus ride and the ink pen slipped from my hand. It fell into the gap between the edge of the plastic seat and the inner wall of the bus and I couldn't retrieve it again. So, I carried on writing with the second one, until I lost it the same way again, rolling off my bag and falling into a crack between a train station's paving and the wall enclosing the lifts. Now tragically, it couldn't be replaced any longer by Anna, as Anna, who knew the source for them, had passed away.

I prepared supper, beef mince and tomatoes, spiced with oregano. I cooked the pasta al dente and added the meat-sauce on top. My spouse ate without saying anything. She must have sensed my tension, the loss of Anna's pens induced in me. "This pasts is delicious," she said finally and looked at me with eyes that expressed the continual headaches she suffered from. I enjoyed my pasta dish too.

Slowly the memories faded again and I looked at the ink pen's shaft with the golden nob, as I had to write down some ideas for a story. I played with the pen in my fingers and recalled my life that had changed since I met H, who became my instant soulmate. What a way out of love that gave me another love I have never questioned, just enjoyed. It seemed that Anna had finally taken leave from me and set me free in mind and soul, to enjoy my new Muse and pick the fruit of mature love, which I thought had become dormant, with new gusto. The pain of losing a lover physically, followed by losing her personal presents, had been a prolonged agony with the loss of these important presents, she had given me when I met her with my spouse for dinner. She told her husband that she'll let me choose one of her writing utensils from her collection. I choose a pen I liked intuitively. I heard her words repeated as rising panic shot-up in my spine and into my head, where it exploded as a flash in my brain and I saw suddenly black spots. "No!" I cried out, the cap must have slid further down into the pocket of my shoulder bag. Warm sweat covered my forehead as I began looking yet again for it, but I couldn't find it. Then I remembered that the black cap of the pen always had a loose cap, probably due to the extensive use of pulling it off and replacing it, while Anna used it.

"I call you an equal," she said as she listened to a recital of one of my poems. "I will give you a pen from my collection." She left suddenly and came back with a box of pens she had collected. "Which one would you like?"

"This one," I said and took a black slim pen that seemed to me most suitable for her in style and appearance. "Oh," she said "that one? I wrote all my poetry with it." She smiled and I felt as if I would have touched the extension of the poet's soul as I held her pen between my fingers, stroking its smooth dark shaft. The cap disengaged too easily, as if the resistance of holding it in place had been worked off by constant opening and closing. I loved Anna's pen and kept it at a special place, in the drawer of my night table. At times I stopped using it, as it did not write properly on the unlined paper of some notebooks. I remembered that Anna had told me that certain ink pens write only properly on certain papers, especially pens with finer nibs. A new series of Italian notebooks favoured the use of my Waterman pen. The more different paper-surface qualities I came across, the more I began to understand Anna's collection of ink pens with different nib qualities, and I began collecting my own set of ink pens. But if I fancied a certain design of a quality ink pen, which I could not resist to acquire, I had to find the matching unlined notebook, whose pages provided the paper, the new ink pen's nib would write upon properly.

However, one day I ran out of cartridges for the French pen, but I had still cartridges left for Anna's black Parker pen. I recalled the paper quality she had shown me, onto which the nib's ink flow would be best. The words I wrote turned into a prose-poem of my life with her, for a short period of 21 days, during which I saw her every late morning. I walked the southern suburbs of Athens searching for the shop which carried electrical appliances at best prices, I intended buying. Anna's pen had a magical effect on me, besides making notes into my pocket notebook, its smooth slender shaft I ran my fingers along, reminded me of her well-proportioned body. Absentminded I stuck her pen into the breast pocket of my shirt, whenever I finished my notes. My initial fear of losing it had evaporated and self-confidence of handling it returned to me with its frequent use.

One August day I set out early in the morning to visit my friends in town, *Kritikos,* in a pizzeria and *Baba Che,* in his ice cream parlour. As closer I walked to the Plaka district, the more light-footed I felt, greeting friends I haven't seen for some years. Of course they immediately recognised me and we exchanged news about our lives. As Che, as I called him, due to his tee-shirt featuring the famous revolutionary, had his shop on my way to the small square, where all eateries gathered around its perimeter, I visited him first.

"Hey Zeni," he called out as soon as I entered his dim lit shop. "Geia sou," I replied in Greek and he smiled with his white teeth showing. He started off with his usual monologue telling me the happenings in his family and the patch of bad luck he had with a health problem. "But now I am cured. It's OK. I am working again part of the week. I lauded him and he continued with the latest reports about Greek politics and the European tragedy of being the end of Greek life, as we once knew it. He closed his monologue as customers came into his shop and he had to serve them from behind the glazed-in ice cream counter. As soon as they paid and started leaving, he carried on telling me about his projections for the foreseeable future. I took my leave having enjoyed his talk he had delivered to me, like the sermon of a preacher, with a sparkling Greek temperament.

Around the corner to the right of the small square the Pizzeria is the smallest, but best eatery tucked away at the end of the street. Already from a distance, Kritikos would wave his hand in greeting, as he rushed about serving food to the tables opposite the café below a shaded outdoor terrace, the extension of their tavern. Any café or tavern in Greece had such extensions under shaded roofs, as their inside spaces were small, usually occupied by a kitchen and storage area, besides the climate was ideal for outdoor eating. "How is life?" Kritikos cannot speak as well English as Che, who worked in the USA, where he acquired the necessary capital to open his shop in the Plaka in Athens, as many Greeks have done and still do. We converse with short sentences and catch-up on the latest news. Kritikos brings me a catalogue of the Cycladic islands, he considers to be best to visit at this time of the year. His eyes open wide as he calls out their names: Paros, Sifnos, Andros – I take my pen and notebook and write all down. Having ordered a small pizza and a carafe of wine, he treats me the same way as his friends, who gather around the tables on the pavement outside the café. He passes to serve the customers on the opposite side, below the shaded terrace with shrubs and greenery, before he casually serves me the wine, and as he passes again, my meal. "I have an address for you," he smiles.

"Write it down please," I reply. The moment he has a break, he takes my pen and writes. "Nice pen," he mumbles. "A poet's pen," I tell him.

"Oh!" He looks at Anna's black Parker pen and his eyes show a glimmer of respect. "Very special," he adds and finishes his notes. He hands me the pen and then recites a poem. "Sounds great," I said, "who wrote it?"

"Iannis Ritsos," he said and I nod. "OH, you know him?"

"No, I know of him," I correct him and he smiles repeating the phrase I had told him once before.

On my way back I had to stop at the New Acropolis Museum. I cannot pass without visiting the top floor to view the Parthenon temple to its real measured extent, as I admire the frieze, which once had been part of its outer walls. The missing original panels show empty spaces and everybody who has visited the museum knows that those panels are the ones deliberately removed for fame and financial gain, still creating bad vibes for an unlawful act amidst loud voices, from art lovers and a chain of cultural ministers, for their return. I love to sit on the low marble sill of the panoramic glass façade and sketch a horse's head or the movement of a body. Anna's pen serves me well and I feel euphoric.

"You have returned," her faint soprano voice sounds in me. "Yes, but you have left!" I gasp. I am talking to you through my former beloved pen. Hah! I have been using it for the last week writing all my journals with it."

"I'm proud of you Zen; you have still time to write your poems. Well, I have learned from you, Anna!"

"Ah, I was just your guide and I am happy of handed you my pen."

"Well, you have inspired me, Anna!"

"Ah, I was your prompter and I am happy of having you placed onto the right track –"

"Of course, it was your doing – your closing act – before made your big leap into the universe…I hope you are content."

"Ah, yes…"

"Damned" I woke from daydreaming as Anna's pen slid from my hand and hit the marble floor. I gasped, but it sounded far off and my own. I knelt down and picked the pen up. It seemed to be all right. I tried writing into my notebook: Today Anna appeared to me as I sat on the windowsill of the topmost floor of the NAM – yes! It still worked. I sighed relieve, but still couldn't find the protective cap for Anna's pen. Finally I gave up and headed for the subway to travel back home.

My euphoric state had turned into despair having lost the cap to her pen. It must have fallen down into the slots of the ventilation grille. I kicked myself for having taken on one visit too many and for exhausting myself. Or perhaps it was Anna's voice that made me doze off in a state of remembrance? I sat in the tram staring out into the horizon of the sea, where the tram runs along the Saronic Gulf for a while. I felt dumbstruck.

At home I took the pen from my pocket and placed it into the bag where I keep all other pens and cartridges. At least part of it remained with me; I mused, but noticed that the tip of its nib had been bent in the fall to the marble floor. It was now defunct, but recalled the times with Anna, when she was still alive. Is this the way to preserve her memory through my own clumsiness?

I hear her voice: "Come Zen, don't cry like a baby, I will buy you another one."

"Yes," I respond, "but it's not the one you wrote all your poetry with! I will write it poems of the now."

"I like that," she replied. Dialogue with Anna has never stopped. The uncovered half of her pen is like the encumbered being of me: Half poet and half artist. The one half writes down all what moves my senses, while the other one seeks out the colours of moods, I feel shifting through me continuously, as if she still has a hand in all of my creative inspirational work. Perhaps she has, her spirit has. I am glad.

*

The Red Packet

What's that red packet on the gate? It looks like a small bomb, but who would want to blow up this pretty house in the leafy suburb of Athens? Just because the name of the street refers to a hero of the Greeks, who was a successful general in a war of freedom against the Turks? It's history and yet I have been recalling the words of my good teacher – History, my dear scholars, history will repeat itself – I have listened to his soft-spoken monologues for a whole year and became lost in thoughts, which made my eyes wander through the classroom windows into the distant horizon of a sky that changed with the seasons. At times it fascinated me much more than the countries engaging with war. I'd rather paint his portrait; I thought and scribbled into my history lesson book, which became a heaven of retreat, and the colours on his stern face changed with the light condition of the seasons.

I checked the packet. The contents were hard and round: It's not a soccer ball, but nobody plays cricket here in Greece. I went inside, Georgio, the Labrador bounced up on me, snapping like a black knight in friendly banter. He smelled the ball. As I peeked inside the plastic packet I saw a red pomegranate. I wonder what it's for. Is it a vitamin shot?

"Have you received the rodi?" Jo called me on my mobile phone.

"Aha! It looked like a bomb from a distance." She laughed; "You look too much at CNN. OK. Today I'll come and smash it."

"Really, whereto?"

"Onto the floor, for good luck!"

"Aha," I replied. She arrived soon after and told me not to step over the threshold of the entrance door to welcome her. Then she entered our apartment with the right foot first. I will draw this into my next painting, I saw it already transformed into poetry. The black knight fighting her entry, the bag snatched back from his teeth and smashed against the wall and all odds to leave blood. It's easy to die, but it is difficult to be reborn, my inner voice cited the famous Gestalt-philosopher's quotation. But I felt reborn at the moment of the dulling sound of the plastic-parcel's impact. Jo hurried away, back to her base. "They start at 12:00 noon," she said, meaning the famous New Year's Concert of the Vienna Philharmonic Orchestra. "Aha," I said, "which channel?" "At 'ERT'," she replied. "OK, I will check it out." I don't know if I am still a rebel inside and prefer vibes from an opposite musical style. It's not easy for me to watch TV, while other ideas from my creative work float around my mind. By accident I pressed the wrong channel, but then recovered it. There it was – The New Year's Concert with the Vienna Philharmonic Orchestra. But right at the end it was announced a replay from the year 2005. I liked Lorin Maazel, but my spouse switched on the right channel and there was the present performance again, another concert, but this time for the New Year 2011. I had already viewed one concert, be it old or new, and I disliked comparisons right now.

I quit, I thought, got up and looked at the smashed pomegranate in the transparent plastic bag, lying at the leg of an old Cape Dutch writing desk, waiting for good luck to happen. "Happy New Year!" My spouse said and kissed me. I couldn't tell if it was her or one of my Muses, went to my blemished laptop and started typing: ZZ, a New Year in the Unmaking. As no new ideas emerged, I stopped typing and saved the page.

On my drawing desk, next to me, the unfinished watercolour still called-out to me to finish it. I started to paint and soon, as I found my groove, I completed the watercolour task. I placed the painting on top of my drawing board, below the fluorescent tube light, to dry.

"It's a woman," the dusky eyed woman in the frame shop exclaimed, as I gave her my watercolour to frame. "What colour you want for it?" Her words broken through her strong accent.

"I think chocolate brown or black would suit the painting. She showed me samples of stained wooden frames. I placed a few corner samples to the mounting I had done in Ingres cardboard. She agreed to one I picked. "Indeed," she agreed. "You painted?"

"Yes, I did. It's more than just a woman," I commented to her initial remark.

"OK, on Monday." I frowned. "No!" I'll need it for Saturday." She returned with the frame samples. "Then you must take something else." She placed another sample into my hands. I pointed to the damages on the sample frame. "Of course not!" she laughed.

"Fine," I said, "how much?"

"Fourty Euro," she replied business like.

"That's for everything?"

"Of course, we need to have a glass."

"A glass?" I recalled an article I had read about framing watercolour paintings. A glazing in front will diminish its translucent quality through less light transmission.

"Yes, It's a watercolour, you know?" She acted a sneeze with rolling eyes "some people will spit on it and it will be damaged." I had to laugh, but knowing her expressions she translated from her Greek mother tongue, I suppressed it and smiled.

"OK," I said. While she scribbled a note, I thought about tomorrow.

The party at Jo was in a good swing, when we arrived. I handed the painting to Jo, who immediately took the wrapping off, placed the painting on the seat of a chair, and let it lean against the backrest. More people arrived and I observed them as they took interest in the painting. Some gave it a glance, others studied it. A tall man came across the room addressing me in English.

"Is it your work?"

"Yes."

"I see the face of a woman, another one, a body…" and he carried on describing what he detected. I let him finish and smiled.

"Is this a watercolour?"

"Yes," I said. He studied the painting again. "I have a friend who paints in oil. He is self-taught."

"OK," what did he expect me to say? I guessed he wanted to know if I could paint with that medium as well.

"It's just another technique," I replied, getting annoyed at the way he carried on.

"Can you paint in oil?"

"Well, I have done some work once, but found the medium to stiff for my way."

"No, he could teach you." Hah! I thought, now I know where the wind blows from.

"My Mom was a well-known aquarellist and my teacher a prolific painter in oil." This seemed to stop his queries and he departed. I thought of him the same, I thought of all people asking questions about finding another potential customer rather, than to enjoy genuine creative work. Jo came and handed me a glass of wine. "Have the cognisanti inspected your work?"

"Well yes, everybody seems to know about art," I replied. "But few understand it," Jo said and carried on to entertain her friends. I sat quietly in a corner and viewed the dancing crowd and the olive eaters. My spouse enjoyed dancing. A dusky woman appeared dressed in black. Ah, the black knight, I mused. "This is a great painting," she exclaimed, "who has done it?" Jo came and introduced her. "This is Thalia, my friend." We shook hands, then Jo pointed to me, "and there's the artist." I talked to Thalia for a while. It was refreshing of having found a woman who had a sense for art and the creative process. She told me that she is painting too.

"You must show me your work one day," I said and she smiled. "Sure, why not." My spouse appeared, who wished to depart, as it was already late. "Well, just another nightcap and some final talk about artists in Greece." She sighed. "I think it's a great party," I said and my spouse frowned. Thalia filled our glasses and we toasted to the brothers and sisters in arms, who were bound together by engagements with art.

The Trinity Children

It was a hot day in August. The sun baked down on this small country town on the Eastern borders of Austria, nestling along a stream, called 'Stoob'. The name had been derived from the village that lay close to its source. It swelled as it flowed along southward and eventually joined a larger stream that headed for Hungarian soil and whose name I have since forgotten. There were many trees along its winding path, mostly willow and poplar, and the grass was tall and dark green along its ragged banks. Close to the village of Felpu there was this ominous high belt of an electric fence erected by the Russian occupied country next door, a mere fifteen minute drive from Felpu. Behind the fence was a minefield, carefully laid out and about ten metres between two parallel running fences. This strip or red and black earth was always carefully tended to, as if a giant comb had groomed its dark, wavy hair of soil, leaving behind ripples of parallel lines. Not the slightest vegetation would be tolerated on this endless stretch of barren field, which oozed an eerie atmosphere, where a wicked ploughman of death had laid seeds of violent extinctions, with mines set below the weaving bands of the earth, meandering off into the horizon to either side of one's view. One had to turn one's head to see its half-circular extent. Like projecting an illusion, it rather looked like land especially prepared to take precious seeds. Yet, just below this agriculturally prepared surface lay personal mines to be triggered off by the weight of a stepping foot, however careful and lightweight the victims tried to cross this no-man's-land, to rush to the other side of the fence and climb, or cut their way through to freedom. One false step and the unfortunate victim was killed, if more lucky, he was maimed, often losing a foot, yet, in desperation risking his life, escaping the repressive Red regime that had all connotations of an inverse ideology to fascism, but not in their deeds that forced so many seeking a life in freedom outside the electrically fenced-in 'paradise'.

This life-threatening belt of terror was called the 'Iron Curtain', closing in doors tightly on all citizens inside, as a cruel worker's regime inflicted an anti-Semitic campaign on their own countrymen, exercising their menacing power that favoured the hoi-polloi. The hordes of weirdoes fighting even their comrades in arms, hysterically struggling in fear to gain and keep an absolute reign, fashioned on the prototypes of Stalin and Lenin. Sacrificing whoever became suspicious, or was reported to be, by jealous men. Nobody trusted anybody. Your neighbour was maybe made to spy on you and the secret police had a field day to pin their accusations on anybody they disliked; burn a free mind on the stakes of this megalomaniac run country. The courts did remind of times in middle aged Spain, where the Inquisition swept mercilessly across a once free society, rich in education of sciences and all arts, like a giant apocalyptic furnace dissolving everything, stone, iron, and human beings.

It was the year 1948, close to that, three years since the end of WWII, with its fierceness and destruction still hovering on everybody's mind; its cruelties still embedded lively in the minds of the people, who had the eyes to see and the ears to hear.

Many soldiers did not return from the front lines, reported fallen, or missing. It was a time of pain, sorrow and of re-building that brought about a certain tiredness of looking ahead on all tasks that lay ahead, dark, huge like mountains of rubble, which grew through the actions of clearing and sifting. Especially in the cities that were the hardest hit by the bombs and shrapnel. The buildings looked blackened by smoke and fire and their ghostly appearances evoked a feeling of hopelessness and destitution: A landscape of destruction, scarred, and with deep wounds of ditches and direct hits, even in places of worship, like St Stephen's cathedral in Vienna and the cultural inheritance of the opera house on the 'Ringstrasse' that was burnt out.

There was a burnt-out camouflage painted tank in front of the entrance to the primary school in Felpu. It had a big red five-pointed star painted onto the side of its movable tower, where the cannon was controlled with. It pointed now to the opposite side, frozen, like when it was surprised by a deadly anti-tank grenade of the German opposition that finally collapsed it. This happened at the end of the war, when fights became desperate to fend off the advancing Russian troops.

Sometimes its massive steel body was gleaming, as if it had come suddenly alive and was poised to shoot just now its deadly rounds at its enemies. It looked indeed very real from a distance to us children and many stories were told about its attack on the village, before its final end at the entrance to the school yard, adjoining the village's main street.

Often the tank would come alive in our minds at the moment we approached the school in the morning's light, its gun erect, aiming at the building opposite 'Friedhofstrasse', as we could hear the heavy noises of its cater pillared wheels rattling, expecting its rounded turret to turn and aim at us; we fled to the sides of main street, just in case it still worked at its deadly games. Such strong impressions were embedded in our minds, having been listening to this specific war story that were shared between the elderly.

Some kids enjoyed climbing into the turret, bust someone closed the access lid and some kids were stuck inside the tank. From when on the access lid was welded close and nobody was allowed even nearby the tank. However, we kids were eager to touch its thick and heavy steel armour as we passed by to access the school yard. It felt cool in the morning, but as summer approached the thick steel became piping hot and was impossible to touch. Friedhofstrasse lay behind it, taking one uphill and below the arch that bridged the railway line above, the one connection for goods and people to the village.

The sombre looking building where we congregated every morning for the roll call, resonated the voices of the children from all four classes of the elementary school, with the girls separated from the boys. The boys wanting to show off to the girls often, climbed the tank outside extending a nose to the girls inside the yard, who would point fingers at them. The boys became skilful in the game of timeous ducking, not to be caught by the eyes of the teachers. Besides, this game extended from a tank climbing competition in presence of the teachers, between the Upper part of the village and the Lower part, into two groups, where gang members were engaged fighting each other in 'war' games. The winning team claimed to be more daring having escaped more often punishment. We, from the Upper village were smarter, but non-members from the Lower village betrayed us to the teacher. Even later, when these two villages were consolidated, the rivalry still remained, probably passed-on from the parents to their children.

One upcoming Friday a school holiday was declared. We all had to attend a young schoolboy's funeral. He became a victim of explosives, left behind around the village in the aftermath of the war. Most of the areas around the villages were neither safe for inhabitants to walk freely, nor for the farmers to tend to their land. Many areas, where grenades or bombs were found, were immediately fenced off and declared off-limits for everybody. Teams of minesweepers extended their search and detonating teams blew up grenades and bombs when found, also those transported to a quarry close to town. I could still hear the siren going off warning about an explosion in five minute's time. One would hear the frequency of the sound and the bang of its explosion, indicating by its noise the size of bomb. One could feel the pressure waves through the air and sometimes the rattling sound on the window frames of our house. On those days my mother insisted that I'd stay indoors.

Friday, when we attended the funeral of a school friend, the sadness from his parents and relatives affected us all. Ferko, a boy with a keen interest in physics and chemistry, perhaps with a curiosity for weaponry he had found, and experimented with a grenade that exploded in his hands, had ripped him into pieces. He was ten years old. The school had ordered a congregation to honour young Ferko, and everybody had to attend.

Most scholars came and congregated in the small schoolyard, a sea of faces, all in dark and pretty clothes. Once all had assembled, the teacher led the way to Ferko's home. There were emotional outbursts by his parents and brothers, and his sisters were in tears, mourning their kid brother. The waves of emotions touched us all. Nicky, my friend showed a pale face and he acted to be uncomfortable in his dark blue suit, and so was I. However, Nicky was a sensitive kid and he looked most of the time anaemic, but today he seemed to be physically and emotionally in a bad shape. He moved away from our group and walked behind a nearby fence to be sick. I went to his aide, but he wanted to walk away as I tried to console him. He wanted to run away from the ceremony, as he couldn't cope with these drawn out ceremonies at all. Helga, a girl from the parallel class was joining us. She was holding his one hand and I held Nicky's other hand. It seemed as if Nicky was close to fainting. I approached our teacher, who was himself under strain that morning, and I offered to take Nicky home together with Helga. The teacher agreed and dispensed us from staying on.

We went off along the path along the winding stream that led us to a lovely spot, just outside the last homes on the edge of the village and Nicky wanted some cooling water for his head and feet. The midday heat was upon us and we trailed slowly along the path that led off into the natural wilderness. At a spot with a group of willow trees, we stopped. The coolness of the air in the shadow of the trees seemed to refresh the pale cheeks of Nicky and Helga offered her handkerchief for a cool watered compression Nicky placed on his forehead.

We felt all heated up, but enjoyed the coolness of the air amidst the gurgling stream that had an unforeseen effect on nus, as if it would guide us with its conjuring sounds to a mystical adventure. I helped Nicky to sit at the low-grassed ground, close to a huge willow tree that provided a sunken flat area close to the riverbank. Nicky sat down and stretched out. Helga asked me to get her handkerchief dipped again into the cooling water at the embankment's side of the stream, and I proceeded. There was a parting of the slower-flowing stream that forked around an island of smooth sand I was looking at. And as I tried to take my shoes off and my dark-blue pants, I slipped off the riverbank and fell into a deeper end of the stream. Coming up for air, more frightened by the sudden fall than the depth of the stream, I gasped for air and my arms came up gesticulating in the air, as if I would be drowning. As if this spot had that unpredictable depth that had frightened me for a moment. I must have frightened Helga too, and Nicky turned pale again in a fright that I might have hurt myself.

I wasted no time to get through to the centre part of the slow current and straight to the island. I rested and gained my composure in the sun-spotted sand, while I couldn't find Helga's handkerchief. I must have lost it in the shock of my fall into the deep part of the stream. I watched the glitter of the sunrays playing ever changing patterns on the flow of the water, as the stream rolled across huge pebbles reflecting below the in the riverbed, fascinated by the sound of its murmurs. What did the stream have to tell me? Time must have stood still. I heard Helga shouting "Zol are you all right?" That brought me back to the conscious world.

"Yes, I am all right," I called back and heard Helga and Nick laughing at my misfortune. "I bet you too are not brave enough to get across to here." I shouted. Nicky seemed to have recovered from his dizzy spells and I saw his slim body getting up and soon he stood next to Helga. They seemed to be in doubt about my challenge. I was wet in my white shirt and dark-blue sailor suit. I undressed and laid out my clothes onto the pebbled area of this island that was fully in the sunlight. I was careful to lay all out as plain as possible, as Mom had tailored the suit for me with lots of effort and I wanted it to dry without crimples smoothing it down now and then.

The air was warm and a breeze flowing across the area dried my clothes rapidly. The groups of willows were surrounding this piece of seclusion as if protecting us in a hushed and densely positioned way. I felt suddenly alone on this island, enjoyed though the sunshine as I lay on my back thinking that Helga and Nicky wouldn't come anyway. The birds were chirping in the denseness of the fresh green and blended into the streams murmur. Suddenly I heard a splash, then another. I turned my torso and looked up, twitching my eyes due to the bright sunlight. I saw Nicky wading through the stream towards me. He was joining me on the island and we soon engaged into some fun, joking about the way things turned out today. When Nicky said we should engage Helga to come also, "she is after all our friend," Nicky said aloud. "Yes," I replied, "we should all be together here, on our island!" I exclaimed enthusiastically. As Nicky was jumping up and down in the shallow water, close to the sandy island indicating his fun, he encouraged Helga to come across. She stood on the riverbank, afraid to join the two boys in their underpants enjoying themselves. Then she undressed slowly, her top and her skirt, shoes and socks. She still stood there on the riverbank against the dark green shadows of the willow trees with her porcelain white skin, hesitating to get across on her own.

"Stay here," I said to Nicky, "while I go and help her."

"No," Nicky said, "we both will help her." We both strode through the slow flowing current towards her, looking at her slim figure and her long legs, stretched out our hands so she could clasp them and we would get her down slowly. Helga would emit a soft cry as she felt the sudden contact with the fresh water on her skin, Nicky on her right side and I on her left. We waded together through the stream to our island. At one spot the water was rushing in the leaping swell of a current, divided by the river sand embedded island that made the current faster where it had carved-out a deeper ravine near the embankment. It was this spot where we wetted our underpants and as we arrived at the island, our underpants were half torn down our thighs from the current. We looked at each other with new interest. Helga was shaking as she felt cold and she wanted to dry her panties immediately. "Turn around," she said and took her panties off, squeezed them out. Turning around, I looked at her body. I saw a fine line between her thighs, but there was nothing else to see. As Nicky turned, Helga sat on the sandbank and she felt better. Her panties placed on the pebbles to dry, she turned and smiled at us. "Why don't you let your underpants dry on the hot stones as well?" She said and looked at us with curious eyes. As we hesitated she added "or are you afraid I might look at your things?"

No," I said to her, and took my underpants off, placed them beside her panties, and sat down next to Helga in the sand feeling just fine. Nicky took longer, but then we sat all together, compared notes, and teased each other. We laughed a lot as Nicky said he had to pee. "Me too," I said and we both walked away from Helga to pee into the stream and entertained her with a competition who could pee the further. Helga was animated by our performance and wanted to pee herself. She squatted down to pee into the sand at a distance. We both watched er. As she had finished she stood up took us by our hands and wanted to take a bath together, but she was afraid of the currents. So, we, the three children engaged in a bath together, holding hands alternatively, while one of us was squirting water on the other two, and then holding hands and using our legs splashing water on each other. As we enjoyed our childish games, there was instantly cracking in the nearby riverbank and we got a fright. Helga was afraid someone watching us and asked us to lie with her together flat on our tummies, closely huddled together on the warm sand of the isle. There we lay still for a while, with only the murmuring of the stream to be heard, but at times one could hear the cracking sound of a foot stepping on a dry branch, as Helga had imagined at first. But suddenly it was gone, only the murmuring of the stream remained.

There we still lay quietly and started falling into a relieved daze, our bottoms getting burnt. We stirred from this uncomfortable lie, getting up one after the other and sat close together with Helga in the middle, who extended her hands around our shoulders. She felt cold and shivered, hugged Nicky and me for comfort and warmth. It was my first time I watched her in her nude hugging my friend and wondered how this would be feeling if she hugged me too. When she did, I felt nothing at first, just the body contact of a girl who was soft and warm, and her auburn hair flowing around my face. She kissed me on the cheeks and laughed. It was a very special moment of intimacy at such a young age. It was then that Nicky and I became real brothers and Helga became our only sister that afternoon.

She wanted to have some fun and Nicky bathed together and played wrestling games, spraying water across each other. I was laying still and as I was gazing into the thicket of the overgrown embankment, where the cracking sounds had been coming from before, I could not observe anything strange, except that in my imagination I saw the face of a man between the moving leaves that I had noticed before. It was only for a split second, and as I had my face buried into my crossed hands supporting my head, I tried avoiding an impression watching the embankment, especially the spot of the bushes, where the noise of something moving came from. As I moved my head up, tired from the strain of holding still in this position, the face disappeared. I saw that clearly, as my eyes had tried to distinguish the darker leafy background against the paler facial features of a man.

Helga and Nicky were lying next to me and she was riding on his back, playing horse and rider with him. I was jealous of Nicky because Helga did so many games with him, I wanted her to do with me. She turned him around, telling him "Nicky come, let me see..." and she looked at his penis. "Oh," she said "it's cold as she touched it with her hands, but soon lost interest in it. She turned her attention to me and wanted a bath with me. She took me to the deeper part and falling she cried out "Oh I will drown, I cannot swim," clinging to my neck with her hands, encircling my waist with her feet, rubbing her body close to mine. In this playfulness I lifted her out of the water and she enjoyed it, as I was holding her close to my thighs. There was a warm current running through my thighs as I let her slide down my body and I brought her back to the sandbank. "Let me kiss you," she said and kissed me on my cheeks first and then on my lips. It felt to me soft, yet strange. I lied down to rest and dry. She was up onto my back straddling me and riding me like she rode Nicky before. Her legs were around my waist and her bum was rubbing against mine, probably in the most sensual game she had been stirred-up to with our togetherness, and it must have been quite a sight to anybody who could have watched us there.

Nicky was resting and Helga, tired of riding me, was now lying along my back playing 'Mother and Father' as she told me. I should turn, she told me, and when she did lie on me, she said that this is how her mother lies sometimes on her father. I found it very pleasant, I told her and couldn't see yet what it was all about. Helga felt smooth and our fingers touched our bodies searching for the secret button that would tell us all about how grown-up couples do this things to each other. Kissing seemed not being the key either. We just lay there and warmed each other, as we began to feel cold. I was this bod warmth and closeness I still remember. It was my first hug with a girl that intimate, as we had fun playing, cajoling in the water, especially as we got heated-up. Helga was always first in this regard, as she seemed to get blushes on her cheeks all the time. I had developed a crush on Helga that afternoon and it seemed she had a crush on both of us. As we la close next to each other, I observed the fine soft short light hair on her arms and gazed over her fine sculpted face into her brunette hair that fell to her shoulders. The smoothness of her skin was something new to me, as she allowed me to touch her, stroke her arms and shoulders.

Her hands between her legs, she turned towards me and smiled, showing her perfect row of white teeth that had just bitten me on my shoulder. She gave me a kiss and she rode me again like a poncho, imitating her father, she said. Then again it was Nicky, and so it went on all afternoon. She had great fun rubbing herself on our skins and let herself fall down on us impressing us with the smoothness of her skin, smiling, and kissing. She behaved innocent and lustful, and sensual at such an early age creating moments of pleasure. We had an innocent children's love-in, one would coin the phrase nowadays. Helga's skin was glowing after a while as she had exhausted herself playing us. Suddenly she seemed to get uneasy and she wanted to go home. She was afraid someone was watching our games and nude bathing, our hugging and her imitations of parental riding exercises on both of us.

Her eyes were illuminated in jade-green as the late afternoon sun played in it, filtered by the willow's hanging twigs, but there was a flicker of fright in her large irises mixed with her smile, as she cuddled closer to Nicky and me. I got up to fetch our underpants, my sailor suit, and Helga's panties. They felt warm and dry. We waded in the shallow part of the stream to the riverbank. Nicky and Helga were first up and they extended their hands to take the underwear and my clothes and help me up to the big willow tree, where we started dressing. I gave Helga my underpants to smooth them over and she gave me hers by mistake. Nicky was already dressed as we heard that slight cracking sound again and he went into that direction to investigate it. Helga and I dressed and helped each other to smoothen-out our slightly crumpled clothes. There was a sound of voices and Helga and I, in a moment of panic, his quickly behind the adjoining bushes taking our clothes with. She was frightened and I held her close to my chest, feeling the little puffs of her breathing that tickled my neck. She held on to me as if it would mean life and death. We saw Nicky emerging from the opposite side of the groove with a man who had a rifle slung around his shoulders. He was a hunter, I gathered. He talked to Nicky asking him many questions, we could hardly hear.

Helga was afraid, her body shaking, pressed against me on the ground. It seemed to me that she knew the man, but was afraid to tell me. She whispered his name into my ear and that he was the official inspector for this area, who controlled hunting and fishing, as I found out later from my mother. Helga then murmured that she loved me, kissing me, as if she would try to divert our attention from the scene and to swear together that we would talk to nobody about this afternoon, which we promised each other. It was impossible to check out Nicky's conversation with the man. Helga was excited and she asked me if we could touch each other's sexes together, as we were alone now and to seal our secret. She took my hand and guided me to her belly. It was the most sensual feeling. She moved her hand across to me and played with my penis that sent out heated signals to my groin as I wound myself in bitter-sweet pain, but kept quiet to avoid detection. Then she stopped and kissed my cheeks. We promised each other under oath not to tell this to anybody. It was our secret forever. The hunter meanwhile nodded to Nicky and left. Only after a while Helga and I emerged from behind the bushes and continued dressing in a hurry. Nicky came closer waving his hands at us and gesticulated as if stung by a bee. Being closer he shouted "We have to get away from here! There's a criminal out here!"

"Tell us Nicky," I replied. "What did the hunting man say?" Nicky told us on our way back to the village that the hunting man is the provincial forest master and he is looking for a man setting snares to catch deer. "You know Zol that he is also getting children like us into trouble?" Nicky gasped. "How?" I said and thought about my earlier observations into the nearby bushes lying on my tummy on the island.

"Well, he is a past criminal, misusing a girl right close to here." He sighed. "The hunter told me that he took her into behind the thick bushes and did bad things to her." I thought about myself and Helga touching our sexes in the bush. I had then a slight feeling that Nicky might ask me what we were doing behind the bushes, but he didn't and I felt happy, because I had loved her small hands running over my body and her kisses on my cheeks and lips. I think my cheeks were red and still burning, but Nicky did not see it. Helga's cheeks were slightly flushed too, but they were often pink.

However it was our secret that she and I swore never to break to anybody. I have done so for 55 years now and I hope Helga agrees with me that it might be the right time to write about this wonderful experience, I treasure to this day and for all my life. I wanted to tell this story to readers who'll join me to enjoy special childhood memories. To enjoy sensual moments one will appreciate only at a later stage in life. Helga asked me about her handkerchief that was missing. "It must have been swept away when it fell into the stream," I told her. When at that instant I became pale and Helga asked "are you all right Zol?" And I said "I knew that he was watching us all the time!"

"Who?" They both enquired.

"The pervert man, the one who takes little girls, feeding them sweets and then doing bad things to them."

"Where?" They both wanted to know.

"In the bush, when we lay in the sun after our nude bathing stints on the island."

"I know," Helga said, "I think I saw his face." So Helga and I agreed on this, as we both detected his face in the bush staring at us. "I thought at first it was a deer and wanted to avoid panic between us, so I didn't bother, but observed." I said. But as Helga told us her impressions, we knew why she felt so frightened and wanted to go home suddenly. As we walked I promised Helga to look for her handkerchief the next day, as I would go for a weekend walk with my parents, along the murmuring stream.

We never repeated our bathing at that spot ever again. We talked about it whenever we were together in hushed voices and felt like the 'trinity children', as we were called by our friends from the on, entwined through this bond of secrecy. But indeed somebody had watched us that day. The grown-ups called him a pervert and a violator of children. I wanted to know more about this man, as I asked my mother the next day, as so much was talked about this violator, but it seemed that I neither could get satisfactory information about him in detail, nor a description of his looks. The chief forest inspector with his rifle slung across his shoulders did see us, but much later that day, when we were already all dressed, especially Nicky, who was the first to encounter him, while Helga and I were hiding behind the bushes.

The episode was only known to my mother and the parents of Helga and Nicky, yet there was never a word said about the details, as we told nothing to our parents about our private afternoon.

I only told my mother, who probed me that it was hot that afternoon and we cooled down. That was all. But it was as if by talk about the violating man, they had laid bare the base of our triumvirate meeting, our secret for all to see, making us feeling repelled by the way all grown-ups talked about this matter. We rebelled against their bickering, their constant spying on us, and their drilling inquisition to find out more about our doings, which he hid jealously.

Nicky, Helga and I finished our primary schooling days in the next couple of months, remaining very best of friends, being called since the episode at the stream 'The Trinity Children', maybe because we all stubbornly didn't reveal any details. In our trinity we were that strong! This name had stuck to us ever since. Nicky left to attend secondary school in Vienna, and Helga attended a technical school to be trained as a bookkeeper. Our ways had suddenly parted and our conspiratorial togetherness came finally to an end. But whenever we met and greeted each other, we talked as if that bond would last forever and nothing in the world could ever put a dent into it. It was like that Russian tank at school that became a symbol for our tightly knit friendship, we felt strong like its steel to keep our secret.

Helga grew-up rapidly to become a beautiful girl with long auburn hair and sparkling green eyes. I reached puberty and dreamed often of her, holding her close and kissing her. I felt that rising warmth I did back then, on the island in the stream, when she kissed me the first time.

But now my behaviour seemed strange and it angered me at times, as every time when I saw her waving at me and we exchanged a 'hello', I blushed. She looked at me and smiled at me with a smile that still held our secret embedded in her gleaming eyes.

I saw Helga again when she was eighteen, as I came to visit my hometown again after years of having studied in the capital. I met her with a boyfriend, a man much to my dislike. Being acquainted with the police force he looked even vulgar to me. He owned a dark painted motorbike and it hurt me seeing her wheeled-off in a hurry as she just smiled and waved a hello to me. The powerful roar of the motorbike was like a show of power of the guy who intended to outdo her bond with me. I had only a glimpse of her well-shaped legs showing from her short tight pants she wore. It was an instant turn-on for me. As she disappeared in a flash of speed down main road, I still could feel our secret bond between us from the episode on the riverbank, even her new friend with his roaring bike could never sever. I sensed that she was inclined to hug and kiss me, as I wanted that too. Soon the hurried take-offs with her boyfriend , whenever I met her, did not hurt me any longer, because I knew from the way she looked at me with her warm smile that she still remembered the time we had at the willow-embedded stream together, and I often wondered if she was perhaps, at times, dreaming about it, as I did. Was she having memory flashes when she was together with her boyfriend? And if she closed her eyes, would she think of me now as how we would be touching each other in our nakedness?

I wanted to tell her about her handkerchief, but the boyfriend who had a strange name, I hardly recall, never allowed us to talk more than a few words. So, I never came around to tell her that I'd found her handkerchief with the small blue bear on it, that afternoon I went for a walk with my parents. Now, after so many years I still have it in my cupboard. Eventually I found out that this not getting to tell her was a sure sign to keep it. Besides she never asked me for it. For years I had a special place for it close to my heart, watching her growing up from a distance, but nethertheless with tenderness inert in me, whenever I saw her.

She always greeted my mother and Helga always asked about me and how I kept. Thus my Mom became a go-between her and me. And I did the same, asking my mother to tell her this and ask her that. This went on for years and I wondered if she eventually got rid of that hideous boyfriend. One day my mother told me "Helga is marrying soon." My heart stood still for a moment. I was thinking if she'll still remember me and would think of me sometimes, as she now entered a new chapter in her life.

Helga became a mother. I lost sight and contact with her as I sailed for Africa, now married myself, yet I often thought of her. Later in life, as I have walked along many avenues of my life and have explored many happenings in my mature age, I think of her again. A lady friend of mine had brought out in me the idea of writing about this story, as I had told her about it. She liked the scenery of us 'Trinity Children' and subsequently I showed her my first draft of the story, she liked. She became my friend and confidante, a tireless mentor for my writing efforts in poetry and prose. I felt close to her and thank her for her help, her deep interest, and constant encouragement for creativity. She showed me a sensuality that opened my heart and let this sensuous story become alive.

For years I wrote to her and we exchanged poetry and interests in the arts. It dawned on me that most happenings in one's life seem to happen in wide and recurring circles, as if there would be a law of nature imbedded in us that reminded of the planets that fascinate us with their interstellar relationships. I wonder if Helga would come across this story and read it one day. Would she be stirred by it, as I was when describing it the first time to my friend, the gifted poetess?

I guess I have to finish my short stories and publish them. I wonder if I ever would visit my hometown again and meet Helga. The other day I looked for Helga's handkerchief, but it was missing from the usual spot I had kept it between my keepsakes. Maybe now, as I have finished the story as well as I have remembered it, I'll have time to look for it. I wonder if we ever would have time to reminisce the story of 'The Trinity Children' once again. Or would we never bring it up when we met at an old age, afraid of destroying the magic that it had spun around us with its memories, the magic that still lingers on right to this day in our hearts.

Fin.

About the author

Born in Eastern Austria, close to the Hungarian border, he witnessed as a young man the horrors of a nation's suppression, erupting in the Hungarian Revolution of 1956. He finished his education in art and architecture in Vienna, married and sailed for the Cape of Africa, an adventure that followed his childhood dreams. He had drawn African animals for his art classes, but the time had come to see them in their natural habitat.

Meeting a varied facet of people and cultures, working as a draughtsman in an engineering office, as an architect for a cultural centre, as a coordinator of craftsmen and professionals, he made good use of his language skills traveling throughout Southern Africa.

During a trip to Lesotho, a native artist showed him rock-paintings with their stark palimpsest outlines and with typified movements of animals and humans. It made a lasting impression on him and influenced his artistic work.

His vast collection of drawings and slides had been lost during a change of domiciles, but further studies of the art of the San-people reawakened his dormant artistic longing for expression of his art, filling sketchbooks with drawings and notepads with poetry and prose.

While revisiting the capitals of Europe, he sensed the bond of art being borderless and free, reaching out across continents into the world.

During a visit to Greece, he was accepted into a circle of artists and poets, who encouraged him to continue his art and a friend introduced him to the works of famous Greek poets.

In South Africa, he joined he joined writing and poetry workshops of *Writers Write.* It was to open the floodgates of his creativity.

He decided to travel through Greece and visit its sites of antiquity, read-up on Classical mythology, and to enjoy translations of Greek poetry and prose.

He settled in 2023/14 in Klosterneuburg-Weidling. Poet Nikolaus Lenau is buried here. Franz Kafka had visited here. Their writings will always be an inspiration.

Other books by the author:
(Available in the BoD-bookshop)

Acropolis – Book I Fervour

Athens Elegies – A Poet's Lament

Educating Pizzy - The Artist Evolves

Fighting Stance – Triangulation in Love

King of Ice – A Poetic Legend

Spleen of Love – Zen & the Lake Moeris Adventure

The Fabricator – Life and Death of a Great Canvas

The Mill Below Owl Castle – Zol's Sentimental Education

Zora's Mistake – The Potential of a Hidden Error.